The Purveyor
of Enchantment

The Purveyor
of Enchantment

Marika Cobbold

St. Martin's Press  New York

A THOMAS DUNNE BOOK.
An imprint of St. Martin's Press.

Library of Congress Cataloging-in-Publication Data

Cobbold, Marika.
      The purveyor of. enchantment / by Marika
Cobbold.—1st U.S. ed.
          p.   cm.
      ISBN 0-312-18160-4
      I. Title.
    PR6053.018P87   1998 $o'|3$
    823'.914—dc21   97-32201
                                                    CIP

First published in Great Britain by Black Swan
Books

First U.S. Edition: January 1998

10 9 8 7 6 5 4 3 2 1

To my parents
with love and gratitude

My warmest thanks to Sarah Molloy, my agent, and to Patrick Janson-Smith, Diane Pearson, Shauna Newman, Catherine Pollock, Katie White and everyone at Transworld for their encouragement and their hard work on behalf of this book, and to Harriet Cobbold for all her help and advice.

Chapter One

'I'm sorry,' Clementine whispered to Mr Scott, 'but I never was very good at carpentry.' She looked out from the attic window, into the night. Below, lit by moonlight, lay the rope-ladder, draped across a rose bush, no use to anyone.

Mr Scott just shrugged his shoulders, sinking down onto the chair by the desk. As he sat, a heavy loose-limbed man, the chair sagged, pushing the spring which pierced through the bottom of the chair right down to the floorboards.

They had heard the sound of glass breaking some minutes after going upstairs to look at Mr Scott's books on African legends. Then a door had slammed shut.

'What on earth!' Mr Scott had turned from the large trunk in the corner of the room, a battered book in his hand.

'Shush,' Clementine placed her finger across her plump lips, smearing it with raspberry-red lipstick. She tiptoed across the room to close the door, her heart beating so fast that she thought any minute now it would sprint right out of her chest and across the room all on its own.

'I think someone's broken in,' she whispered, and it was then her gaze fell on the rope-ladder that she herself had given to Mr Scott some weeks earlier in case of fire or some other emergency just like this one. From down below came the sound of china crashing to the floor. Mr Scott flinched and his old face seemed to drop off its bones.

'I'll climb down the ladder and run for help. The curtains are all drawn so he won't spot me.' She had gathered up the coiled ladder from the floor and looped it onto the hooks in the window-sill, the very same hooks she had put there herself, and then she had watched as they slipped from the wood as easily as if they had been oiled, falling to the ground with the ladder.

'Sorry, sorry, sorry,' she mumbled, her large hands flapping. 'This simply wasn't meant to happen.' And it was all her fault. Who was it who had introduced Derek Fletcher, in his guise as plumber, into Mr Scott's house, although he fitted to a tee the description of the man wanted in the latest Aldringham burglary? Who was it who had prattled on about the importance of security, only to install a rope-ladder which turned out to be no more use than a shredded parachute? And who had insisted, in spite of the lateness of the hour, that they go up to Mr Scott's attic study to search for his books on African legends? Clementine, Clementine, Clementine.

She turned away from the window with a last look at the rope-ladder below. 'It's a terrible shock when something you've always expected to happen actually happens,' she whispered, tears welling up in her eyes.

Mr Scott leant towards her, taking her hand and giving it a little squeeze. The loose flesh on his jaw quivered as it set in a determined clench. 'I've been in much worse scrapes than this. Whoever it is down there won't come up this far, I'm sure of it. He'll grab what he can from downstairs and then he'll be gone, you'll see.'

Clementine tried to look reassured. It was the least she could do, but her heart was pounding as hard as ever.

'Why don't you sit down?' Mr Scott whispered, nodding towards the wing chair in the corner of the room.

'Did you hear that?' Clementine's knuckles whitened as she clasped the dusty brocade of the armrest. 'Was that a door?'

'Now there's no need to panic,' Mr Scott's voice was barely audible. 'I'm sure we're quite safe up here in our little tower. Anyway, I'm expecting Nathaniel back any time now.'

Nathaniel. The pale face and green eyes of Mr Scott's only son appeared before her. Mr Scott spoke again in the same crackling whisper.

'Maybe this is not the time, or maybe it is precisely the time, to ask you why, when you loved my son and he loved you, you abandoned him?'

*   *   *

'A life lived in fear is a life half lived,' Ophelia proclaimed. She stood in the middle of the small sitting-room, a red and white china elephant in her hand, her eyes fixed on Clementine. 'Turning the house into a fortress is just ridiculous. We'll end up burning alive instead, unable to get out. That's what happens when people install all these bars and locks.' She gave the elephant a long look. 'This is revolting. Give it to a white elephant stall or something.'

Clementine looked up from the box she was unpacking. 'Now a child would say, "But you can't, it's a red and white elephant." '

Ophelia raised her eyes to the ceiling. 'What I'm saying is, this isn't New York City, it's Aldringham. Ease up. Even an old lady like Aunt Elvira didn't go in for all that kind of stuff.'

Clementine lifted a cornflower-blue glass paperweight up to the reading lamp, twisting it this way and that, admiring the shards of colour thrown out into the light. 'Well there you are,' she said; 'I'm not so like her after all.'

'To my beloved great niece, Clementine Hope, in whom I see myself, I leave my cottage in Aldringham,' Elvira Madox's will had read.

It was a wonderful thing to inherit a house, especially for a divorcee on a limited income, Clementine was aware of that. But it was a shock to find oneself described as the mirror image of a woman commonly referred to as 'poor old Aunt Elvira'. In fact, Clementine thought now, her great aunt had probably been known as poor old Elvira even as a tiny child in pigtails.

'How could she think I was like her?' she complained. 'I'm totally different. My life has been totally different. I ask you, what similarities are there?'

Ophelia was rummaging through the boxes, searching for a hammer, and with a little grunt of satisfaction she sat back on her heels and contemplated Clementine. 'Well,' she said, 'what springs to mind is that you're both dead.'

Clementine blinked against the light as she looked across the room at her sister. Sister; everyone had preferred that they dropped the half. 'You haven't lost a father, children, you've gained a little sister,' Grace, Clementine's stepmother, had dimpled when the nine-year-old Clementine had first seen the newborn Ophelia. Clementine's father had stood by looking proud. At the time, Clementine had not felt that she needed a sister. There were four children already: Roger Junior, Juliet, Timothy and Clementine. They were an expense as it was, always needing new shoes at the same time and not fitting comfortably into a normal car. And now there was another one.

But they all came to love Ophelia, and here Clementine was, about to share her house with her. Right now though, she was feeling hurt.

'I've lived a quiet life, I admit,' she said, 'but so have

12

lots of people. You don't find them accused of being like Aunt Elvira.'

'And you don't find them inheriting her house either, so stop whinging.'

Clementine had to admire the way Ophelia said things so straight. She, personally, wrapped her sentences in so many layers of excuses and explanations, sub-clauses and nervous little laughs, it was hard, sometimes to find the meaning in what she said. She unwrapped a Staffordshire shepherdess from its newspaper parcel and, dropping the paper back into the box, she walked across to the fireplace. The mantelpiece was already crowded with Aunt Elvira's Beatrix Potter figures.

'Now there's a difference for a start,' she said, giving Tom Kitten a little shove to the back of the shelf and putting the shepherdess in his place. 'Aunt Elvira was mad about Beatrix Potter ornaments, and I'm not.'

Ophelia did not reply, she was busy banging a picture hook into the wall by the south-facing window. 'I thought this would be a good place for my still life,' she said instead. 'That's all right isn't it?'

I hate that still life, Clementine thought. Everything in it is dead; dead and brown. 'You know when you're little,' she said, 'and you wonder what the inside of a cloud must be like . . . ?'

'Nope,' Ophelia said. She hung the picture on the hook and stepped back to admire the effect.

'You've never wondered what the inside of a cloud looks like?'

Ophelia shook her head. 'Just go and sit in some steam.'

'I never thought about it in that way,' Clementine admitted. 'Anyway, I thought I'd like this house to be just how I imagined it.'

Ophelia turned from her picture to face Clementine, arms crossed over her child-like chest. Clementine looked back at her with all the nervous admiration of a tall woman with a generous bosom for everything that was dainty and fragile.

'You imagined the inside of a cloud as a two-storey cottage with a double-aspect sitting-room and north-facing kitchen?' Ophelia wanted to know.

'Not entirely,' Clementine admitted. 'More sort of cosy and light and softly focused; but not brown and dead.'

'Who's talking brown and dead? Anyway, you just have to get rid of some of this junk.' Ophelia gesticulated at the cluttered corners of the room. 'All those papers that sit in heaps everywhere, they'll have to go for a start.' She nodded towards the cardboard boxes stacked on the rosewood table by the window.

'No, absolutely not.' Clementine hurried across the room and put her large hand protectively on a baby-blue folder. 'These are Aunt Elvira's fairy tales. I can't throw them away. They're our childhood. Well, mine.'

'It's just notes, reams and reams of notes that never came to anything. She never wrote the stories down, you know that. She was just like you, grabbing at any excuse not to get on with things.' Ophelia had a knack of putting the fool into other people's gold. Clementine was beginning to regret having offered her lodgings.

'I have plans for those notes,' she said. 'Unlike Aunt Elvira I *will* do something with them.'

'What?' Ophelia asked.

Now there was a question. Clementine gathered her hair in a twist, piling it on top of her head before letting it cascade loose down her back again. It was like smoking a pipe, she thought, having long hair: it bought you time while you fiddled. 'Do we know that Nero really did fiddle while Rome burnt?' she said. 'Or did he simply fiddle with something? I don't suppose it matters, the thing being that he didn't help.'

She knew the kind of look Ophelia would be giving her, right then, so she looked in the opposite direction, out at North Street, contemplating the view that would

14

soon be as familiar as the sight of her own face in the mirror. 'I intend to publish six volumes of fairy tales, one for each continent and with each story retold my way, showing its relevance to life today,' she said, turning back to Ophelia.

Ophelia looked surprised. So did Clementine. 'Well,' Ophelia said finally, 'that's the first I've heard of it.'

Clementine should, in truth, have said, 'Me too,' but there was Ophelia, so young, so sure, so fair, so elfin. And there was Clementine, so, well, so middle-aged, so big, so vaguely brown and sure of nothing but her own uncertainties.

She was about to say, 'I might well travel,' before remembering that Aunt Elvira had been quite a traveller herself, so she decided to quit while she was ahead. Returning to the box, she fished out the last package, the portrait of herself set in a heavy silver-plated frame, which Aunt Elvira had given Clementine and Gustaf as a wedding present. At least, Clementine thought, unwrapping the picture, we don't look the least alike. Elvira was smiling that slightly buck-toothed smile at the world which never seemed to smile back.

'No, not a bit alike,' Clementine muttered. Elvira's hair was dark and curly; Clementine's was light brown and wavy. Elvira's eyes were hazel; Clementine's were dark brown. Elvira's nose was large and hooked; Clementine's nose might be a little wide perhaps, but no-one could call it big, not really. She wandered across to the grand piano that took up a good quarter of the room, and popped Aunt Elvira down on the black lacquered surface. She gave Elvira one last look. Elvira peeped back a little nervously.

Elvira Madox had gone through life like a last-minute substitute, born in 1903 in place of a brother who had died. The brother had been a perfect child, as beautiful as only those who live in the memory can be.

But Elvira would have palled even against a less formidable rival than the tiny waxen baby who had died when his hands were still like starfish and his eyes were the dark blue of a northern summer night. Elvira was not a pretty little girl. She grew up big-boned and given to clumsiness. She would rush up and embrace her mother with such indelicate abandon that the poor woman had to steady herself against the wall and rearrange her dress. She would play with the puppy and step on its long ears. When she admired the cranberry glass vase her mother had been given for Christmas, she picked it up and held it between her large hands, twisting and turning it in the light, misting the pink glass with her excited breaths, only to put it back down on the edge of the bureau where it tottered before falling to the floor and breaking into miriads of pink slivers. Slivers that caught the light from the tree and the tears that rained down from Elvira's flushed cheeks.

Graceless was the adjective most often affixed to Elvira. She never married. Once a young man employed at her father's linen factory, the very same young man who had come up with the slogan, 'Madox Fine Linens: wraps you from cradle to grave!' stood ready to propose when the dinner bell sounded. Later in life he drew much laughter when recalling how he was once, quite literally, saved by the bell.

Graceless Elvira became a teacher at an undistinguished girls' school in Hampstead. She lived in a small flat in Highgate, and every working day, Saturdays included, she taught English and History to young charges whose minds were as resolutely empty as their purses were full.

Every year she removed her savings from the local branch of Lloyds Bank and then she travelled, and on those travels – Bargain Breaks, Super Saver Deals, Back of the Bus with Shabby Single Room kind of holidays – she collected fairy tales the way other people might collect pottery donkeys or Spanish flamenco dolls. On her infrequent visits to her brother, George, and his family in Aldringham, she would tell the children her stories and to them she was no longer big-boned, graceless Elvira, but a purveyor of enchantment.

But the children grew as children will, and soon they saw Elvira through grown-up eyes. She continued to visit, but the visits grew shorter and even less frequent now that there was no-one to listen to her stories, only adults with barely polite smiles stretched across their impatience. Then the oldest boy, Roger, married and had children of his own. Once more, Elvira would be greeted by whoops of delight as she arrived with her old suitcase filled with ill-assorted gifts: a dried sea urchin, a free sample of Chanel No. 5, a crocheted doll. Again she would tell the fairy tales to children sitting spell-bound at her feet.

Those children too grew up and they grew faster, it seemed to Elvira, than any other children before them. The time came for her to retire from teaching, and she bought a little cottage in Aldringham to be ready for the new children. But while she waited, her stories, like old bank notes in a biscuit tin, began to lose their value. 'But I've seen *Sleeping Beauty* on video,' Juliet's boy squirmed. 'Do you know which is the fiercest of the gladiators? I do.'

Elvira's death some months ago, in the first week of February surprised everyone but her immediate family; few had realized that she was still alive.

And that, Clementine thought, was the woman who saw herself in me.

Chapter Two

Clementine looked at her watch, trying to tell the time by the pale moonlight shining in through the attic window.

'Do you think it is Derek Fletcher down there?' she asked in a voice so quiet that Mr Scott had to ask her to repeat what she was saying. 'He does fit the description of the man in the paper, the man who burgled and beat that poor old woman in East Street. And he's been to the house so he knows the layout and what kind of things you've got.'

Mr Scott just shrugged his shoulders. At least we've been introduced to Derek Fletcher, Clementine thought. He was an acquaintance, however casual. The thought was oddly comforting, like being scared alone out on the streets at night and feeling happier at the sight of another human being approaching; just as comforting and just as illogical.

Clementine looked towards the door, listening. How stupid she had been. She leapt from the chair. There was a perfectly good lock on that door and she had not thought to use it.

'Don't,' Mr Scott hissed, but it was too late, she had turned the key.

'What do you mean don't?'

'It jams. We're locked in.'

Clementine tried to turn the key but Mr Scott was right, it was jammed tight.

'But that's good,' she whispered. 'He won't be able to get in, unless he breaks the door down.'

'I've got my heart pills downstairs in the bedroom.' Mr Scott's voice barely reached her across the room.

'Oh Lord, I'm sorry.' Clementine fiddled with the lock, trying to turn the key, but it would not budge, not one millimetre. She prayed that Nathaniel would not be long. But what if he did return while the intruder was still in the house? He might be attacked. Clementine buried her head in her hands. It was a while later that Mr Scott spoke again.

'I haven't asked you about what happened between you and Nathaniel before, as I have a horror of interfering in other people's lives. However, in a situation such as this, one might be forgiven the odd transgression.'

Clementine marvelled at how he maintained the formality of speech, sitting there locked in the attic with a burglar rummaging through his house. Of course, Toby Scott had been a missionary. He was an old hand at passing the salt whilst mortar shells crashed through the wall and men with large knives waited at the door. Whatever was going to happen that night, there was some comfort that she was spending it with a man who was not only the father of the only man she had ever truly been in love with, but also a man of impeccable manners.

*   *   *

'If you walk down the High Street in Aldringham you'll find a left turn just after you've passed Lloyds Bank. That left turn takes you into North Street. North Street is flanked on both sides by large red-brick Georgian houses, homes to dentists and lawyers and the odd affluent shopkeeper. As you walk on up the street though, you'll find a little terrace of odd houses. The first three are of Elizabethan origin. An elderly woman, cat-ridden and hard of hearing, lives in the first. The second one stands empty, spurned by its owner who is said to be settled abroad. The third one is mine. The house next to mine is the end one. As yet, I do not know who lives there, but it's a funny-looking house, tall and narrow, as if its creator had tried to squeeze it in, and yet there's a full ten yards between that house and the next.'

'What are you doing day-dreaming,' Ophelia said. 'You're meant to be finishing unpacking. It's almost ten o'clock. I'm starving.'

'I wasn't day-dreaming I was writing a letter to a very dear friend in Sweden.'

'So where's the pen and paper?'

'I was writing it in my head,' Clementine said. 'It saves postage. Anyway, you're always hungry. I thought being in love was meant to stop you eating.' Ophelia had recently become engaged to William, who ran an art gallery in Winchester. At the moment though, he was travelling round South America, collecting native sculpture.

'Concentrate,' Ophelia hissed as Clementine broke an egg, complete with bits of brown shell, into the mixing bowl. She paced round the kitchen, stopping now and then to peer over Clementine's shoulder as she was scrambling the eggs. 'You're overdoing them,' she said finally.

'Salmonella,' Clementine explained.

Ophelia groaned but Clementine ignored her, stirring the mixture in the pan until it was pale yellow and crumbly, just the way neither of them liked it.

'Salmonella can be very serious, as well as most unpleasant,' she said, defending herself against Ophelia's glare. Wanting to be loved, even by Ophelia, she added, 'Let's have some wine,' and she brought down a bottle from the wine rack on top of the china cupboard. Ophelia had to stand on tiptoe just to get the glasses from the middle shelf. She was twenty-seven, a waif with blond urchin hair. Clementine had been tempted to have her own hair cut in the same way but, thankfully, she had stopped herself. It would never have worked. She was altogether too large, too milk-and-meat fed to make a decent urchin. No, the best Clementine could hope for was a large mermaid. She handed the wine to Ophelia who uncorked it expertly.

'It's two years since the divorce and I bet you haven't seen anyone. What you need is a new man in your life.' Ophelia took her plate and raised her glass to Clementine.

Clementine winced. 'I loath that expression.'

'What?' Ophelia paused with a large forkful of eggs halfway to her lips. 'What expression?' Clementine looked at her and marvelled at how such a tiny mouth could accommodate such a large amount of scrambled eggs all in one go. And there weren't even little dribbles of crumbs down her chin.

'"New man in your life," that expression,' she said. 'I also hate, "Can I introduce you to the new man in my life."'

'Have we finished ranting?'

Clementine had swallowed a large gulp of wine the wrong way and spilt some more down the front of her white shirt. 'You remember the story of Prince Hat Underground?' she asked, dabbing at the stains with her paper napkin.

'Can't say I do,' Ophelia said, picking up the wine bottle. 'One more for the shirt?'

Clementine put her glass out. 'It always was my favourite of all Aunt Elvira's stories. Prince Hat is blind, and he lives in his kingdom underground, hence the title Prince Hat Under . . .'

'I got that.'

'Well, Prince Hat sits by a stream in a garden full of

lilies and roses. Larks perch in the branches of the lemon trees, and kingfishers, their tails cobalt-blue flashes, dive in the sweet water below.'

'Underground?'

'Underground,' Clementine said firmly. 'This is a fairy tale, after all. So Prince Hat sits by the stream and plays his lute, and his playing is so sweet that the birds themselves pause in their singing to listen. A lock of dark hair falls across his forehead which is high and as smooth and white as alabaster. And his eyes, sea-green and luminous, are the saddest eyes you ever saw.' Clementine lifted her glass to her lips and drank from it, slowly, dreamily.

'They wouldn't be, you know,' Ophelia said. 'If he was blind, his eyes wouldn't be luminous.'

'You have the soul of a French merchant,' Clementine said, putting her glass down with a little bang. 'And by that, I mean a very tight little soul indeed.'

'So tell my tight little soul, what has this luminous Hat got to do with whether or not you get laid this year?'

Clementine frowned at her. 'Would you care to rephrase that?'

'So what has it got to do with anything?' Ophelia said obediently.

'Everything,' Clementine answered, getting up and putting her plate in the sink.

It was midnight by the time they had unpacked the last of the boxes. Tired but satisfied with the evening's work, Clementine looked around the little sitting-room. She stiffened. What was this now? Her things looking so at home amongst Aunt Elvira's Sanderson chintz curtains and sofa. In fact, the room looked just the same as before, just more crowded. Even the indolent nude sprawled on a day bed, a bunch of white roses placed on her rounded belly, looked just right above Aunt Elvira's walnut bureau.

Had Elvira been right? Was Clementine really the very image of her, the woman known as the sheep of the family because, Clementine's father had said, she was not interesting enough to earn the prefix black.

'You're not keeping those?' Ophelia pointed to the shoebox filled with letters and cards sitting on the coffee-table.

'Gustaf's letters,' Clementine sighed and shrugged her shoulders. 'I just can't seem to bring myself to get rid of them.'

Ophelia's pointy little face softened and she padded across the rug in her stocking feet, reaching up to put her tiny hand on Clementine's shoulder. 'You loved him a lot didn't you?'

Clementine's big brown eyes softened in response. She looked down at her hands, inspecting her long fingers, counting the ones on her left hand first, then those on the right. It would be a lie to say she was surprised to see them adding up to ten. She rested on her heels and wiggled her toes. She gazed across the room.

'No,' she admitted finally.

The small wooden squirrel Ophelia had picked up from the table slipped from her hand and rolled across the floor, coming to rest under the embroidered piano stool.

'No, I don't believe I loved him nearly enough,' Clementine said, kneeling down on the floor to retrieve the squirrel. A sound as if something heavy had fallen, came from the other side of the wall, followed by a man's voice, cursing. There was a moment's silence and then the soft tones of an old ballad played on the guitar reached Clementine, who was still kneeling by the piano.

Standing up she said, 'Our neighbour? A schizophrenic obviously.'

'Don't change the subject,' Ophelia threw herself onto the armchair, the way you can when you are petite. If Clementine threw herself onto an armchair, all five feet eleven and three quarters of her, it would probably collapse. 'Did it just not work out, or did you never really love him?' Ophelia looked at Clementine, her head cocked to one side, her eyes alert.

Clementine sat down neatly on the sofa. 'It worked out fine for a long time. Gustaf wanted a wife and I don't think he was particularly fussy about what kind, and I . . . ?' Her voice drifted off into silence.

'Can't you ever finish a sentence?' Ophelia snapped.

'He didn't sing "Oh my darling Clementine" at me,' Clementine said. 'It made him stand out from other men.' She closed her eyes, trying to summon up a picture of the man she was married to for thirteen years. The best she could do was a view of his back, the way she had first seen him. He had been browsing round the fiction section of the bookstore where she was working during the holidays; a tall, fair, slightly stooping figure. He had turned round, scanning the shop for assistance, and there she had been, Clementine, perched on a set of library steps. She had tripped as she came down. She always was clumsy; pretty, she knew that now, but clumsy. Until she met Gustaf, it had not seemed an irresistible combination. Her family had done their best, trying hard to boost her confidence. Take her thirteenth birthday dance. Juliet had been determined to make her little sister feel good about herself, so she paid three of the boys a pound each to fight over Clementine. Being fought over was all the rage at the time. The group of friends, all from the same progressive weekly boarding-school some ten miles outside Aldringham, had been having parties – what their mothers embarrassingly insisted on calling dances – at each other's houses for some time already. The fashion was for the boys to go up to the most popular girls and jostle and shove and posture until all but one gave up. The remaining boy got to dance with the girl. Those parties had made

Clementine understand what her father meant when he talked of, 'man's incurable optimism'. It was all about turning up to horrible party after horrible party because you still believed that one day Prince Charming would arrive with a size-eight slipper. And there she was, even giving a party of her own. She was wearing a cream trouser suit with flares. Her mother had chosen it, oohed over it and bought it. Clementine had been seduced by it. She knew the moment the first guest arrived that the suit had been a mistake. In their group there were girls who were fashionable and girls who were not. Clementine was not. Nothing good would come from trying to change. Then, suddenly, there were three of the most popular boys standing right in front of her, shoving and jostling, asking for a dance. Her mother had been right about the trouser suit after all. And about other things. Had she not told Clementine that one day she would grow into her features? Clementine had just not expected it to happen so quickly. Still, she had read more than enough novels to know how to cope with rival suitors. She had the words all prepared; gracious but commiserating for the loser, gently encouraging for the lucky winner, when the boys withdrew, each one trying to shove the other one forward. 'You have her.'

'No, you take her.'

'Nah, it's OK.'

'Bloody hell, that was three quid I gave you,' Juliet screeched as the boys scurried off to help themselves to cheese and pineapple cubes and cauliflower florets with Mexican dip. Clementine remained on her chair, sitting very still, scuffing the toes of her loafers against the soft-pile emerald carpet (not even her mother had been able to persuade her to wear platforms, not at five feet ten).

By the time she was fifteen she had reached her full height of five feet eleven and a bit. The bit was most probably an inch, but she tended to be a bit vague on that point. Her hands and feet were well-shaped, but not small. No boy could hide her hands in his, but she could lend them her gumboots. But in the end, her mother had been proven right, as mothers usually are. Clementine had turned from large and plain to large and pretty. Well, pretty on the outside. On the inside she was still plain. The wicked fairy had nothing on young boys when it came to lifelong curses, she thought. How many pretty women got up each morning and grimaced into their looking-glass. 'Mirror mirror on the wall, I really haven't changed at all.'

She played make-believe. She picked out a boy, decided she was in love, charmed him, because now she found she could, and then she stayed determinedly in love until she got bored. The boys got confused. No sooner had they congratulated themselves on how much that sweet shy girl adored them, than that sweet girl flittered off. Maybe drifted, was a better word, Clementine thought. She was too big to flitter. She had meant no harm. She was just so stuffed full of romance and unfocused affection that she had to have someone to love or she feared she would explode and spill all over the shiny school corridors and the tidy small-town streets of Aldringham.

In the summer of '79 when the tarmac got so hot that the dogs walked on tiptoe, she loved her sister Juliet's boyfriend. She watched Robin from her bedroom window on the second floor as he strode up to the front door to collect Juliet for a party or the cinema, or a weekend away. Then she would hurry downstairs on some trumped-up errand, and when he passed her in the hall she wanted to tear her heart from her chest and present it to him like some Aztec sacrifice. What she actually did was smile.

Robin smiled back, giving her a little pat on the bottom as he passed. 'Always happy aren't you, Clemmie?'

In August Juliet went away to Israel, but Clementine

still watched for Robin from her bedroom window. She sat cooling herself in the evening air, brushing her hair that was long and light brown, when any fool knows that the princess who gets her prince is invariably fair, like Juliet. But one evening Robin's maroon Renault pulled up outside the house and Clementine flew downstairs to greet him. She was wearing a swirling cotton dress and she could feel the beads of sweat trickling down between her breasts. She stood in front of him, and then and there she decided to stop fighting the wantonness that she had kept locked up inside her like a high-security prisoner ever since she had been told that girls were good. She flung her arms around his neck and pressing her lips against his cheek she wept, 'I love you, I love you, I love you.'

If only she had waited a few minutes she would have found out that Robin had arrived to tell her mother that he and Juliet were engaged and that he was on his way out to join her in Israel. As Clementine's father always said, 'timing is all'.

A week later Gustaf had walked into the Treasure Trove Bookshop.

'I was so utterly unsuited to youth,' Clementine confessed to Ophelia who had just returned to the sitting-room with two mugs of hot chocolate. 'I simply had no idea how to go about being young and carefree. Nights at the disco, backpacking holidays, parties that go on until dawn and end with breakfast in a nearby inn; Gustaf rescued me from all of that.' Clementine fell silent, before adding, 'And all-absorbing, turning-the-world-upside-down passion.'

A month after their first meeting Gustaf proposed to Clementine. Clementine accepted. Her parents were surprised; it was all so sudden, she was so young, only twenty-one, but Gustaf was a good man and an artist. Clementine's father approved of Gustaf being a painter in much the same way as other fathers might approve of a stockbroker or a doctor for a son-in-law. Six weeks after their engagement Gustaf returned to Sweden, his mother's country, to finish his work for a planned exhibition. Clementine remained in Aldringham, enjoying the attention given to a bride-to-be. Even her stepmother, Grace, looked at her with new interest and gave her a copy of *Bride* magazine. During the two months that Gustaf was away Clementine loved him like she had never loved him before and never would again. It was November now and she was teaching music at St George's, the local kindergarten. In her spare time she lay on her bed in her mother's house and thought about Gustaf. She had not realized until he left, quite how warm his smile was or how kind the look in his blue eyes. He was taller than her, fair and really quite good-looking, especially in profile. She decided that she could hardly wait to start her life with him in his house in the village of Abbotslea, some miles outside town. Her passion lasted right through to the day of their wedding although she did begin to wonder, as she sat in the car with her father on their way to St Andrew's church, why she was not feeling happier. They spent their honeymoon in St Jean de Luz. The first morning, the hotel porter had called their room to wake them. 'Bonjour, Madame Hope,' he had twinkled down the line. His voice had carried such expectations of fulfilled young love, and annoyingly her eyes had filled with tears. Tiredness, Clementine had told herself. She got plenty of rest during the next three weeks. She spent hours lying on the large brass bed in their little hotel room, a model for her husband's work rather than an object of his desire, but that was all right. She lay still, she was good at that, and dreamt a lot.

'You know Ophelia,' she said, 'those early years of marriage were the happiest of my life; all cosy and chintzy and rosy.'

Then came the move to Sweden and the grey and white painted wooden house on the edge of a lake. It was a beautiful house, old, low-built and with tall windows facing the lake. Clementine continued to teach music. For her own pleasure she played for hours every day, seated at the large black grand piano by the French windows. Sometimes, reluctantly, she took part in local musical evenings or performed in small concerts. But Gustaf painted less and less, spending most of his time lecturing to the art students at Uppsala.

'Those tiled stoves,' Clementine said; 'I really miss them.' The tiled stoves were indeed beautiful, each room housing a different one, blue and white, pink and white, green and white. 'Very Carl Larsson,' she said. 'I think Gustaf wanted to be Carl Larsson actually, and when he couldn't be, and when we couldn't have children either, well I suppose that was more disappointment than he could take. "Just carry on trying," that doctor said. "Relax and enjoy yourselves. Eat a good dinner, drink some wine, but not too much mind, put on some music." It was all very well, but then poor Gustaf slipped a disc to the strains of Schubert's *Wiegenlied*. It made him feel old, I think, all that hobbling around. All things considered I really can't blame him for falling in love with that student. She told him he was greater than Carl Larsson had ever been and she was just a child herself; no, I can't blame him.'

'Such a shame you never had those children,' Clementine's mother, Lydia, had muttered when she arrived from her home in Cape Town to pick over the pieces of her daughter's life.

'Those children,' Clementine had muttered, as if they had somehow been there the whole time, standing off-stage in their neat school uniforms, waiting.

But Lydia had not been listening. When Clementine's father walked out on her all those years ago, Lydia had said she'd rather he had died, but now, happy on her own, she seemed to get a certain grim satisfaction from Clementine's newly single state.

'Men are a bore,' she stated as they went through the house, packing up what belonged to Clementine. 'Now what do you think I should wear when your ghastly mother-in-law comes? I want to give the right message, you know, I'm glad that my daughter is rid of you all, yet I appreciate the seriousness of what has happened.' She had skipped upstairs, at seventy-one she was surprisingly light on her feet, and returned wearing a simple but beautifully cut navy-blue silk jersey dress. It was, as Clementine often pointed out, not that her mother was selfish, it was simply that while most people suspected that they were the centre of the universe, Lydia knew she was.

'You are in love with William aren't you?' Clementine asked Ophelia as they prepared to go to bed. 'I mean really in love,' she nagged.

'To quote our own dear future King, "What does in love mean?" But yes, of course I am.'

'Grace must be so excited about the wedding,' Clementine felt her stepmother's name on her tongue as if it was a slice of lemon.

'Yeah!' Ophelia nodded. She accepted the adoration that had surrounded her since birth with the ease of someone who was both parents' child. To Clementine and her sister and brothers, that was Ophelia's mark of distinction. It was to her home the half-brothers and sisters went when seeing their father. It was her mother, not theirs, who sat at the head of the table. Ophelia was the whole child, and the others envied and revered her status.

'Actually, she's driving me insane,' the whole child complained now. 'The wedding is five months away and yesterday she rang me up to say I absolutely had to come up to London this week to discuss the flowers, or it would all be a disaster.'

Clementine was not really listening. It was a bad

habit, she knew that: drifting off into your own thoughts when someone was addressing you. Truly wonderful people, 'people persons' concentrated their whole being on their companion, fixing him or her with an unwavering gaze, responding to every word that was spoken; that is how they got loved. Clementine occasionally had the ambition to be a wonderful people person, but she knew as she looked out at the dark rain-washed street, that she was a lost cause. A solitary car drove by, the street light reflected in the spray of water thrown up by the wheel. The darkness of night was infectious, she thought. You had to ward it off with light and sound and bustle, lest it seeped inside you, filling you with melancholy. Biscuits, she thought, biscuits and a mug of warm milk with honey, that should do it, and an old-fashioned detective story to read. One of those where everyone disliked the victim, so that real emotion never got in the way of a jolly good puzzle.

She carried the small tray upstairs to her bedroom. It was only two days since she had arrived at the house from the cottage in Sweden where she had lived since the divorce. Ophelia had moved in at the same time, and they had agreed that Clementine should have Aunt Elvira's old bedroom with the *en suite* bathroom and that Ophelia should have what used to be the spare room. Maybe, Clementine thought now, it had been a mistake. It was no good going on about how unlike Aunt Elvira she was, only to slip into her life as comfortably as she slipped into her old dressing-gown. She stood in the bedroom, hating herself for feeling so at home amongst the William Morris wallpaper, the moss-green curtains and the solid walnut furniture. With a little shudder she placed the tray on the foot of the bed; Aunt Elvira's bed, narrow with a padded headboard to match the curtains, and hurried back along the landing and into the tiny boxroom where she had put her new tool-box. She had been out shopping that morning and she paused briefly to admire the fire-engine-red metal box with its compartments containing hooks and eyes and nails and screws, a hammer, two screwdrivers and a serious tape-measure in a heavy metal casing with a red button which you pressed to snap it all back up inside again. She picked up the tool-box together with the large green and white carrier bag standing next to it.

Ophelia was sitting up in bed reading Proust. She had almost finished the third part of *Remembrance of Things Past*, and that alone, Clementine thought, was enough to annoy anyone. At least she was not reading it in the original French. Clementine smiled at her sister.

'You wouldn't like to swap rooms would you? I just feel this room is more me, if you see what I mean. And you would have your own bathroom. You'll probably come home late a lot of the time and the last thing I'd want is for you to have to go all the way across the landing to wash and things when you're tired.'

Ophelia glanced up from the book. 'No thanks, I'm fine here.' She continued with her reading.

Clementine looked at her thoughtfully. How amazing Ophelia was. 'No,' she had said. 'No, I'm fine here thanks.' No dithering, no excuses.

'I'll put your ladder up then,' Clementine said, fetching the carrier bag and the tool-box from the landing.

'What ladder?' Ophelia called after her.

'Your rope-ladder,' Clementine said holding the bag up, then she went straight to work, drilling holes in the window-sill for the two large brass hooks. 'I've got one for each of our rooms.' She pulled a tangle of rope from the bag and fixed the eyes to the hooks. She turned round with a pleased smile to find Ophelia staring at her, the open book resting on her knees.

'In case of fire or burglary or other emergencies,' Clementine explained brightly. Ophelia continued to stare at her. 'We won't be trapped,' Clementine went on.

Ophelia snapped the book shut. 'You're serious?'

Clementine nodded, determined to maintain that bright, just-rinsed look. Ophelia patted a spot next to her on the bed. Her bed was wider than Clementine's. 'Sit down.'

Clementine sidled up to the bed and sat down on the edge. 'You know, Clementine, I reckon you believe that by fretting away like this, you'll somehow render yourself immune to all the scary things out there. Is that not right?'

Clementine knew she was being patronized, and by her little sister too, but it was kindly meant; it was a form of concern, and Clementine was a sucker for kindness and concern.

'Well I don't exactly choose to worry,' she said, moving further onto the bed, making herself a bit more comfortable. 'I mean it's not as if I enjoy it.' But she knew what Ophelia was saying. There was that time she had been asked to give a concert in Uppsala. She spent weeks beforehand imagining disaster; far more time than she had spent practising. She had foreseen her fingers going dull right at the point when she hit the first note. She had imagined a hall empty but for Gustaf and his mother sitting alone in the centre front row; next, an auditorium packed with a fidgeting, coughing audience whose clapping at the end was so lacklustre that it barely saw her out through the stage door. On and on the conveyor belt of disasters had rolled past her mind's eye. Yet, if any of it had actually happened, no-one would have been more unpleasantly surprised than Clementine.

'You see, I believe that the opposite is true,' Ophelia said. 'I think that the very act of constantly worrying draws all this negative energy towards you until, in the end, your greatest fear does come true.'

Clementine flinched, feeling like the baby at the

christening, gurgling happily in its crib, only to find the wicked fairy smirking down at her. 'How can you?' she gasped, moving so far out on the bed that she almost fell off. 'How can you be so . . . so unhelpful?'

'What do you mean unhelpful?' Ophelia had opened her book again.

'Because it is! You say, "Do stop worrying because worrying will bring calamity." Well, thanks. That's all right then. Now I never need worry again.'

'C'mon, take it easy,' Ophelia put her hand on Clementine's arm.

Clementine shrugged it off. 'What you're saying is that fleeing through the night from a passing psychopath, I will crash my car and burn to death, my body racked with cancer, previously undiagnosed through some NHS mix-up, a slip of paper confirming a positive HIV test clutched in my charcoaled hand, after which, what's left of me is taken and scattered to the winds, everyone congratulating themselves on having saved on a cremation.'

'Now calm down. All I said was stop worrying so much.'

'Yeah, sure. And this little chat has been really helpful. You try *not* to think about something. Take pink. Say to yourself, Whatever happens, I will not think of pink. Instantly, I tell you instantly, your mind will flood with it: pink Cadillacs, pink elephants, Barbara Cartland . . .'

'Christ, Clementine, chill.'

'And don't blaspheme. That kind of casual taking of names in vain is just the kind of thing to provoke God on a bad day.' Then again, she thought, closing her eyes, when was there ever a good day for provoking deities? In the Fifties maybe? In the white-gloved and hatted days of the Fifties, God must have been in a good mood.

She opened her eyes again. 'Say fuck, or shit, or something, if you feel you must, but don't blaspheme.'

'Well fuckadoodle doo, Clementine, chill.'

'That's better.' Getting up from the bed, Clementine gave her a pale smile. As she walked from the room, Ophelia called her back. 'Clementine! Is there anything you're not afraid of?'

Clementine turned in the doorway. 'Of course there is, silly.'

'What?'

Clementine opened her mouth to answer, then shut it again. She thought. Finally, she answered. 'Doris Day. I'm not scared of Doris Day.'

'Christ Almighty, Clementine.'

Clementine winced, but this time, she did not protest.

She ran a bath, hoping the warm water would calm her down. Rummaging through the bathroom cupboard, she found a half-finished bottle of bubble bath in a cupboard: gardenia. It was too much. She and Aunt Elvira even had the same taste in bubble bath. 'No!' she yelled. 'No, no, no. No way!' And she poured the contents of the bottle down the lavatory.

It was a mistake to flush. By the time she had finished mopping the soapy water from the linoleum floor her bath had gone cold. She washed quickly and wrapped herself in her white towelling dressing-gown before hurrying back into the warmth of the bedroom. Seated at her own art deco dressing-table, brought from Sweden, she brushed her hair and put cream on her face and neck. 'Never forget the neck,' her stepmother, Grace, had told her once, showing a rare interest. And Clementine never forgot. This particular cream boasted an ability to neutralize free radicals, making it sound as if it was working undercover for some Fascist junta. She screwed the lid back on the jar before turning to her sponge bag and searching for the condom. She found it, and once in bed, placed it carefully under her pillow before putting the light out on a long day.

Chapter Three

'I know I worry a lot,' Clementine whispered to Mr Scott. 'And right now, it all seems to have been the most cruel waste of time, but then again, how can people not worry? I know that sleeping with a condom under my pillow might be thought of as going a little too far.'

Mr Scott stirred in his chair. 'Would that be some modern version of *The Princess and the Pea*?' he asked.

Clementine shook her head. 'Rape,' she hissed. 'The thought is bad enough as it is, but if you add the risk of contracting Aids.'

'I think it might be a little optimistic to expect an intruder with rape in mind to agree to protect you against sexually transmitted diseases?' Mr Scott suggested.

It was a new experience for Clementine: being accused of over-optimism. 'Well I thought it might be worth a shot,' she mumbled.

'Clementine my dear, you cannot walk through life wearing both braces and a belt. You can't live life to the full without freedom, and with freedom comes risks.'

'I would like nothing better than living life to the full,' Clementine said quietly, 'but I don't know the first thing about how to go about it and now it could well be too late.'

* * *

Aunt Elvira had not been much of a gardener, it had to be said, preferring instead to stay indoors in melancholy half-gloom, reading and writing. No wonder her eyes got so bad near the end. Clementine looked around the tiny garden. It was a good shape, like a mushroom, narrow at the top and growing into a semi-circle at the bottom by the high brick wall. The lawn too was promising; it was there and it was green. Two climbing roses grew up the back wall of the cottage: one pink; Albertine, Clementine guessed, and one wine red. She did not know the name of that one, but it smelt delicious, like . . . Clementine buried her face in the dew-drenched blooms, searching her mind for just the right word to describe the sweet scent . . . roses, that was exactly what it smelt like. She straightened up, moving into the early morning sun. Some years before she had tried her hand at writing poetry. This kind of thing was precisely why she had not persevered; all the good metaphors were already taken. No matter, she would create poetry in her garden; an exclamation mark of lupin here, a dawn of pink and yellow there, a blood-red drop of fuchsias right by the sundial at the bottom. She skipped inside before remembering what a mistake it was for a large woman of thirty-six to try to behave like Christopher Robin. Come to that, she thought, as she landed on the doormat just inside the French windows, it had been a mistake by Christopher Robin to behave like Christopher Robin.

'I'm about to hang the new curtains,' she told Ophelia, who had come into the room at just the wrong time. She had draped the curtains over the back of the sofa the night before, and now she looked at them fondly. She was not a good seamstress, but who would notice when the material was so pretty; golden background sprinkled with roses and cornflowers.

'You know all that banging and shouting from next door the other night,' Ophelia said. 'It was the old boy's son. Veronica at the college knows him. He's a news photographer and apparently he has a major drink problem so he's staying with his father to dry out.'

'Mr Scott is a sweetie,' Clementine said from the top of the ladder. 'We always nod to each other when we meet outside the house.'

'How exciting for you,' Ophelia said. She was still in her nightclothes (one of Clementine's T-shirts) and her short blond hair was standing up in a little quiff at the front.

Clementine finished the first window in silence before moving on to the French windows at the opposite side of the room. They had been in the cottage for almost two weeks now and their colonization of Aunt Elvira's home was almost complete. A fair number of the original inhabitants had been driven out: an old armchair with fleas nesting in the seat; a teaset, cracked and stained; two embroidered cushions, moth-eaten and smelling of cat's pee (it was odd that they did, because as far as Clementine knew, Aunt Elvira had not kept cats) and five antimacassars. Gone too, were the old sitting-room curtains and a chair with a brown vinyl seat. They had stamped out disease, dry rot, damp on the back wall in the kitchen and wood-worm, and only the other night they had amused themselves by poking fun at the indigenous culture, mainly in the form of a stack of romances they had found in the cupboard under the stairs.

Having finished hanging curtains Clementine stepped down from the ladder and looked around her with a little sigh of contentment.

'It's amazing to see', she tried again, 'how different this place is to when Elvira lived here.'

Ophelia too looked around the room. 'It looks much the same to me,' she said. 'Different stuff, of course, but essentially it's the same feel to the place.'

Clementine's smile faded. Her shoulders a little hunched, she put away the steps. Still, she could not help arguing.

'But look at how different it all is.' She gesticulated at the black lacquered grand piano which took up a good quarter of the room. 'Elvira was tone-deaf for heaven's sake. And my embroidery,' she grabbed a Berlin stitch canvas which she was working on and held it out for Ophelia to look at. 'Hers were all floral. Look at this. It's a pug. Aunt Elvira wouldn't have liked it at all. She hated animals.'

From next door came the sound of a guitar and Clementine fell silent and listened. After a few minutes, the melody broke into some crazy-sounding chords and then, abruptly, it stopped.

She wandered across to the piano and, still standing, picked out the notes of the ballad. 'Pretty,' she said.

'Do you realize we haven't had breakfast yet?' Ophelia replied.

Clementine felt happier once she was sitting in the freshly painted blue and white kitchen. It would not have been to Aunt Elvira's taste at all. Actually, it was not really to Clementine's taste either.

She had explained exactly how she wanted the room done to the decorator, Mr Cook. 'If we paint the walls creamy white and then I thought it would be rather fun to do the windows, skirting and the cupboard doors in a soft grey-blue . . .'

'Say no more,' Mr Cook had interrupted her, putting a paint-smudged finger to his nose. 'I've got this knack for knowing what my clients like. Pete's sixth sense, my wife calls it. For you it has to be exactly the right blue, I can see that. You know, Mrs Hope, the problem with today's tradesmen is that they take no pride, no real interest. To them it's just a job of work. Me, see, I'm old school. To see the pleasure on the face of a lady like yourself when I'm done, now that's what gives me my satisfaction.'

39

That's how Clementine had ended up with kitchen cupboards in the bright baby blue of acrylic knitting yarn.

She handed Ophelia the plate of hot cinnamon bagels and picked up the local paper. Ophelia was reading the *Independent*. For a while they read on in silence, then Clementine sighed, a loud deep sigh meant to be heard.

'What?'

'Just listen to this,' Clementine waved the paper at her. ' "An elderly woman was taken to hospital suffering from severe shock and a broken hip following a burglary at her home in Canal Street in the early hours of yesterday. The woman was in bed at her sheltered accommodation bungalow when she was disturbed by a masked intruder. As the woman confronted the burglar she was pushed to the floor and beaten with a heavy metal object. The man, thought to be in his early twenties, tall and strongly built with fair hair and heavily tattooed arms, got away with cash and jewellery worth around two thousand pounds." ' Clementine shook her head. 'It's too bad, really it is. And it goes on. Just listen. "Eight Black and Decker power drills and a barbecue de luxe grill were taken in Sunday night's raid on Harper's Hardware. At Iceland, youths disconnected five of the store's main freezers, leaving . . ." '

'Are you going to do this every Friday?' Ophelia interrupted.

Clementine looked up. 'What?'

'Recite the week's crimes. You did it last Friday, and the Friday before.'

'But it's so awf . . .'

'And then you talk about how awful it all is.' Ophelia stretched across the table and picked another bagel from the blue and yellow pottery plate she had made especially for the new kitchen.

'Do you realize,' Clementine said, 'that by the time

you get to be thirty-six, which, contrary to the general belief amongst twenty-seven-year-olds, most of us do, unless we get murdered or struck down by some horrible disease, you won't be able to eat two cinnamon and raisin bagels for breakfast any more; you'd get fat.' She realized it was not much of a comeback, but right then, it was the best she could do.

'The waif thing's dead, you know,' Ophelia bit into her bagel and wiped a dribble of melted butter from her pointed chin. 'Flesh is in.'

'Now I would be the first to celebrate that particular piece of news,' Clementine said, 'if I didn't know that what you mean is that young flesh, equally divided across the body, is in. A lot of it in bumps around the stomach and thighs, I think you'll find, is not.'

'All I'm saying', Ophelia leant across the table for some more butter, 'is that if you're going to freak, why don't you read a decent newspaper and freak about the big stuff.'

Clementine looked at her over the top of the *Aldringham Gazette.* 'Because, you unknowing child, it is what's happening here that I find so especially scary. What you call the big stuff has always been happening in bad places and big cities, but all of this . . .' she waved the paper at Ophelia, 'all this mindless, brutish destruction of people and property is happening in pretty little, butter-wouldn't-melt-in-its-mouth Aldringham, amongst the coffee-shops and the cobbled walkways. While we sleep behind these four prettily decaying walls with the wind rustling the branches of the maple tree, thugs go about their business outside.' She sighed. 'I remember when it was the muffin man.'

'No you don't,' Ophelia said. 'I doubt that even our parents would remember a muffin man.'

Clementine liked Ophelia's brisk certainty. She envied it too, and sometimes she tried to borrow it, like a warm cardigan, against the chill winds of doubt that swept through her mind and heart unceasingly. No, Ophelia could be comforting. A bit like a medieval monk. Clementine always thought you could not get more certain than one of those: 'On we trundle, the world is flat and God is in his heaven. Trust Him, know your place and all will be well in the end.' That was the sort of thing she imagined a medieval monk might say, if he was having breakfast with her. Ophelia was not a bad alternative. Just look at the way she ate a banana; peeling off the skin and digging her small white teeth into the flesh without ever bothering to check for bruises or that little stalky black bit at the end.

'We've pretty well finished the work on the house,' Ophelia said now, pouring herself another cup of tea. 'So what are you going to do with your life? Get one, maybe?' She topped up Clementine's cup.

'Thanks,' Clementine said automatically, but she thought how typical Ophelia was of her age, asking only rude questions because they think they know the answer to everything else.

After a moment's thought she said, 'There's too much doing as it is, and doing, in my view, is very much a double-edged sword.' She warmed to her subject. 'In fact, if we all did less of it, doing that is, the world would not be in such a mess.' She took a gulp from her tea, dripping some down her cream jersey. She finished wiping herself down before concluding, 'Anyway, if I did more, I wouldn't be able to do half the things I do now.' She picked up her paper again, feeling that she had spoken well.

Ophelia buried her head in her hands.

'All right, all right,' Clementine said testily. 'I am doing things. About things. I've ordered some fliers to advertise my piano lessons and I'm about to begin work on those fairy tales. Just because Aunt Elvira never did anything with all that material, it doesn't mean I have to be the same.'

'I know it's a cliché,' Ophelia said, 'but if trouble wants you, it'll find you. Don't go looking for it. Just try to take each day as it comes, because before you know it you'll have run out of days and there you'll be, having wasted all that time worrying.'

'Like finding a Bugatti, a yellow Bugatti, polished, engine gleaming, and with just a thousand miles on the clock, hidden in the garage of some just-deceased old dear,' Clementine said, wanting to show willing. After all, it was nice of Ophelia to take such an interest.

'Something like that,' Ophelia said. 'You know I could spend the time that William is away fretting about all kinds of things: Is he safe? Does he spend his evenings alone or with someone else? Does he still love me? You know the kind of thing. But I just don't give in to thoughts like that.'

It did not seem fair that forceful people like Ophelia had such easily controlled passions, whereas weak people like Clementine had such wilful ones? Or was there a flaw in that argument? She gazed out of the window, absent-mindedly crumbling the last of her bagel between her long fingers.

'The thing is,' she said, looking at her sister again, 'I find it rather difficult to leap around being life-enhancing and taking each day as it comes, when each day comes loaded with so much misery, maybe not my own, but someone's all the same. It's like: Take care of that suffering, it's someone's son of a bitch. Just think of that poor old thing who was burgled. Close your eyes and imagine.

'"There she was, Violet Hopkins, product of an idyllic pre-war childhood in the Hampshire country-side with her parents and five sisters and brothers. Hers was not a wealthy family, so on leaving school, the young Violet took up a post as governess to the youngest of Sir Buster and Lady Granger's children. The Granger family became attached to the young girl and included her in many family activities, especially tennis, as her backhand was much admired. Violet's dancing was as good as her tennis and one warm summer's evening in August, amongst the heady scent of the Pemberton roses, Freddie Granger, the oldest son of the house, handed her one perfect shell-pink rose and asked her to marry him. Freddie was tall, his hair was thick and fair and his eyes were blue and just a little surprised looking. Violet never forgot the look of delight in those eyes when she said yes. Freddie gave her a ring of amethysts and diamonds and the date for the wedding was set, but before that day came war broke out and Freddie joined his regiment and sailed for France. Even on that last morning as he held her in his arms, Violet felt that they had all the time in the world, all the time in one last kiss. She never saw Freddie again. He was killed at Dunkirk. Violet struggled on, immersing herself in war work, but she never married. After the war she worked as a civil servant until her retirement and, through the years, she comforted herself with the thought that hers and Freddie's sacrifice had been worthwhile. A new generation was growing up in peace and prosperity. For Violet money was tight, but she was good at making do, and now and then she would sell a piece of jewellery, or a silver spoon, whatever she had of any value. But nothing could make her part with the ring Freddie gave her, nothing that is, until a young man broke into her home, wrenching it from her finger, and leaving her broken on the floor.'" Clementine looked across the table at Ophelia. 'Have a nice day,' she said.

'How do you know all that stuff. It wasn't in the paper was it?' Ophelia reached across the table for the *Gazette*.

'No, it wasn't. I guessed.'

'You made all of that up?' Looking at her watch, Ophelia got up from the table. 'I must go. Class starts in half an hour.'

'Ophelia,' Clementine called her back.

'What?'

'Why do you think all the females in our family are named after women who died horrible deaths?'

Ophelia just rolled her eyes and went on her way, leaving Clementine with the dishes, as usual. In every relationship it was like that, Clementine thought, one person striding off to some nine to – goodness no, I can't possibly get home before – eight-thirty, I've-got-a-meeting job, and the other person being left with the dishes. Clementine was invariably cast in the latter role. Even when she had a job to go to and Gustaf was at home thinking about a painting, the dishes had been stacked in the sink waiting for her. It was her own fault, of course, but since when did knowing something was your own fault ever help. When she had finished washing-up, she turned her attention to the cooker, a huge old gas stove bought by Aunt Elvira when she had first moved to the house. Truth be told, Clementine rather liked tidying up. If you can't conquer the chaos outside, creating order in your home offered some little relief. It was Clementine's theory that behind every really clean and tidy house there sheltered a frightened woman. She rubbed the white top of the cooker with enamel polish until it shone. There was just one stubborn mark left, right by the simmering ring. She rubbed hard at it, emptying nearly half the bottle of polish onto that one small spot and wrapping a cloth round the point of her index finger and scraping at it. Things were getting personal between that spot and her. The phone rang, and still with the cloth wrapped around her finger, she went to answer it. It was her friend Jessica, confirming their meeting later that morning.

Back at the cooker, Clementine bent low, peering at the shining enamel. The spot had gone.

There was a troll in one of Aunt Elvira's stories, a small Finnish troll who had tried to clean away the sunbeam that fell across the tree-stump table in her grotto. The troll had gone on cleaning until the sun had moved right round to the west. Suddenly the streak of sun was gone. Tired but well-satisfied the little troll went to bed only to wake up the next morning and find the sunbeam stretched out right where it had been the day before.

At least, Clementine thought, putting the polish away, I'm smarter than the average small Finnish troll.

On her way out to meet Jessica, Clementine gathered up the bags of old clothes she had put aside for Mr Scott's charity sale. Her neighbour, with the son who drank and yelled and played the guitar like an angel, had been a missionary in Africa and now, a widower in his seventies, he had retired to end his days back home. Every other Saturday, he had told her, he organized a jumble sale in the church hall with the proceeds going to his old mission in Kenya.

Clementine stepped out into the dusty July sunshine and walked round to Mr Scott's house to knock on his door with her bags full of clothes. Inside, Mr Scott bustled around, taking the bags from her and riffling through them like a child with a Christmas stocking, exclaiming delightedly at each new find. While Mr Scott was busy, Clementine looked around her at the small clubby sitting-room. Wine-coloured velvet curtains hung in the leaded windows and a sofa and two armchairs were all upholstered in a green and wine red chintz. The walls were covered with English water-colour landscapes and a pair of Staffordshire dogs sat on the mantelpiece. So where was Africa?

'Coffee, a glass of sherry maybe?' Mr Scott offered.

'Sherry would be lovely, thanks.' Clementine had never believed in drinking on her own, with the result that she jumped at every offer to drink in company. Then she remembered the alcoholic son. Would not Mr Scott's sherry be safely hidden and locked away. She should have known better than to say yes to sherry. 'Then again, I'm very happy with coffee.'

Mr Scott paused on his way out of the room and looked at her, sandy eyebrows raised. 'If you would like sherry . . .'

With a small sigh, Clementine sank down on the armchair by the open fireplace. 'Sherry then, thanks.'

Mr Scott returned with two glasses. 'You've given me some wonderful things. Enough almost for a little sale on its own. Oh yes, this is my best haul yet.'

'That's because I've got by far the worst conscience, I wouldn't mind betting,' Clementine said. 'I've got money I haven't earned and I buy far too many clothes that I don't really need.'

'It's the larger lady especially who will find your things invaluable,' Mr Scott beamed, fishing out a pair of black velvet trousers. 'I believe the larger lady has real difficulty finding clothes to fit in the shops.'

With each 'larger lady,' uttered so enthusiastically by Mr Scott, Clementine winced. How was it that the word large, however innocently spoken, carried such a wealth of insults on its back?

'They're mostly a size twelve or fourteen,' she could not help protesting. 'They're just all rather long.' She finished her sherry and stood up to leave. An explosion of music hit them from upstairs. REM, Clementine thought. Then again, maybe not. What did she know?

'My son likes his music on rather loudly, I'm afraid,' Mr Scott said.

Clementine smiled reassuringly. 'Young people are like that. I know my sister Ophelia has only just grown out of that stage and she's twenty-seven.'

Walking with her to the front door, Mr Scott said curtly, 'Nathaniel is thirty-nine.'

Having nothing better to say, Clementine smiled and muttered, 'Boys will be boys.' She should learn to shut up.

Out on the street she looked up towards the window where all the noise was coming from. Through the gap

47

in the curtains she glimpsed a pale face framed by dark hair. Realizing she was staring, she turned away and walked quickly down the street.

She was meeting Jessica at the Chocolate House at half-past twelve, and at a quarter to one there was still no sign of her. Clementine had got a table by the window and she was quite contented waiting, looking around her at the people, comfortable in the light breeze from the open door a few feet away. Behind her a woman on her own was striking up a conversation with the mother of a small girl in a pushchair seated at the next table.

'Lovely smile she's got,' the woman said. The mother mumbled something back. 'She's got your colouring I think, hasn't she, or is your husband fair as well?'

Again, the mother mumbled something before turning demonstratively to the small girl in the pushchair.

The woman rummaged round the large red nylon-mesh shopping bag by her feet, fishing out a packet of boiled sweets. Leaning across, she offered one to the little girl, but the mother shook her head. 'She doesn't have sweets.'

Clementine ordered a cup of coffee. Jessica was nearly always late, but it was no good counting on it and being late yourself, because that would invariably be the occasion on which she was punctual. It was like expecting an important phone call, Clementine thought. You would wait and wait and wait and nothing would happen, and then, just as you had snuck into the loo and sat down, your knickers round your ankles, it would ring. She looked around the room and her glance fell on the woman with the red mesh bag. The woman, thin and tanned, with her dark speckled hair gathered in a bun high up on her head, sat straight-backed on the small hard chair, knees apart and her feet planted firmly on the floor. She sat quite still apart from her head which moved and twitched like that of a bird watching for its prey. A plump waitress with short bleached hair sauntered across with Clementine's coffee, but as she passed the woman stopped her. 'It's getting full,' she observed. 'If you run out of tables I shan't mind sharing. I'm like that,' she added as if she was passing on a piece of privileged information. The waitress told her that she hoped it would not be necessary and prepared to move on when the woman stopped her again with a light but precise touch on the arm. 'I haven't seen you here before.'

'No, I'm just filling in during the busy time.' With a determined look, the waitress moved on with Clementine's coffee. There was still no sign of Jessica so Clementine picked up a volume of poems by Yeats. She was very fond of the idea of always carrying a book of poetry with her wherever she went. The only problem was that she was less fond of reading it. Halfway through *The Ballad of Father O'Hart*, her eyes began to wander.

'Reading are you?' a brisk voice enquired. It was the woman with the mesh bag. 'I'm a great reader myself,' she confessed. Clementine nodded and smiled. 'It's not surprising really. My father was headmaster – head, they would say these days – of Billsbourgh Grammar, you've heard of Billsbourgh? A wonderful man, my father . . . My name is Stephanie Granger by the way. My father, of course, was James Granger.'

'Really,' Clementine said. Her neck was beginning to hurt with the effort of keeping her head turned towards the woman. Her coffee was getting cold. Each time Stephanie Granger drew breath Clementine resolved to turn back to her book, but it never happened that way. The woman would look at Clementine expectantly with those small round eyes and Clementine would end up saying, 'Fancy that,' or 'You don't say, how fascinating,' and off Stephanie Granger would go again, prattle, prattle, prattle.

Half an hour late Jessica arrived in a flurry of excuses, notebooks and bags. Clementine forgave her; after all, she wasted far more of her own time than anyone else could ever hope to. Anyway, Jessica was always late, just like Clementine was always anxious. That was how it was. Clementine could not remember a time when she had not known Jessica. She had been there when Jessica was smacked on her bare bottom by her nurse for tipping a plate of spaghetti in tomato sauce on the floor. She had stayed at Jessica's house more than her own in the months after her father left. Jessica had hated Grace as much as Clementine did. It was Jessica who stole Clementine's first boyfriend and it was Jessica who jumped on a plane to Sweden to help her through the separation from Gustaf. In short, she was Clementine's best friend. She had been married to Michael, a barrister, for five years, and they lived in a large Georgian red-brick house on the outskirts of the town. They had two black Labradors and a donkey to keep the grass down in the paddock, but as yet no children. To Clementine it seemed that her friend's whole life was dedicated to disproving the outward conformity of her life. There was the time she left home to join the Greenham Common protesters. She had sent Clementine a video of a news clip showing Jessica squatting in front of a dank-looking fire, grinning at the camera and making a victory sign. When Clementine had next spoken to her she had said that if she had to choose between all-out nuclear war or using those latrines one more time, she would have to go for the war. After that she had joined the Euthanasia Society, but then her mother had got upset and told her it was tactless. Last year she had begun a course in photography at the art college, and by the time Clementine arrived back in Aldringham, she thought herself a writer. Clementine loved her but she did not understand her. Her life was safe, comfortable and normal, everything that Clementine strived for, yet Jessica never stopped trying to turn it upside down.

Jessica finished her quiche. 'Of course, writing fairy tales is just your usual way of refusing to face up to reality and the emptiness of your life,' Jessica said, rather as if she had taken lessons from Ophelia.

Clementine shook her head. 'Not at all. It's a tribute to Aunt Elvira who gave me her house and her inferiority complex.'

Jessica was blowing a small trench in the froth of her cappuccino. She looked up. 'Now my work is all about confronting reality. If Gregory – you know, the guy at the art college – hadn't suggested I write my Book of Life I would never have realized that my father abused me.'

Clementine almost dropped her cup. The coffee spilt over the rim of the cup and over her hand. She grabbed a napkin and wiped the hot sticky liquid away. 'That dear sweet man abused you?'

Jessica looked at her from under curly lashes. 'Well, when I say abused I don't exactly mean abused . . . not in the sense you might think anyway.' She leant forward in her chair, lowering her voice. 'But I know it's what he wanted to do. You remember the way he was always so distant? The fuss he made once when I kissed him good night on the lips.'

'Yes . . . ?'

'God you're dense sometimes.'

'Don't blaspheme, it might bring you worse things than your father not abusing you in an abusing kind of way.'

'You think this is funny. Gregory reckons it's at the root of everything. Why I'm always searching. Why I can't settle down to anything. Writing my Book of Life could be a complete rebirth for me. I'm telling you, my father wanted me. He thought of me as a sexual being,

51

but because of his upbringing and the kind of man he was . . .'

'Honest and upright, that kind of man,' Clementine said, remembering a kind and rather shy solicitor father.

'Absolutely. The way he carried on about me covering up and not showing cleavage at the same time as he made those really creepy remarks about my friends. Like, "That young lady is certainly well-developed for her age." Oh what the hell let's have some chocolate cake.'

Clementine could not quite decide whether or not a quick 'hell' counted as blasphemy or not. Did it offend the devil in much the same way as it was meant to offend God when one took his name in vain? In that case it was a good thing to say, because offending the devil was what it was all about. Then again if it was seen as invoking hell, then it was obviously the wrong thing to say. But by that token, saying God, or Christ, or Jesus, should be seen simply as ways of invoking the powers of God and would therefore be a thoroughly public-spirited thing to do. Clementine's head was beginning to ache and Jessica was looking at her as if she was expecting her to say something.

'Oh well,' she tried, 'that does seem a bit odd. "That young lady certainly is well-developed; let's have some chocolate cake." I suppose it could even be seen as a bit kinky, I do see that, but then again, in all fairness, he might just have thought this particular friend . . . who was it? Kate I wouldn't be surprised, looked nice and bonny and reminded him of chocolate cake.'

Jessica was staring at her, her cup halfway to her lips. 'I know you're meant to be intelligent. All our teachers said so, but is it possible that they were wrong? Now are you going to have some chocolate cake or not?'

Clementine brightened. 'Oh me? Yes, why not?' She smiled at June Challis, the owner of the Chocolate

House, who had appeared ready to take their order. Mrs Challis smiled back in that way she had of conveying a previous existence more waited upon than waiting on, a life bravely led below her expectations.

'And how is Abigail?' Clementine enquired. All that talk of plumpness had led her thoughts to Mrs Challis's daughter. Clementine sometimes worried that asking after such a disappointment as Abigail Challis, was an unkindness to her mother, but in the end, ask she did. Abigail had grown from a small disappointment to a large one in the years that Clementine had been away. When the Chocolate House had first opened Mrs Challis had offered regular customers the chance to see what the overweight, bushy-haired child who skulked in a corner behind the counter, had once been. Pointing to a large silver-framed photo of a chubby, rose-bud cherub astride a furry rocking horse, she would say, 'And that's my Abigail when she was a baby.' Then, with a sucking of long teeth and a glance at the present and infinitely less pleasing incarnation, she would hiss, 'I know it's hard to believe it's the same child.' Back then though, it was clear from the way she kept tying ribbons in the poor child's hair and fitting little white pointy shoes on her large square feet, that she had not altogether given up hope. But nowadays, apart from asking Jessica where she had had that nice colour done on her hair, or Clementine how she kept so slim at her height, she seemed resigned. The photograph of Abigail's brief flowering was still there, but pushed back now, behind the display of chocolate novelties, and its silver frame had lost its lustre.

'Abigail is very well, thank you, Mrs Hope,' Mrs Challis's frosted pink smile tightened. 'She's got herself a young man. She hasn't brought him home to meet her mother yet, so I dare say she knows I won't approve.' She leant closer to the table. 'In fact, I'm sure he's a bad influence. Just last night, when I asked if she really felt she needed a third piece of leftover chocolate gateaux, she just tossed her head and said her Derek likes a bit of flesh on a woman.' Mrs Challis shuddered delicately. 'Of course, the last person they listen to at that age, is their mother.'

'My grandmother gave her daughters just two bits of advice,' Clementine said. 'Never allow the sun on your face, and always wear the best quality foundation garments you can afford. Awfully good advice I've always thought,' she added brightly.

'Really.' Mrs Challis's voice lacked warmth. 'I'll bring your cake right over.'

'Have I told you the story of the changeling?' Clementine asked Jessica as she watched Mrs Challis clip-clop her way towards the counter on high-heeled patent pumps of the kind that only bits of Abigail's feet would fit into.

Jessica shook her head.

'Well,' Clementine said, sitting back in her chair, 'once upon a time, in a country far away in the north, a daughter was born to the king and queen. The little princess was so beautiful and her smile was so bright that the sun itself stayed up late to watch her sleep in her golden crib. And although the princess was just an infant, young men travelled from far away to ask her father, the king, for her hand in marriage. But in the same land there lived an old troll woman and she too had a daughter, as vile and cross a troll brat that ever lived. One night, driven to distraction with jealousy over the fuss made of the little princess, the troll woman grabbed her child and set off for the palace. She crept into the room where the little princess slept and snatched her, leaving her own brat amongst the silken sheets.'

Clementine shot a glance at Mrs Challis who was standing behind the counter weighing a small pink and white striped box of chocolates. 'I always think that particular story was put about by a woman with a lot of explaining to do.'

'Gregory saw it immediately, about my father I mean,' Jessica said. She patted her red notebook. 'It's all here.'

Clementine smiled at her. 'You really shouldn't believe everything you write you know.'

'Gregory says that these notebooks are my stepping-stones to a greater understanding.'

Clementine waited for her to tell more. 'Of what?' she asked finally.

'Myself, of course.'

Clementine shuddered. 'Now you really shouldn't do that; try to understand yourself, I mean. Untold problems arise from people running around trying to understand themselves, and when they succeed . . .' she rolled her eyes heavenwards. 'I myself live in constant fear of one day really getting to know myself. How could any of us live with such knowledge? No, mark my words, nothing clouds the horizon more than a clear view of the world.'

'You know,' Jessica said, 'it wouldn't surprise me if I was the only follower of Zen in Aldringham.'

Clementine looked around her. A heavy young woman wearing leggings and a T-shirt struggled through the door dragging a pushchair with a tiny baby slumped inside like a drunk over the railings of a ship. At the counter an elderly man was fumbling with his change and two women with matching steel-grey, set and back-combed hair were picking up their shopping bags and making for the door. She sighed. 'I'm sure you're right,' she said.

'Flow time,' Jessica exclaimed.

'Flow time,' Clementine agreed reluctantly. Flow time was Gregory's idea. You spent an hour just writing down whatever came into your head, no pause, no interruptions of any kind.

'It has to be completely spontaneous,' Jessica kept

telling Clementine. 'You should capture thoughts as fresh as the first covering of snow. You'll be amazed, at the end of a session, when you look back at what you've written.'

Clementine went along with it because she valued their friendship more than she valued her time. Obediently she picked up her own notebook which was large and black with a red spine and thin pages that crackled when covered in ink. She twiddled her pen between her fingers and beat a tattoo against her front teeth with its thick black tip. She finished her coffee.

'Another cup?' she whispered.

Jessica looked up from her writing with a frown. 'Yes, all right then.'

Clementine signalled to Mrs Challis, holding up her empty cup and making as if she was pouring her thumb into it. A posse of leaves rattled past the glass-fronted door at odds with the bright summer clothes they were all wearing. 'Quite autumn-like for July,' she mumbled. 'All that early heat.' Then she wondered how many pointless remarks like that she had made in her life and how she would be perceived if she never opened her mouth except to say something worthwhile. She would be perceived as very silent indeed, that's how. She shifted in her chair. Very quietly she tapped the tips of her fingers against the table top. She had read somewhere that it stimulated the function of the brain.

Jessica looked up with a glare, but she kept on writing. Clementine was impressed. If Jessica could write while glaring, she, Clementine, should be able to write while bored. She picked up her pen again and nodded a silent thank you to Mrs Challis who had arrived with their fresh coffee.

A few minutes went by. 'Jessica,' Clementine whispered, 'do you ever wonder why, if the Aids virus can't live outside the body, there's such a fuss about dental equipment and cuticle scissors and even hair-dressing combs?'

This time Jessica did stop writing. 'If you're going to insist on talking all the way through flow time, you might as well speak in a loud enough voice for me to hear. And no, I don't know why.'

Clementine mumbled an apology and began to write:

    puy lentils
    tagliatelli, fresh
    mushrooms, large field
    carrots
    celery
    lemon
    bananas

This time the look that Jessica gave her was encouraging. Clementine smiled back, covering her writing with her arm.

Half an hour went by. Clementine looked at her watch and stood up. 'I must go,' she said to Jessica. 'I've got graves to visit.'

They kissed goodbye and Clementine paid for the coffee and cake on her way out. At the door she walked straight into Abigail Challis and a large young man with blond hair shaved up his neck and tattoos running down his bare arms all the way to his knuckles. Clementine stopped dead in the doorway. Slowly she turned her head and looked at the couple as they stood at the counter talking to Mrs Challis. That young man, where had she seen him before? And why was she feeling so ill at ease?

Chapter Four

'There I was, face to face with a man fitting to a tee the description of that burglar,' Clementine whispered. 'The thing is, I just know it's him downstairs. He's been here already, remember, so he knows the layout.'

'What do you mean he's been here?' Mr Scott's voice was barely audible and he kept wiping his forehead with a large white handkerchief that seemed to move by itself, back and forth in the faint moonlight.

'He's the plumber. Remember he was over at my house and then he came in to look at your heating. I just knew something like this would happen. I just knew it.'

*   *   *

Clementine standing at the foot of her father's grave, tried to recall how old she had been when she first realized that it was possible to die before you were a hundred. Probably far too old, she thought with a sigh. She had been a deluded child, getting to be nine before finding out that Father Christmas, who called every Christmas Day at teatime with a sackful of presents, was actually Aunt Elvira. Even then she had only worked this out because minutes before Father Christmas's arrival, Aunt Elvira disappeared with the words, 'I'll just pop down the road and get some cigarettes from the machine,' when the black onyx case on the table was brimming with Benson and Hedges and, anyway, there were two boys to run errands.

It had been a shock to find out about Aunt Elvira being Father Christmas; all those lies fed to her, Clementine had thought, who could she trust? But finding out that you did not necessarily live happily ever after until you were a hundred, but could die well before, in fact, at any time, was terrible. She knew that the little match girl had died young, and Judy in *Seven Little Australians* too, but those were stories. In real life you grew up, married, had children, and then died when you were a hundred. But she had been wrong again, and ever since she had looked at life and happiness with suspicion, all too aware that it could be snatched from her at any moment.

It was family knowledge how one Christmas, Aunt Mabel, as ever wanting to outdo her sister, had wrapped up a host of expensive toys for her two children watching the excited oohs and aahs as the gifts were handed out, only to gather them all up on the twenty-seventh and return them to the shop. Clementine had been told that story as part of the explanation as to why cousin Digby had a nervous twitch, and also why it was all right to lie and say that Mummy had just popped out, when Aunt Mabel phoned.

Clementine grew up thinking God was a lot like Aunt Mabel.

'I don't know why you are so unsure of yourself, child,' Clementine's father lamented one day as he dropped her off at her mother's house. 'Look at your brothers and sisters, even little Ophelia has more confidence in her little finger than you have in your whole body.'

Of course she did, Clementine had thought. She was the whole child. She probably still thought you lived until you were a hundred.

'And does Juliet creep around with her shoulders hunched apologizing for her existence?'

That particular day, Juliet had just borrowed Clementine's best blouse without asking, so Clementine said, 'Maybe she should.'

'I don't think you could say Clementine creeps, Roger dear,' Clementine's mother had said. Her parents were friends again now, some years after their divorce. 'Runs, more likely. And listen to her, she never stops chatting. No, I don't think it's fair to say she lacks confidence.' She paused. 'But if she does, I'm afraid we both know why that is.'

Well, they were fairly good friends.

'No, I'm pleased to say that all my children are outgoing and popular,' Clementine's mother went on with what Clementine had thought at the time was a truly impressive disregard for the truth. 'Just look at all those boys hanging around our little girl. And now she's grown into her size, almost, and that lovely hair.'

Clementine had listened to her mother and then she had gone up to her room and lain on her bed. Her parents were enlightened. They had vowed never to inflict on their children the kind of narrow discipline and petty dictatorship that had blighted their own childhoods. So Clementine had been left from an early age to the terrors of her own judgement. 'I have no worries about my children,' she would hear her mother boast to her friends. 'For a start, I always know where they are and who they're with.'

Yeah, sure! Big deal! Clementine had wanted to shout at her. Like the evening when she met Dieter, one of those nice boys whose parents were friends of some friends of her mother. Dieter had a head like a bullet and a body that his mother undoubtedly referred to as strong. But he was undeniably a boy, and everyone knew that even an ugly boy was worth more than the prettiest girl. Clementine had ended up in the spare-room bed with Dieter on top of her, fumbling with her bra. Going halfway, that is, allowing a boy to do whatever amused him with your top half, was acceptable. Going the whole way was a sin, so Clementine had lain on the quilted bedspread counting the little white dots that formed a pattern around each yellow rosebud on the wallpaper, putting up with this boy kneading her breasts because, at least, she was wanted. It was the curse of women, Clementine had often thought since: needing to be wanted. Men seemed to assume that they were. Maybe it was some ingrained reaction, a reflex apology handed down the generations from mother to daughter, in response to the countless men who had turned away from their newborn girl child with a small grimace of disappointment, 'Oh, a girl.' Maybe it was stored in the collective female psyche that the birth of a royal princess only merited a six-gun salute, whilst the birth of a son was cause for the full twelve. Baby girls, Clementine thought, were born with an apology on their lips for the pain and inconvenience caused; baby boys just thought how lucky their mothers were to have them.

Dieter had been kneading and rubbing for what seemed like hours, his breath was coming faster and faster, when suddenly he sat up and began to laugh. Clementine too had sat up, confused.

'That hair,' Dieter pointed to her naked breasts, 'that hair looks just like it's growing from your tits.'

'It's from my head,' Clementine had shrieked.

'I know,' Dieter shrieked, slapping his thigh with mirth, 'but it looks just like . . .'

Clementine blamed her parents. What right did they, did any parent have, to trust their child? What right did they have to allow you the freedom to be used and humiliated? 'Have fun, darling, and remember, I trust you.'

'Well don't!' Clementine had wanted to scream. 'Oh please don't,' she had whispered as, with a heavy heart, she walked out the front door to be young and have fun on yet another Saturday night.

At Jessica's sixteenth birthday party the gramophone played 'Those Were the Days', and all five bedrooms of the large house were occupied. Christopher had arrived on his moped. He was tall and dark and gentle, a doctor's son who demonstrated against the war in Vietnam. When the second spare room became empty, he and Clementine had gone there and made love. Alone, back in her own narrow bed, she had lain dry-eyed after hours of crying and thought of the unfairness of it all. It was God at his most Aunt Mabelish, she thought bitterly. First He gave you holy virginity and then He gave you hormones. He must have known there would be tears after bedtime.

'I trust you, I trust you implicitly,' her father had told her from behind his newspaper the next morning.

'Well you shouldn't have,' Clementine whispered to her father's grave. 'Loved me, yes; disciplined me, that too; but for heaven's sake, what induced you to trust me?'

Today was her father's birthday, which is why she had gone straight from lunch with Jessica to the florist, and then on to the churchyard. Her father's grave lay just to the right of the vestry door. His headstone had barely passed the planning laws, decorated as it was with the masks of comedy and tragedy as well as a squirrel and a wreath of stone roses. It had taken a march to the council offices by the whole of the Madox Theatre Company and an all-night candlelit vigil to make the parish council withdraw its objection.

Clementine knelt down and placed the bunch of blue and white freesias on the grave. 'From me and mother,' she mumbled. Lydia would be pleased to hear there were fresh flowers on the grave. Her love for Clementine's father had survived him ceasing to be her husband, and then ceasing to be anything at all. Now she lived in a cottage in the grounds of her oldest son's property in Cape Town where she enjoyed ill-health and her memories.

After a moment's thought, Clementine pulled a stem from the bunch and wandered off to place it on Elvira's grave. Aunt Elvira rested a little removed in the newly opened extension, sidelined in death as she had been in life. There were rules, it seemed to Clementine, as to how much grief was suitable for each death. Her father's at eighty-five, and after a long illness, was classified as a merciful release. The vicar had told the mourners that Roger Madox had had a jolly good innings and the whole tone of the service had made it clear that it would be ungrateful and rather churlish to display too much sorrow at his passing. When Gustaf's sister Ulla had died, poor thing, aged only fifty-one, her passing had merited anything from stoical grief to complete breakdown. Aunt Elvira had had the kind of funeral where everyone had a frightfully good time at tea afterwards.

Back at her father's grave, Clementine bent down and smelt the freesias. Her father had adored the scent. Once, when she was very young, Clementine had tipped the contents of her stepmother's bottle of Joy down the loo and replaced it with her own careful distillation of freesia petals in water. After all, had not Grace said just the night before, as she sat at her dressing-table dabbing scent behind her pearl-studded ears, that she liked to smell nice for her husband. Making the scent had been meant as a lovely surprise. Grace and her father had not seen it as such and Clementine had been sent to bed without her supper. She had stood there looking up at her father's outraged face and listening to the angry words that rained down and she had given up trying to explain. When you are eight years old and told you are a wicked nasty girl, you tend to believe there is something in it.

Clementine lingered by her father's grave, looking

around her at the small churchyard. This really was much the best place to rot away eternity, she thought. It was overgrown, moss infested, higgledy-piggledy. It was possible to believe that one or two graves had been mislaid, like a sock or a biro, but it was a place that had character and its own kind of melancholy charm. The graveyard equivalent of the executive property with full central heating and double garage was the Memorial Gardens on the outskirts of town. It even had its own crematorium and that, Clementine felt, said it all. She knelt down and pulled out some weeds. Soon there was a small mound of them. Her father had despised gardening but he would not like weeds growing all over his grave. He had been a man of strong views, and not only on gardening, a man so full of certainties that there often seemed no room for his family to have any certainties of their own. He had been a large man. His body, six feet five and seventeen stone, was impressive, his personality was enough for a good-size town. Clementine used to imagine him trying on different towns for size, like a pair of combinations, before settling for Aldringham. London or Birmingham, too big, they flapped around him in empty folds that he could never hope to fill. Alresford or Odiham, too small, the fabric strained and pulled until his limbs burst out from its constraint. So in the end it was Aldringham, fitting snugly, caressing his ego. He had been born into the theatre. His grandfather and namesake was Roger Madox, the Shakespearean actor. His father, Aunt Elvira's brother, was George, juvenile lead in countless West End comedies until the day before his forty-second birthday when the run of *The Errand Boy* finished and he switched to the wireless. He had died at the age of eighty, 'A voice which was a friend to millions,' as the obituary had put it. Clementine's father had founded the Madox Theatre in an old grain store on the outskirts of Aldringham, and home-counties couples came from all around to enjoy Shakespeare, Shaw and Coward, and once, but never again, Osborne. The Madox Theatre was still there, still giving its audiences what they wanted and a fairly decent dinner as well if they wished, but was no longer managed by a Madox. Timothy did take over from his father for a short while, but he had not lasted long. It had all been too safe, too predictable, and he had fled to the West End. How unlike his sister he was.

Clementine sat back on the damp grass, her back resting against her father's headstone. Roger and Lydia; their children: Roger Junior, Juliet, Timothy and Clementine; a handsome family and they knew it. Tall, straight, athletic looking, they all resembled each other, as if they were the products of some incestuous relationship, their parents looking more like brother and sister than man and wife. Our family, she thought wistfully; handsome, confident, enviable. She had photographs to prove it; albums full of them: the family alighting from Roger's old Bentley on the way to an opening night, leaving church on Christmas Day, smiling into the sun on some Cornish beach. Roger always had his arm round his wife's shoulders, and the children clustered around the parents like the fruits of their loins that they undoubtedly were.

'You don't tell me who to see or when, do you hear! I told you I'll stay and I meant it, now for heaven's sake stop your infernal whinging and let me get on with some work.'

Clementine had been on her way down to breakfast, one tall step at a time, when she heard her father's voice coming from the hall. As she turned the bend in the staircase she saw him grab her mother by the arm, giving her a little shove towards the large gilded mirror on the wall by the door. 'Look at yourself,' he hissed; 'every line on your face is one of dissatisfaction. Is it any wonder I turn to more congenial company.' He let go of her shoulder and marched into his study, slamming the door behind him. Clementine stood on the stairs looking at her mother, who stayed staring into the mirror for what seemed a very long time. She wondered if maybe her mother was playing the same game that she herself did, imagining herself going through the glass Alice like, on her way to an adventure. Then her mother turned round and saw Clementine standing there. She looked as if she was about to cry, but instead she smiled and said, 'Good morning, darling, I didn't see you there. Come along now and have some breakfast.'

Clementine had tried to smile back at her mother. 'Were you and Daddy fighting? Is that why you're sad? Are you going to cry?' She walked carefully down the last few steps.

'Oh, darling, we weren't fighting. You know Daddy and I never fight. That was just a little disagreement, that's all. And I'm not sad. What would I have to cry about?'

Clementine had thought for a moment. 'I cried yesterday,' she said finally, 'because Timothy took my new doll and swung her round and round his head until I was sure her arm would come off.'

But her mother was not really listening. 'Breakfast,' she said again. She turned away from the mirror and hurried ahead into the dining-room.

After breakfast Juliet had looked after their mother's disappearing back and said, 'Had another fight have they?'

Clementine had shaken her head vehemently. 'Mummy and Daddy don't really fight, they just have little disagreements.'

Juliet had looked at her with scorn and shrugged her shoulders. Clementine looked away, fixing her eyes on a picture above the sideboard of a man with his hands in the air trying to keep up the heavens.

That night Timothy had sung to Clementine. She was crying again and it annoyed him. 'Oh my darling, oh my darling, oh my darling Clementine, you are lost and gone for ever, dreadful sorry, Clementine.' Timothy's voice was as sweet and clear as only a seven-year-old boy's could be. The nursery was dark, but not too dark for shadows. High up in the far corner of the room Clementine could see the hawk. The others said it was the handle for the vent, but Clementine knew it was a hawk, just as she knew that her parents had really had a fight. The hawk simply made itself look like a handle during the day, it was clever like that. Clementine did not like Timothy's song either so she cried even louder. In the end, she climbed out of bed and was on her way to the door when the Girl, who had been listening to records in her room, came clomping into the nursery covered in irritation and the sweet, boyfriend-attracting scent of musk. She told Clementine not to be a silly baby and finally, when that did not help, she pulled the blanket down ·and smacked her hard on the back of her legs.

'Now if I find you out of bed again or hear one peep out of you, you'll be sorry, do you understand? And there's no point thinking you can go running to Mummy because she's not here. She's gone away for the night.' The Girl looked down at Clementine, her face alive with glee. 'For good if she has any sense.'

Timothy sat up in his bed, waiting, listening to the silence, his blond head to one side. Then he climbed out of bed and padded across the floor to Clementine. Grabbing the ribs of her high-sided bed with his small strong hands, he dragged the bed, with Clementine in it, right across the polished nursery floor to the corner where the hawk was waiting.

'You'll be sorry if she finds you out of bed again,' he singsonged, then he turned and ran back to his own bed.

'Oh my darling, oh my darling, oh my darling Clementine, you are lost and gone for ever, dreadful sorry, Clementine.'

Clementine stood in the churchyard, her fists clenched and her mouth clamped into an angry line. If Timothy had turned up now, a tall, slightly stooping, prematurely balding theatrical agent of thirty-nine, his sister might well have punched him. The sins of older brothers might be forgotten, but often they are not. Right now though, Timothy was safe in his office in the West End. With a little shiver, Clementine looked up at the darkening sky. She pulled a powder-blue cardigan from her large tan handbag and put it on. A twig snapped somewhere behind her. She looked around, but there was no-one there. She was all alone in the churchyard with an ever-darkening summer sky threatening rain, and she scrambled up from the ground with her bag. Remembering the weeds, she bent down quickly and picked them up. After all, where would it end if *nice* people went around littering churchyards? Looking around for a bin she spotted a wire-netting basket right by the hedge which divided the church grounds from the canal. As she got closer she heard a man's voice humming and, raising herself on tiptoe, she looked over the hedge.

He sat quite still on the grass verge that ran down from the footpath to the water, long legs stretched in front of him. In one hand he was holding a bottle of whisky, in the other a glass. A very nice cut-crystal glass, Clementine noticed. He was humming, in a pleasant baritone, some melody she knew but could not place. Feeling he was being watched, the man went silent and turned round. Clementine dropped the weeds. There before her sat Prince Hat. Granted, this was not a kingdom underground but the canal footpath, and granted that it was a bottle of whisky in his hand not a lute, but his hair was dark and wavy, falling untidily across his forehead which was wide and as pale as alabaster, and the eyes that smiled at her in a slightly unfocused way were large and luminous. She could not see their colour from where she was standing, but she knew they were green.

'Hat,' she gasped.

The man smiled amiably, waving the glass at her. Clementine dived down behind the hedge, gathering up the weeds that lay scattered across the gravel path.

'That's right, Nat. Well done!' The man had got to his feet and was peering down at her from the other side of the hedge. 'But to be absolutely brutally honest, I prefer Nathaniel. You don't mind do you?' Swaying slightly, he frowned with concentration as he looked at her. Clementine put the weeds in the bin and was about to walk off when he exclaimed, 'You're the girl from next door, that's who you are. I've seen you.' He sounded triumphant, as if he had just solved a major question in his life.

Clementine turned back. 'You're Nathaniel Scott?'

'Absolutely,' he said. He seemed delighted at the thought. Looking around him, he leant closer to the hedge. 'I came here to drink.'

'Oh but you're not supposed to,' Clementine could not help saying; 'you're not drinking any more.'

'Oh yes I am,' Nathaniel exclaimed, holding up the bottle and the glass. His eyes – green eyes, she had been right – focused. He looked intently at her, then he pulled his mouth down in a little half smile. 'You're right. I'm a prat.'

'I didn't say that.'

'I did. Don't argue with me.'

Clementine felt she ought to take offence, but the trouble was she felt no real inclination to.

'I'm coming over.' With great care, Nathaniel handed first the bottle then the glass to Clementine. Then he started to try and heave himself over the hedge.

'You won't do it,' Clementine said.

Nathaniel dropped back down onto the footpath. 'You're right,' he said again. 'Look after these,' he pointed at the bottle and the glass, before wandering off up the path towards the churchyard entrance.

Clementine could not make up her mind whether to stay or not. Was he really Nathaniel Scott? Had he actually said he was or had he just gone along with her suggestion that he was? He could have made up having seen her next door. After all, it was a pretty safe bet that she would live next door to someone. Maybe he was just a very good-looking psychopath? And there she was, waiting for him, holding his glass and bottle even. She was just about to leave them on the gravel and run for it when she spotted him ambling through the lych-gate and up the path towards her.

'I have arrived,' he called, waving his long arms in the air. 'I think I shall walk you home.'

Clementine could hear the defence council at the rape trial. 'So, Mrs Hope, let me get this straight; alone in a churchyard, having tended your father's grave, and what a laudable deed that was, if I may say so, you were approached by a complete stranger in a state of intoxication who proceeded to ask you to wait for him to join you?'

'I just hate being rude,' she would explain. 'I really hate it.'

'Come on, come on, come on,' Nathaniel said impatiently. 'Are we going or not?'

'Actually,' Clementine said, avoiding his eyes, 'I've got some shopping to do.' She handed him the glass and the bottle.

'All right, that's fine with me,' Nathaniel swung round a little unsteadily and wandered back down the path. At the gate, he turned and waved before disappearing from view.

Clementine waited a moment before walking out onto the street. A car alarm began its insistent wail as, with a look at the dark sky, she crossed Canal Street. The lights of a white Ford Granada were flashing, the alarm kept on sounding, and as she passed, Clementine looked into the impassive face of a veiled

70

woman sitting alone in the passenger seat. Cars drove by, shoppers and children on their way home from school hurried past, but most did not even glance in the direction of the Granada. There had not been that many alarmed cars around Clementine's house by the lake, so maybe that was why she stopped and walked the few steps back. Pressing her face against the window she mouthed, 'Is everything all right,' at the woman inside. The woman looked at her and then she gave a little nod, before turning her face away.

As Clementine straightened up, a raindrop hit the tip of her nose. She brought her umbrella out from her bag and went on her way. She looked back a couple of times and by the time she had reached the pedestrian crossing at the top of the street the alarm had stopped sounding. A couple came up beside her. The man had his arm around the woman's shoulders, and as she looked up at him and smiled, he bent his neck and kissed her; a deep, lingering kiss, for all the world to see. The light changed and Clementine hurried across. She was keen to get home before it began to pour. It was sadly indicative of her personality, Clementine thought, this reluctance to get even a little bit wet. She yearned to be the kind of woman who stood, head back, hands outstretched, laughing at the sky, telling it who was boss. You met them all the time in the television ads, stepping out of dinky cars and into an admiring circle of men with slicked-back hair and more than their fair share of teeth. But it was the life-enhancing acceptance of whatever was thrown at you which Clementine envied so.

It was raining heavily by the time she turned into Wagon Lane. The street ahead was deserted. Clementine slowed down. Looking around her, she tilted her umbrella back like a parasol and lifted her face to the sky. A fat raindrop exploded in her left eye. Rain trickled from her hair down her face. Clamping her eyes shut, she made a half-hearted twirl, and then

71

another, more assertive this time, coming to a halt right by the window of Pandora's Box. She opened her eyes to meet the stony gaze of the sales assistant inside. Clementine grinned apologetically; the assistant did not smile back. Clementine raised her umbrella once more and continued her walk.

Twelve years ago, when the shop had first opened, Clementine had looked around the rows of suits and floral silk frocks, the racks of shoes and the handbags and hats stacked on high shelves, and she had asked the owner, conversationally, 'Aren't you being a little hard on yourself?' She just wanted something to say while she was trying on a large black hat with a huge velvet bow at the front. The woman had looked at her blankly. Maybe, Clementine had thought at the time, she was busy wondering, as shopkeepers must at times, why women always try on hats but hardly ever buy them and, equally mysteriously, whatever happens to the ones that are bought, because they tend never to be seen again.

'The name of your shop,' Clementine had explained. 'You know, Pandora's Box, whence all the evils of the world were released? No?' By then, even Clementine had not found her comment very amusing.

It had been two years before she had dared to go into that shop again.

'What makes you think the woman will remember you for a day, let alone years,' Gustaf had said to her one day when she had flatly refused to go into Pandora's Box to look for a present for his mother. 'That really is having a rather inflated idea of your own importance.' He had said it kindly, though, in a smiling, fatherly sort of way.

Home truths, Clementine thought now as she trundled through the rain, she had never cared for them. After all, when did you last hear a nice one?

In the High Street she passed the couple that had been kissing at the pedestrian crossing. They were standing at the bus stop, and it was quite obvious to anyone looking that they would be quite happy to wait for ever. They were standing facing each other, talking, smiling; his arms around her waist, hers around his neck. The look in the woman's eyes as she gazed up at the man sent Clementine scurrying across the street, blushing with envy and longing. She, Clementine, would most probably die without ever having looked at anyone with eyes like that.

She felt restless as she arrived home, and her heart was beating just a little too fast. She tried to concentrate on putting the shopping away neatly, in just the right places. She drew the curtains although it was broad daylight still, and made herself some tea. After a moment's hesitation she went to the cake tin and brought out the lemon sponge cake, cutting herself a generous piece. Still her heart was beating uncomfortably fast. She was probably just tired, she decided, as she pottered across to the dresser to fetch Mrs Granquist. The book lay in the bottom drawer. It had once belonged to Gustaf's mother who had given it to Clementine on her wedding day. It was bound in pearly grey with pink letters saying in Swedish: *Mrs Granquist's Guide to Graceful Living.* Underneath the title was a photograph of Mrs Granquist herself, blond hair set in loose curls and tucked behind her pearl-studded ears; red lips smiling just right, not too much so that she showed all her teeth, but not too tightly so that she looked mean. Mrs Granquist was wearing a blue and white gingham skirt, a white blouse and a pretty white apron with a frilled edge and, all in all, she could give Doris Day a run for her money any day. Clementine put the book together with the cake and the tea on a tray and brought it into the sitting-room. With a little sigh, she sat down on the sofa and opened the book at the chapter headed: 'Banish that Monday morning melancholy'. As her eyes scanned the well-thumbed page, she felt herself relaxing. It was not

Monday or even morning, but as always, Mrs Granquist was such a comfort. 'Even I', Mrs Granquist admitted, 'have at times fallen victim to that Monday morning feeling, but, as all true devotees of graceful living know, the answer is not to give in. No, get busier than ever around that haven, your home, and make those little improvements your family is sure to appreciate when they return from their busy day. Is every room a showcase for nature's bounty? Are your vases filled?' Clementine shook her head. 'No-one', continued Mrs Granquist, 'who enters a home filled with flowers can fail to recognize its mistress as a woman of true taste and refinement. Whatever the season, there is sure to be something on offer at Mother Nature's table. So, reader, what are you waiting for?'

Clementine was just waiting for her tea to cool down sufficiently to drink, and then she nipped out into the garden, fetching the secateurs from the small shed. It had stopped raining and the sun was making a tentative return through the clouds. As she put her hand in amongst the branches of the climbing rose, the water trapped amongst its leaves drizzled down on her and she turned and shook herself. The sparrow taking a bath in a puddle on the gravel path looked at her with his black button eyes and shook himself right back. She picked some catmint to go with the pink and the red roses and then she went back inside and arranged them nicely in two vases.

Chapter Five

It was a good ten minutes now since they had heard any sound from downstairs. 'I think he's gone,' Clementine said finally, but she was still whispering, just in case. Mr Scott just nodded, his face glistening in the moonlight. 'It's getting cold,' Clementine shivered and pulled her cardigan closer around her neck, yet Mr Scott seemed to be sweating ever more profusely.

'I remember Nathaniel telling me about your first meeting,' he said, his voice a little stronger. 'There he was, standing in the kitchen doorway, hiding the bottle behind his back like a naughty child. "I've just met a very beautiful woman," he said, "and she lives next door."'

'He barely said hello the next time I saw him,' Clementine said. 'He just muttered something as he hurried on down the street.'

'If it's the drink problem that's worrying you, I think maybe you're making too much of it. I had a problem myself once. A lot of us did out there. I got over it. Nathaniel will too, I'm sure of it.'

'It was much more than that,' Clementine looked unhappily at him across the dark room. 'I had a perfectly good life. My nice little house, my family and friends, my work, the fairy tales. I was quite content for me.' She wrung her large hands. 'I was quite content,' she repeated, and she buried her head in her arm, stifling her sobs with the sleeve of her grey cardigan.

*   *   *

Clementine slept in her narrow bed, her long hair fanning out across the white lace pillow. A crack in the curtains allowed a shaft of light to find its way through the room, shining straight onto Clementine's face, waking her. It was just as well; she had a busy day ahead, she thought self-importantly as she bustled down to the kitchen in her dressing-gown, filling the kettle, fetching the post. Well, busy for her, not, she suspected, for the Chair of East Hants Council, or a stockbroker, or a mother of four children under five, but busy for her, Clementine Hope, an occasional visitor to reality.

'I've got three new pupils starting this week,' she told Ophelia over breakfast. 'A little girl this afternoon. I think she could be interesting. For a start it sounds as if she's turning up by her own free will. The mother told me that Beatrice, that's the child's name, had been in tears for a week after her previous teacher, Miss Hoffman, retired to Cornwall. I'm picking up quite a few of Miss Hoffman's former pupils.' She raised her teacup in the air. 'So rejoice, we'll eat another day.'

'Don't be ridiculous,' Ophelia glared at her through unadorned eyes. It was seven in the morning and Ophelia had not got to bed until two. She was wearing no make-up, Clementine noted enviously, and she still looked gorgeous.

'Are you really not wearing any make-up, not even the tiniest little bit of Mac's malt-coloured eye-shadow?'

'You haven't got a mortgage and then there's the money from Daddy, so please don't pretend you have any worries in that direction.' Ophelia reached across the table and helped herself to another slice of whole-meal toast.

Clementine looked downcast. Ophelia was right. But she had just wanted to try the phrase out. She had thought it might sound sort of hip and laid back, a brave smile and a, 'Hi, it's OK, we'll eat another day.'

'I know people who worry about where their next meal is going to come from,' Ophelia said, rubbing it in. 'It's obscene for you to talk like that.' She reached over for the honey.

Clementine hung her head. She agreed with Ophelia in every way. It had just sounded nicer than the truth: 'Oh goodie, even more money to add to the totally unearned and not inconsiderable amount I rake in every month.'

She topped up her blue and yellow breakfast cup with Darjeeling tea. 'Sometimes I feel you can't sink much lower than being middle-class, middle-wealth and middle-aged. I suppose I'm middle-aged,' she added, reluctantly, hoping to be contradicted. She was not. 'Middle-class and struggling, you even get your own literary genre,' she complained. 'Filthy rich, of any background and at least you're interesting, if only as a hate object. Working class, you're always pretty interesting. If you've made it, you're admired and if you haven't, you have theses written about why not, and questions asked in parliament. If you're a member of the aristocracy you're a cherished symbol of our national decline.'

'Stop complaining and get real yourself,' Ophelia said.

'Ha! How?'

'Life is a bowl of cherries,' Ophelia said, not really concentrating it seemed to Clementine. 'Dig in.'

Clementine thought life was more like a bowl of custard, and she herself just a fly glopping around on the surface, so lightweight, so insignificant that she did not even leave a footprint. All around her people lived real lives, surrounded by family and colleagues and money problems. Of course she had a family: mother, stepmother, sister, stepsister, brothers, nephews, nieces, but they were extended family and that meant that they stayed as far away from each other as they could without the family bonds snapping altogether.

'Maybe I should give away my unearned income?' she said.

Ophelia looked appalled. 'Of course you shouldn't. What you earn is nothing like enough to keep this place up and live decently. You'd have to sell the house and then where would we be?'

'Carving out our own small corner of reality,' Clementine tried. 'It would probably make me grow as an artist.'

'Artist? Oh, you mean your music.'

Clementine felt that the day, which had started so positively, was taking a distinctly depressing turn. 'Well, I have to get a move on,' she said without moving at all. 'I've got to post these fliers.' She showed Ophelia the contents of the large brown parcel which had been delivered earlier that morning. 'Individual tuition in Piano and Harpsichord. Pupils of any age and levels of skill welcome. For further details contact Clementine Hope on Aldringham 57236,' she read out. For reasons of safety she had not given her address. They still had not caught the man who had robbed and beaten poor old Violet Hopkins. Clementine saw before her a leering face beneath close-cropped fair hair. Maybe he had moved on; maybe he kept moving from one burgled, vandalized, murderous town to another; then again, maybe he was still in Aldringham, lying low, waiting. With a shudder of unease she remembered Abigail Challis's boyfriend.

Ophelia took one of the fliers, glancing at it before standing up. 'Nice,' she said. 'I won't be back until late.

I've got an installation to finish.' She was off and Clementine was left with the dishes, again. Her day was obviously still not busy enough.

On her way out she stopped by Mr Scott's house. She wanted to ask him if he was sure her giving lessons would not disturb him.

'I hear you've met Nathaniel,' Mr Scott said.

'So it was him!' Clementine exclaimed. 'He said he was, but I wasn't absolutely sure.'

Mr Scott looked confused. 'Is it your experience that people turn out to be someone else?'

'No. Not really.' Then, because Mr Scott looked in such a kindly way at her, and because he was not sneering or laughing at her like Ophelia and Jessica, she went on. 'It's like all the worrying has carved a groove through my mind, so that now all my thoughts run in the same direction. I see something and I think, That's lovely, but wait a minute, where's the snag? Where's that problem hiding, I know it's there somewhere?'

'My old nanny used to say "Don't trouble trouble until trouble troubles you,"' Mr Scott said.

'It's my experience that most nannies do,' Clementine said, 'but I never found it all that helpful. The last nanny to say that to me, well she was more of a mother's help really, left us to become a patient in a mental hospital; I don't know whether or not that had anything to do with it.' She stopped, realizing that she was keeping poor Mr Scott standing on the doorstep in just his stocking feet.

'I actually just came over to make sure that my giving piano lessons won't disturb you too much. I can hear music faintly from your house, but it never comes across very loudly, so I hope it's the same way this end.'

'Of course, of course. Anyway, I enjoy listening to you. Don't give it another thought.'

And that was that. Now she should take her leave,

but she did not. She hung around waiting, waiting for what? She craned her neck, looking past Mr Scott into the hall. Mr Scott looked expectantly at her. Clementine smiled.

'Oh well,' she said at last, 'I'd better be off. I've got a busy day,' she added, feeling that Mr Scott would be more receptive to that kind of talk than Ophelia.

The sun was shining and out on the street the Japanese cherries bowed towards her in the wind like so many geisha girls aiming to please. She strode down the road, back straight, head high, just in case Mr Scott was watching ready to pass comment to his son. 'Handsome girl that Clementine,' she would like him to say; 'big but handsome.'

As she wandered on, she glanced approvingly at the gas-pipe marker that stood like a tiny tombstone a few yards from the house. The sight of it always cheered her up. It was a sign of order and cooperation. You sink a gas pipe into the road, and then, thoughtfully, you mark it. Like when someone pulled up their car to allow you to pass on a narrow stretch of road; a nod, a smile, a hand raised in thanks: it gave you hope. 'Order and cooperation,' she mumbled to herself. She walked down the High Street thinking about her collection of fairy tales. How different she was from poor old Aunt Elvira. There was Clementine with her plans for six volumes of stories, her untried heart, her quiet life in Aunt Elvira's house, her undisturbed nights in Aunt Elvira's bedroom. How utterly the same. With a little cry of dismay, she aimed a kick at the black bin-liner left outside the pub. Then she looked up to meet the disapproving gaze of a passing matron, shopping basket firmly in place in the crook of her arm. On top of it all, Clementine thought, I'll soon be a passing matron. A tall, wild-haired matron maybe, but a matron just the same.

She arrived in the square, a bunch of the fliers in her hand. She looked around at the pretty shop fronts with their wrought-iron signs and geranium-filled hanging baskets. Between them, those little shops could provide you with practically everything: American patchwork quilts, pot-pourri, gold bangles, Waterford crystal, Guerlain scents, doormats with geese and Home Sweet Home woven onto them, anything in fact, as long as it was not strictly useful. A couple of years earlier the recession had come to Aldringham. Each time Clementine had come back to visit another shop had closed. It had started with the sports shop. The row of look-at-me trainers thinned out, and the shoes themselves took on a dusty, seen-better-days air, that made you feel you might as well go somewhere else entirely. They stopped stocking ski gear, and there were no more waiting-lists for the £180 croquet sets. The clearance sale followed like the last precipitous stage of some contagious disease, and the shop was gone with its lycra feel-good message and bouncy young staff. Next it had been the turn of Life's Little Luxuries. It had not come as a surprise to Clementine. In the four years of its existence, right next to the Chocolate House, she had never seen its stock vary: tights and stockings, knickers but no bras, tartan umbrellas and fake leather bags with initials all over them. On Clementine's last visit, just before her mother's move to South Africa, she had found the greetings card shop gone. Clementine had been sorry to see it go. The couple who ran it kept a German shepherd dog with ears like a rabbit in the back room, and it was the only place Clementine knew of where one could buy a badge with '63 today!' on it. Now new shops were appearing. Only the other week The Flying Carpet, specializing in oriental rugs, had opened its doors. Clementine decided to start there. A pink slip of paper advertising the Aldringham Players' production of *The Merry Widow*, was already posted in the far corner of the window, right above the public seat outside in the cobbled yard.

Stepping inside was rather like entering a bedouin tent, or at least, Clementine thought, the Turkish delight version of one. The walls were hung with rugs, every inch of floor was covered, and rugs were flung across chairs and tops of tables and dark wooden chests. As the door shut behind her, a wind chime alerted a small man who came bouncing out from behind yet another rug that hung like a tent flap across the doorway at the back of the shop.

'Good morning,' he beamed, rocking back and forth on his heels. 'I'm John Melchett, owner of this establishment.Welcome,' he added, as if that had ever been in doubt. He pushed a shock of blond hair from his lined forehead. 'And what can I show you?' he made a sweeping gesture across the expanse of rugs.

Clementine hid the bunch of fliers behind her back. He looked so hopeful, as if Clementine visiting his shop was what he had wished for all week. 'Just looking around,' she smiled, slipping the fliers into her bag.

'Go right ahead,' John Melchett said. 'Enjoy,' he added, but he seemed less bouncy all of a sudden.

'Beautiful carpets,' Clementine tried to cheer him up again.

A woman with a baby in a pushchair backed in through the door; she wanted to know the price of a small rug in the window. It was £800.

'Eight hundred,' the woman shrieked. 'I only want it to cover a stain.' She turned the buggy on its heel and marched off towards the door, waiting for John Melchett to hold it open for her. 'Eight hundred pounds,' they heard her mutter as the door closed behind her and the chimes played.

Clementine had planned to leave, but the resigned look on the little man's face kept her there, wandering around the shop, admiring the rugs, making interested noises. Again the chime tinkled and an elderly couple wandered in. John Melchett excused himself and hurried across to greet them, arms outstretched. 'And how can I help you?'

The woman glanced around her before turning to her husband. 'No, dear, I don't think this is at all the type of thing we are looking for. I told you, Randalls.' Her husband nodded and followed her to the door. 'I said all along we should try Randalls,' her voice complained above the tinkling chimes.

John Melchett stood looking after them as they disappeared down the square, his manicured hands caressing a small rug arranged across the back of a chair, as if he was trying to comfort it for failing to please.

'Such a nice name for a carpet shop, The Flying Carpet,' Clementine tried. 'Oh and isn't that a gorgeous one, this one here, the yellow and red one. Normally I don't care for yellow and red together. Yellow and red tulips for example; horrible. But this, this is lovely, like a sunrise. Over the desert,' she added for good measure.

John Melchett had stopped stroking the little rug and had joined her in front of the large Persian. 'I have to admit that it's one of my particular favourites,' he said, but with a furtive air, as if the others might hear and feel slighted. 'It might end up in my little flat if it doesn't get sold.'

'How much is it?'

'One thousand six hundred pounds, that one.'

'One thousand six hundred pounds,' Clementine repeated, feigning nonchalance. 'Right.' She had practised for years until she could stand in any shop, anywhere, and be told any price and remain seemingly unfazed. It had started when she went into a gift shop in Bond Street to buy Gustaf an engagement present. 'Now that's lovely,' she had said to the assistant, pointing at a bottle-green leather desk set. 'How much is it?'

The assistant, a middle-aged woman with steel-grey

hair that sat like a hat on her head, had glanced up at her from a ledger, taking in Clementine's duffle-coat and wind-blown hair. 'It's very expensive. Top of the range,' she said nasally.

'But how much?'

The woman had told her the sum with a triumphant little smile, waiting for Clementine's blushed exit.

The price of the desk set was about as much as Clementine's entire monthly salary, but she had smiled back at the woman and said, 'That's fine, I'll take it.'

But poor John Melchett was different. He looked at Clementine, just waiting to be told what a fool he was for imagining he could sell his rug here in Aldringham. An as good as hand-quilted bedspread for £300; yes, Clementine thought, there would be a taker for that. She had seen a woman buy £100 worth of very realistic silk flowers, but she could not envisage a buyer for this £1,600 rug, although it did look like a desert sunset.

'It's just a little bit more than I had planned to spend,' she said, reminding herself that she had not planned to spend anything at all, 'but it really is the most beautiful rug. I can just imagine some sloe-eyed beauty sitting cross-legged right there in the centre of that garland of flowers, telling stories to a hushed circle of listeners. She probably found most of the stories right here in the rug.' She pointed to the bottom right corner where a posse of huntsmen on horseback chased a panther across a pattern of rushes. The hunter closest to the fleeing animal had his spear raised high above his head, ready to strike, and the panther was looking back, right at him, fear showing through the whites of his eyes.

'Of course, that's no ordinary panther,' she said. 'I'm quite sure it gets away. I suspect it metamorphoses into a bird and takes off right at the moment when the spear flies through the air.'

'There are four hundred knots to the square inch,'

John Melchett said, his baby-blue eyes opened wide. 'Now if you look here', he got down on his knees and turned a flap of the rug over, 'you can see the knots.' Clementine knelt down beside him, feeling the roughness of the unvarnished floorboards through her tights.

'Now a lesser rug would have just a handful per inch, but this rug would have been worked on for at least a year and by three, even four women. And then people are amazed at the cost.'

'Maybe they're not so much amazed as not very wealthy,' Clementine tried to soothe him.

He did not seem to have heard. Getting up from the floor, he said, 'Now I'd love your opinion on this one. It's not as colourful, but the design is most unusual.'

Clementine scrambled up from the floor with her bag full of fliers. 'I'd love to have a look,' she said, basking for a moment in his delight at having found such a keen customer. Basking that is, until she remembered that she had no intention of buying a rug. Embarrassed, she followed him across the shop. This rug was smaller, dark-hued with a dull-gold thread running through it. Draped over an old oak barrel at the back of the shop, it seemed to carry its own light. 'It shines like an amethyst,' Clementine said.

John Melchett nodded. 'It has rather a sad story attached to it. It used to belong to a very prominent family, owners of a string of quite glorious hotels. I knew one of the sons from a winter holiday. He was a quite wonderful skier. Very naughty in the evenings but always up bright and early on the slopes the next day. He committed suicide, or so his parents were told. The father suffered a stroke on hearing the news; he, too, died. Their daughter, a university lecturer, is in prison, but no-one has heard anything from her in years. The last remaining child, another son, works as a bellboy in one of the hotels his father used to own. The mother sold it to me. This rug was practically the only possession she had left from her old life.' His face brightened. 'I should love you to have it. You'd appreciate it properly. I'll give you a very fair price.'

Clementine glanced at her watch, feeling trapped. She had been in John Melchett's shop for over half an hour, leading him on like some Fifties college girl in the back of a Cadillac, and now she was about to smooth down her hair, pick up her purse and abandon him, right at the point of fulfilment. There was a name for women like that, she thought. Making a quick calculation in her head she worked out that she had a little over £500 in her current account and about £2,000 in her savings account. A fair amount of that was needed for the month's housekeeping and then there was the outstanding tax and the telephone. . . Maybe she could sell some shares or another painting?

'Let me go home and take some measurements,' she said at last, 'and go through my accounts, just to make sure,' she continued, as the smile died in his eyes. 'Maybe you could put the amethyst one on hold for me, just until the end of the week.'

That did it. John Melchett's face brightened once more and he walked Clementine to the door.

'Certainly I'll keep it on hold for you,' he said as the chime tinkled above their heads.

'Of course, if someone comes in and really wants it you mustn't think of not selling it to them.'

'Absolutely not, Mrs . . . ?'

'Simpson.'

'Mrs Simpson. Now don't you worry. It's yours.'

Clementine smiled helplessly at him and hurried off down the square. She had to have two large cups of milky coffee to get over the shame of leading poor John Melchett on in that way. And then there was the problem of how to get past his shop for the next weeks and months without being recognized. She would have to wear dark glasses and a scarf, that burgundy and gold one her mother had given her two Christmases ago. She paid for her coffee and handed a bunch of fliers to Mrs Challis. 'Would you mind leaving a few of these on the counter?' she asked.

Mrs Challis looked approvingly at the papers in her hand. 'I'd be delighted, Mrs Hope.' She smiled her frosted smile. 'I like to think of myself as a supporter of the arts. Anything that keeps these young hooligans off the streets and doing something sensible like learning the piano has my approval.'

Clementine wondered whether it was worth pointing out that nice as the thought was, precious few hooligans came along asking for piano lessons. One thought led to another and she found herself asking Mrs Challis, 'How is Abigail? And Derek? Does he go out a lot at night, late, on his own?'

Mrs Challis looked a little surprised. 'Abigail has never complained about it to me. I think they stay in most nights. Derek likes the television. He's especially partial to the *Antiques Roadshow*, she says. *Antiques Roadshow*, who would have thought it, great big lump as he is.' Mrs Challis glanced round the shop, making sure there were no customers waiting before continuing. 'He has a temper though. He ranted on for hours the other Sunday when Abigail forgot to tape it for him. "Tell that Derek to tape his own programmes," I said. He's got one of those video recorders in every room, so he boasts.'

Has he now, Clementine thought as she hurried along to the bookshop; has he really. She posted her fliers in the bookshop and the music shop and then she made her way to the supermarket.

As she approached Safeways she heard a tangle of badly played guitar chords and an unmelodious voice accompanying the playing. The sound, making passers by frown and wrinkle their noses as they hurried on, came from a scruffy man, half hidden behind the pillars at the front entrance to the supermarket. A beaten-up bowler hat lay upside down on the ground at his feet. Clementine looked away, all around her, upwards, scanning the sky, such an interesting place, while she attempted to dislodge a trolley from the back of a row. As the man broke into a loud rendering of 'The House of the Rising Sun', she managed to yank her trolley free and back in through the large mechanical doors of the supermarket.

She concentrated on her shopping list. 'Apples, crisp ones,' Ophelia had added in her small even hand. Clementine felt annoyed. You can't go around despising other people's lives and then expect them, just like that, to buy you apples whenever you wanted some. Anyway, with large chunks of humanity suffering – here her thoughts returned uncomfortably to the dishevelled busker, before hurrying on – with people knifed to death over a pittance and children being beaten to death by their parents for the sin of having been born, Clementine's life was pretty damn good. In fact, it would be downright indecent, provocative in fact, to try for more. Feeling decisive, she stopped at a display of Golden Delicious, putting three in a bag, although she knew full well that Ophelia had meant those pea-green Granny Smiths. It was a funny name, Granny Smith, for an apple as hard and sharp tasting as that, she thought as she manoeuvred her trolley along the fruit and vegetable aisle. If Clementine knew anything abut women called Granny Smith, it was that they liked their apples rosy and mushy and kind to dentures.

The busker had moved on by the time she got out of the shop, once more leaving a clear view of the black and gold neo-Dickensian rubbish bin. The sun was still shining, but the wind was picking up, shoving her along from behind, catching in the plastic bags, blowing her hair all across her eyes.

As she turned into Canal Street, she thought she saw Nathaniel Scott. The man, tall and dark, dressed in a black leather jacket, with a large black bag slung across his shoulder was striding up the road. She admired how straight he was walking. No swaying now.

'Oh dear, is that the time,' Clementine muttered, pretending to herself that her hurrying had nothing to do with wishing to catch-up with Nathaniel.

Chapter Six

'I'll never forget you turning up on our doorstep that day,' Mr Scott said. 'Out of breath, your hair tangled across your face. What was it you said? Oh that's it, "I just wanted to let you know that Golden Delicious are on special offer at Safeways."' He chuckled, covering his mouth with a veined hand to muffle the sound.

He probably need not have worried. An hour had gone by and still there was no sound from downstairs. No, the intruder was gone all right, but they were stuck in the attic until Nathaniel returned and, by now, Clementine was more worried about Mr Scott's heart than anything else. The thing to do was open the window and shout out for help. But like the baptized Vikings who sacrificed a bit on the side to their old Norse gods just in case, Clementine hesitated to abandon herself entirely to her belief. After all, the man might just possibly be lurking there still. Maybe he was having a break. The best thing to do for the moment, she decided, was to keep Mr Scott calm; to take his mind off their predicament. Nice normal cheerful conversation was the thing.

'It's a real blessing, don't you think,' she said, 'that the HIV virus can't survive for long outside the body.'

*   *   *

90

By the time Clementine reached her own black wrought-iron gate, Nathaniel had already disappeared inside his father's house. But instead of going home herself, Clementine walked right past the house and up to Mr Scott's front door, as if pulled along by an invisible rope. It would be nice, she thought as her hand pressed the doorbell, to be able to blame some spell cast over her for her silliness, but not, it had to be admitted, in the slightest bit realistic.

'Clementine,' Mr Scott beamed at her. 'How nice to . . .'

'Apples,' Clementine interrupted breathlessly. 'I just wanted to let you know that Golden Delicious are on special offer at Safeways.'

If Mr Scott was surprised, he did not show it. Instead he thanked her for her thoughtfulness and asked her in for coffee. Clementine accepted, thinking that what she would really like was a nice poisoned chalice to end her humiliation.

Nathaniel was in the kitchen, standing reading the paper which was spread right across the Formica table top. 'Clementine came over to tell us about a special offer at the supermarket,' Mr Scott told him.

Nathaniel looked surprised and he showed it. Clementine closed her eyes, imagining herself sinking silently right through the linoleum, down, down, down. Damn! Who should she see when she hit the bottom? Prince Hat, with his remarkable resemblance to Nathaniel Scott.

'You're tired,' Mr Scott said, his voice all warm with concern. She opened her eyes. 'Come and sit down. Take the weight off your feet.' He bustled up to the sink and filled the kettle.

Clementine did what she was told, wishing, as she sank down on the pink and blue patchwork cushion, that it was as easy to take the weight off one's mind. Nathaniel smiled at her and folded up the paper, putting it away neatly on the window-sill behind the table. Clementine wondered for the hundredth time why it was that she felt it was her duty and hers alone to break a silence. Even with twenty people in the room, it was the same thing; it all hinged on her to rescue the situation, make an effort, make a fool of herself. But not now. This time she would be serene and relaxed. If she had something to say she would say it, otherwise not. She looked around the kitchen, counting the chipped mugs lined up on the old oak dresser by the glass-fronted back door. There were seven. The silence grew. A handsome mahogany-cased clock ticked away the seconds on the wall above the door. She gave up.

'I can hear you play your lute . . . I mean your guitar through our sitting-room wall. Not that you're disturbing us or anything. No, it's actually very nice. Then I expect you've heard me play too.' She gave a little laugh. 'Not that I expect you to enjoy that racket. It probably annoys the pants off you.' She stopped, feeling herself blush, as an image of Nathaniel without his pants appeared before her eyes.

'I told you we love listening to you playing.' Mr Scott joined them at the table bringing a tray with three mugs of coffee and some milk and sugar.

'Absolutely,' Nathaniel agreed. 'Of course, if you could keep it down just a little during *The Bill*.'

'He's joking, of course,' Mr Scott said.

Clementine looked at Nathaniel and he looked back at her in that pleasant, remote way of his. She searched his face for a flicker of recognition. Surely, if she had recognized him from so many dreams, he had to know her too. Deep down in his subconscious there had to be an image of a large brown-haired princess? But there was no recognition in Nathaniel's green eyes, just detached amusement. She sipped her coffee and made small talk as best she could. Nathaniel told her he had been to Stockholm.

'I did a piece on the city following Palme's murder.'

Clementine shook her head. 'No place is safe any more.'

'Not many places were,' Mr Scott said.

'But it's the mindlessness, the brutishness of it all,' Clementine's voice rose. 'An upstanding citizen beaten senseless for the hell of it, here; a young girl set upon and raped, there. A pensioner bashed to the ground for the sake of a pound . . . Where are we all going?'

'I'm a fatalist,' Nathaniel said, rather stupidly in Clementine's opinion. 'If your number is up it's up. You can't spend your life worrying about it.'

Wanna bet? Clementine thought. She gazed at his pale face and his distant eyes, and the yearning to reach out and touch him was so strong it made her fingers twitch. Pulling back against the back of her chair, she said, 'But you can lengthen the odds; having rope-ladders in a couple of upstairs rooms for example, in case of fire or burglary.' She turned to Mr Scott. 'You should have at least one you know.'

Mr Scott smiled and shook his head. 'I can't really see myself scampering down a rope-ladder, whatever the circumstances,' he said. 'No, I think I'd rather take my chances with the fire or the burglar.'

Nathaniel fiddled with a packet of Marlboro which he had pulled from the pocket of his khaki-coloured corduroy trousers, drumming it against the edge of the table. 'You don't mind if I smoke do you?' he asked Clementine.

Of course she minded. Had he never heard of passive smoking? And her hair would smell for hours, and then when she woke in the morning her pillow would smell too, unless, of course, she washed her hair, but that really took for ever and she had not planned to wash it until the next day.

'Of course not,' she smiled. 'You go right ahead.'

'So,' Nathaniel inhaled deeply, leaning back in his chair, 'you teach the piano.' He made it sound paltry somehow. She would have preferred, 'You teach music,' or better still, 'So, you're a musician.'

'Amongst other things,' she answered airily. There was a pause while she waited for him to ask, 'What other things?'

'What other things?' Mr Scott said.

'I collect fairy tales.' Was that a smirk on Nathaniel's face?

'I'm afraid I've never had much time for fairy tales,' Mr Scott said.

'Quite,' Nathaniel agreed, shifting in his chair, crossing one long leg over the other.

'Fairy tales', Clementine said, feeling her cheeks turn pink with irritation, 'are distillations of age-old truths and dreams dreamt through centuries. They span time and continents, they deal with the strongest human emotions: love, aspiration, fear, greed, courage. What you should ask yourself is, with the short time allotted to us, can we afford not to read fairy tales?'

With a nod to Nathaniel she carried on, feeling like a novice skier hurtling down a black run, 'In my opinion it's photography that's the real enemy of truth. You capture a moment in time, isolating it from its past and its future, and then you call it reality when it's simply a twitch with aspirations to be a grand gesture.'

'If you say so,' Nathaniel smiled amiably at her.

The man was a marshmallow, nothing made an impression; a moron, blind to anything other than the bottle; blind like Prince Hat, she thought, softening already. Now she thought about it, he looked awfully tired. She had upset him, or maybe simply bored him. She drained her mug and stood up, narrowly missing hitting her head against the pewter lamp that hung above the table.

'Nathaniel made the cover of *Time* magazine last year, Rwanda,' Mr Scott said.

'Oh. How wonderful.' The large brown-haired princess retreated in confusion.

94

Ophelia was returning from college just as Clementine reached the front door. 'So what's he like, our drunk?' she asked.

'I have no idea,' Clementine said crossly, 'other than that I should report him to the advertising standards people for being packaged like a prince and acting like a prat.'

'You'd never win,' Ophelia said pushing the door open and stepping into the hall. 'It's being done all the time and they're getting away with it.'

The doorbell rang at four o'clock. Clementine, after a quick glance in the mirror and a smoothing down of her hair, opened the door to a woman and a small solemn child.

'Mrs Hope?' The woman smiled, a measured smile as if she was charged by the width. Clementine nodded and smiled back and the woman stepped inside, pushing her daughter in front of her. 'I'm Helen Jones and this is Beatrice. Beatrice is very pleased to have found a new teacher.'

The child, Beatrice, looked up at Clementine, sternly, as if to imprint on her the seriousness of her undertaking.

'I'll pick you up in three quarters of an hour, Beatrice,' Mrs Jones said.

'I can walk back myself. Angela is allowed to walk home from ballet and that's further.' Beatrice did not whinge or beg, her voice was as matter-of-fact and as solemn as her expression.

Her mother considered for a moment. 'Well, all right then. But you go straight home, and what do we say?'

'Don't talk to strangers,' the child carolled.

Mrs Jones directed another of her tight little smiles at Clementine. 'Maybe I'm a little overprotective.'

Clementine warmed to the woman. 'No,' she smiled back. 'No, I don't think so at all. I know that when I was looking after my sister's little boy for a month I just couldn't stop fretting about him. No sooner was I rejoicing in his laughter or in the feeling of his little plump arms around my neck than my stomach would tighten with worry at all the awful things out there just waiting to strike: perverts, drunk drivers, leukaemia. Once we were out walking, just him and I, and suddenly there I was in floods of tears, as in my mind's eye his little white coffin was brought out of church, so light it took just one man to carry it. The poor little chap put his arms around me and asked me why I was crying. Well, I could hardly say I was crying at his funeral now could I?'

Grabbing her daughter's hand, Mrs Jones took a step back towards the front door. 'Of course, it's vital not to frighten ones children, making them over-anxious,' she said coldly. 'One has to be sensible.'

'Oh dear me yes,' Clementine nodded vigorously, wondering if she was the only person in the world whose speech could bypass her brain entirely. 'Sensible is the word, absolutely. For example, it's worth remembering that we live longer today than ever before in history. Well, some of us. Just as long as we don't fall victim to violent crime or cancer or Aids . . . and after all, why should we?' She laughed a little shrilly and put her hand out to Beatrice. 'Shall we make a start then?'

Mrs Jones seemed reluctant to let go of her daughter's hand, so Clementine tried a smile that would convey common sense and a measured enthusiasm for the task ahead. Mrs Jones took another step towards the door, still holding on to Beatrice. Clementine stopped smiling and this seemed to reassure her. She let go of her daughter's hand and allowed Clementine to usher her outside. 'Don't be late now Beatrice,' she called as Clementine closed the door behind her.

'Beatrice Aurora,' Clementine said to the child as she led the way into the sitting-room. 'Goddess of the rosy dawn and inspiration to poets. If I had had a daughter, that's what I would have called her. Actually,' Clementine smiled apologetically, 'I decided it would have had to be just Beatrice. The Aurora might have got her teased.'

'My name is Beatrice Catherine,' the child informed her as she settled on the stool, jigging about to adjust its height.

Clementine sat listening to her playing. Her technique was basic, not much above what you should expect from a talented ten-year-old, but musically, she was exceptional. The expression on the small face barely changed as she played her piece. She sat upright and unusually still, no swaying, no unnecessary raising of the hands.

'Your mother doesn't have to tell you to practise, I imagine,' Clementine said as Beatrice finished playing.

Beatrice shook her head. 'She says she'll put a padlock on the piano if I don't spend more time doing my school work. She says a musician's life is a miserable one and that I should treat music as a hobby.' At the word hobby, her small nose wrinkled in distaste.

Clementine thought for a moment before saying, 'I'm not one to advocate taking risks, but maybe when it comes to your music you should. It might be a miserable life being a musician, but if you really care, not as miserable as not being one. I wouldn't dream of contradicting your mother, but if you have a gift you must use it or it atrophies and ends up a terrible burden.' She got up. 'Now, let's swap seats, and I'll play you the piece I'd like you to work on next.'

'I think you play better than my last teacher,' Beatrice said when Clementine had finished, 'but not as well as my uncle. He's the one with the miserable life Mummy doesn't want me to have.'

'Thank you,' Clementine smiled. 'That sums it up rather well. I'm good, but not good enough to be miserable.'

'Do you want to be?'

Clementine told her no. 'Anyway,' she said, 'there are thousands of ways of making oneself miserable, one to suit everyone. Have you read the Pollyanna books?'

Beatrice shook her head.

'Pollyanna was a little girl in turn-of-the-century America and she was always cheerful, because she played this game of finding something to be cheerful about, however glum the situation. She wanted a doll more than anything, but instead she got a pair of child-size crutches. Did she complain, no siree, she did not. Instead, she swallowed her disappointment and said, "What a lucky girl I am, not to need them there crutches," or something to that effect. Well, I play that game too, but I've changed the rules a bit. In my game, you have to find something to be glum about, however happy the situation.'

For a moment it looked as if Beatrice was going to smile. Her dark eyes lit up and the thin little mouth softened. The moment passed. She asked, 'Do you still play that game?'

'I'm world champion,' Clementine said.

Beatrice nodded. 'You're a worrier, aren't you?'

Clementine thought for a moment. 'Let's have a biscuit.' She walked across to the mantelpiece where she kept one of her favourite possessions: a rose-patterned blue and pink enamel biscuit barrel. Lifting it off the shelf, she added, 'And something to drink.' She opened the tin and handed it to Beatrice before going into the kitchen and fetching a can of Coke from the fridge. Back in the drawing-room, she beckoned Beatrice across to the sofa. 'Come and sit down.' She gave her the can of Coke and a glass.

'When I was young, a year or two older than you maybe,' she began, 'my great aunt told me the story of a small anxious creature who lived in a very beautiful house on the edge of the sea. The little creature should have been happy. In the autumn the woods were plentiful with nuts and mushrooms, and the branches of the apple trees bowed low enough for her to reach the fruit. In the summer the ground was carpeted with wild strawberries, and raspberries shone like rubies in the thickets. In the winter the house was warm and cosy, and in the summer the trees ushered in just enough sea breeze through the open windows to keep her cool. The house was filled with beautiful furniture and china, and on the walls hung pictures of the lovely house and of her mother and father and brothers and sisters who were pretty and plump-cheeked and happy, whereas the little creature herself was all elongated with worry. She told everyone that she felt the presence of something dark, something dangerous. Maybe it came from the woods? But the branches of the huge trees just whispered gently to each other. Maybe it came from the sea? But the sun just carried on playing with the waves. Sometimes she thought the trees were moving closer, threatening to crowd right up to her beautiful house. Sometimes she thought that maybe one of the gentle waves would grow until it rose, a giant from the sea, washing everything away in its wake. But of one thing she was sure; sooner or later there would be a calamity.' Clementine fell silent.

'Did it?' Beatrice looked intently at her. 'Did the calamity come?'

'I don't know,' Clementine shrugged her shoulders, 'Aunt Elvira never finished the story. I expect we were called to supper or something.'

Beatrice gave her a stern look. 'I don't think you should be telling stories you don't know the ending of.'

'You're right,' Clementine sighed and reached out for another biscuit, holding the barrel out to Beatrice first. 'You're quite right and I'm sorry.' She looked at her watch. 'You should probably be making your way home now, or your mother will worry.' She walked Beatrice to the door. 'I'll ask her if there's any way she

99

could allow you to practise a bit more. You're good. In fact you're as promising as anyone I've ever taught.'

At last the child smiled. It was as if the little solemn face had been waiting to find just the right thing to justify such an upheaval of features.

Clementine was making herself a cup of tea when the doorbell went. She opened up, leaving the chain on, and peered out. 'Oh,' she said, on seeing Nathaniel. 'Oh,' she said again, taking the chain off and opening the door fully. 'One can't be too careful,' she excused herself as he stepped into the hall. 'Especially not when one's a five feet eleven, athletically built grown-up living in a small town.' Looking up at Nathaniel and seeing the polite but vacant expression on his face she added, 'That was supposed to be amusing.'

His face cleared, 'Ah, right.' He had a way of turning his mouth down at the corners in a wry little half smile, that made Clementine suddenly ache to kiss him. 'My father suggested you might like to join us for supper tonight. He's making curry and he always makes too much.'

'And I look like a girl with a strong healthy appetite,' Clementine continued for him.

Again that half smile. 'Well, anyway, we'd love to see you if you're free, about eight?'

Clementine considered playing hard to get but the danger of that was always that one was not got at all. 'I'd love to,' she beamed at him. 'I'm looking forward to it,' she toned down the beam to a polite smile. 'Eight o'clock then.'

Clementine was going through her wardrobe, deciding what to wear, when Ophelia sauntered into the bedroom. Throwing herself down on the bed, she rested her Doc Martin boots on Clementine's white lace duvet cover. She was wearing a short, black and white flower-sprigged skirt and a thick black woollen jumper and her black tights looked as if they had been brushed with a pan scourer. Her fair hair was plastered to her cheeks and her eyes were smudged with mascara. She did not seem able to stop smiling. 'I've had a fantastic time; the best.'

'Good day at the college?' Clementine sat down at her dressing-table, still not sure what she should wear for dinner.

Ophelia stretched out on the bed and giggled. Clementine turned round and looked hard at her. 'You're drunk.'

'Sort of.' Ophelia looked even more pleased with herself. 'I didn't go to work today. I've been with Max. I've spent the whole day in bed with Max.'

'When you say Max, you mean, of course, your fiancé, William, to whom you are engaged to be married?'

'Nope. When I say Max, I mean Max.'

Clementine got up from the dressing-table. 'I'd love to hear more,' she said, 'but I'm getting ready to go out.' She moved towards the bathroom, but Ophelia called her back, a slurred and softly insistent voice. 'Dear old Clementine, going out eh.' She sat up. 'He's totally brilliant, Max is.'

'Fancy that,' Clementine said politely, her hand on the bathroom door.

'His name is Max.'

'You said.'

'He's got an enormous dick.'

'How nice.'

'God, I hope I'm not in love.'

Clementine turned in the doorway, her expression softening. 'If you are, you must put a stop to all these wedding arrangements. Is Max in love with you?'

Ophelia looked a little surprised at the question. 'How could he not be? I'm young, blonde, gorgeous and incredibly talented.'

There she went again, Clementine thought, the whole child. 'Sorry,' she said. 'Silly question.' She went into the bathroom and shut the door behind her.

'Max says that if you spent your life being chased by mammoths and having to scrabble for roots for your supper, you wouldn't have time to worry about everything. Worrying is a disease of the spoilt modern mind.'

Clementine flung the door open. 'You've spoken to this Max person about my private thoughts?'

Ophelia had got up from the bed and now she did a little pirouette, coming to a wobbly halt with her back to Clementine. 'Yup,' she said again, and just as smugly.

Suddenly, humiliatingly, tears flooded Clementine's eyes. 'Well you're a little bitch and your Max is a silly ass who should mind his own business, if he has any.' She slammed the door behind her and turned the key in the lock. Through the door she heard Ophelia's voice.

'Max says that what you probably need is a good f . . .'

'Shut up!' Clementine screamed. 'Shut up, shut up!' She turned the taps on, all of them; bath and basin. Ten minutes later she emerged from the bathroom, wrapped in a towel, to find Ophelia had gone. She opened her closet once more, as always in the hope that this time some mix-and-match fashion fairy really had waved a magic wand and turned a cupboard full of ill-assorted bits and pieces into a workable wardrobe. But no such fairy had paid a visit, so Clementine pulled a short black skirt off its hanger and put it on, together with a pale-blue twin set. She had bought the twin set the other day, refusing to listen to the small inner voice which told her that twin sets might well be this season's 'must have' on every fashion editor's list, but it turned Clementine into a frump. She pulled the clothes off again, leaving them in a heap on the floor. She finally emerged from her bedroom wearing a green knitted dress which she had bought a couple of years earlier because her mother

102

had told her it was too short. As she walked downstairs she heard Ophelia call. 'Want a drink?'

'No, thanks,' Clementine yelled back, 'I've got to practise. I've got a ten-year-old to keep up with.' In the sitting-room, she seated herself by the piano. She lifted the lid and wiggled her fingers. Her hands were large and soft, pale-skinned and long-fingered like the hands of the Nazi killer in the black and white newsreel. It was over thirty years ago that she had watched that film and still she remembered those hands.

She had been told that she could stay up late with the others that evening to watch the film about the war. She had been excited at first because she liked staying up late and she liked films on television. She had wondered if there would be sweets. Sometimes, if there was a special programme her mother bought sweets to be eaten in front of the television. This was obviously a very special programme. Then, at half-past nine, just as it was about to begin, Aunt Mabel telephoned. In her rush, Clementine completely forgot that if Aunt Mabel called and it was before six, Mummy was out shopping, and if she called after six, Mummy was in the bathroom. 'Sorry Aunt Mabel,' Clementine had twittered, 'Mummy is out shopping.'

'Are you mad child?' Her voice was so sharp Clementine had to move the receiver from one ear to the other. 'I said, are you mad?'

Clementine had considered the question seriously, coming as it did from an expert on the subject.

'No,' she stated finally. Listening to her aunt, she hoped madness was not catching, like chickenpox or measles.

'Do you hear me, child? I wish to speak to your mother. Now where is she? And what are you doing up at this hour? When your cousin Digby was your age he was in bed by seven-thirty sharp, every night without fail.'

Maybe some wicked fairy had put a spell on Aunt Mabel, Clementine had thought, or maybe Aunt Mabel was a wicked fairy herself. The thought was exciting.

Aunt Mabel's voice made Clementine move the phone back to the other ear again. 'Now for the last time, Clementine; this is Clementine isn't it? Is your mother home or not?'

'I'll get her,' Clementine had dropped the receiver on the carpet and ran into the drawing-room.

She had heard her mother's voice. 'As you very well know, Mabel, I'm every bit as strict as you are, but I feel it's absolutely essential that the children grow up with an awareness of what happened and what being Jewish . . . all right, part Jewish, means.'

At last they had settled down to watch. There had been no sweets. On the screen, young men like Uncle Timothy – the Uncle who had died in the war and whom her brother was called after – ran across a beach, their hands thrown high in the air as they fell into the wet sand. Houses burnt black against an orange sky. Women wearing head scarves and shawls and heavy black coats walked along endless dusty roads, their children, looking like no children Clementine had ever seen, tagging along behind. One such child, a little girl, stepped out from a train, and a uniformed man with granite eyes put a soft, white long-fingered hand on her shoulder. Pillars of smoke rose into leaden skies as skeletal bodies were shoved into ovens that spewed out the flames of hell.

Apparently, Clementine had screamed. She could not remember that part herself, but according to her mother she had gone on screaming for quite a while. She did remember her mother muttering, 'For once maybe bloody Mabel was right,' as she put Clementine to bed with a mug of warm milk. Clementine had mumbled her prayer, the way she had been taught to do every night. 'God who loves little children, look down at me. Wherever I go my happiness lies in Thine hands. Happiness comes and happiness goes, but he whom God loves is the happiest of all.'

Clementine had never really listened to the words before, she had simply mumbled away at them in an unthinking nightly ritual; a kind of insurance policy handed to her by her parents. Now she read them over and over to herself. 'Happiness comes and happiness goes, he whom God loves is happiest of all.'

So how could you make sure that God loved you? So far, Clementine had been all right, but what if He changed His mind? What if He stopped loving her? Would she have to leave her room and her house and all her toys to tramp along the roads with her brothers and sister, their mother pushing the large Silver Cross pram piled high with saucepans and chairs and blankets, or worse still? She had pulled her blankets over her face, shielding herself against those huge staring eyes and the gaping flaming ovens.

Clementine hit the first note of the *Warsaw Concerto*, hard on the piano. She carried on playing for half an hour, wanting only to immerse her fretful mind in music. Finally, exhausted, she stopped playing and looked at her watch. It was time to go. She was about to fetch a bottle of South African red wine from the rack in the kitchen, when she remembered that Nathaniel was supposed to be a reformed alcoholic. Instead she brought out a box of Marabou chocolate she had brought with her from Sweden and, after a moment's pause, she pulled off the black velvet ribbon which held her hair back in a pony-tail and wound it round the box instead. She grabbed her handbag and a black knitted wrap against the cold night air and set off for next door.

105

Chapter Seven

The moonlight had dimmed with the thickening clouds. From her chair, Clementine peered anxiously at Mr Scott. He kept telling her he was fine, but there he went again, she could just see through the darkness, wiping his forehead with his large red and white spotted handkerchief; the kind that little boys tie in a bundle on a stick when they run away from home. The colder and more worried she was getting, the more irritable she became. She walked up to the attic window and held her watch up to the faint light. It was one o'clock.

'I thought Nathaniel was meant to be home by midnight,' she muttered.

'He is almost forty years old,' Mr Scott pointed out mildly. 'I don't put a curfew on him.'

'No, of course not,' Clementine agreed with bad grace, 'but if you say you're going to come home around midnight, you should come home around midnight, for just this kind of reason.'

'I don't want to be seen to be overly defensive of my son,' Mr Scott said, 'but it seems a little bit unreasonable to expect him to foresee that his friend and his father would get themselves locked in an attic room while hiding from a burglar.'

But Clementine was not in a mood to be reasonable. Life was utterly unreliable; the only reliable thing about it being that it would be taken from you. So, given that indisputable fact, people turning up at midnight when they said midnight, was the least one could ask for.

'The perimeters of existence are so utterly haphazard', she said, 'that the only way of coping is to raise one's own secure borders against the chaos outside. Nathaniel is the enemy of secure borders, he really is, in fact, he thinks a secure border is a come on.' She sighed and threw herself down on her chair.

'How, I ask you, can anyone as insecure as I, someone who doesn't gamble on the National Lottery in case she wins and gets murdered for her money, make a life with a man like Nathaniel?'

Mr Scott did not answer.

*   *   *

There it was, Clementine thought; after years of emotional slumber you meet the man of your dreams and then you find that, quite frankly, you have nothing whatsoever to say to each other.

The oak refectory table in Mr Scott's dining-room could seat twelve people comfortably. By implication it should seat three people even more comfortably, Clementine thought, but things did not work like that. Mr Scott, Nathaniel and Clementine sat at one end of the table with Mr Scott at the head. Further along were the empty seats where all the witty and fascinating guests should have been dining. The wine-coloured chintz curtains were drawn against the summer evening and the room was lit a little harshly by one of Mr Scott's pewter lamps. The walls were covered with water-colour landscapes, most of them Italian, it seemed to Clementine, with their green rolling hills and exclamation-mark cypresses. Returning to the face that had gazed back at her through a thousand fantasies, she said, 'We've had such a good summer, haven't we?'

'Absolutely,' Nathaniel agreed.

'We all love the sun,' Mr Scott said, refilling their glasses with elderflower cordial. They had started dinner with a spicy mackerel pâté and thick triangles of toast, and now it was time for Mr Scott's curry. Picking up a plate from the sideboard with one hand, he gesticulated with the other towards a large dish edged with wedges of hard-boiled eggs.

Nathaniel too got up from the table. 'Clementine, would you like some wine?'

The answer to that, of course, was yes, she was dying for some, but she had manners, she knew the form.

Mr Scott's grip tightened on the plate.

'I'm very happy with this,' she smiled, holding up her glass of cordial.

'Not for me either, dear boy,' Mr Scott said quickly, as he began to dish out. He placed the plate in front of Clementine. The curry smelt of coconut and cardamom. Nathaniel was rummaging through a drawer in the sideboard, when, with a little grunt of satisfaction, he pulled out a key and unlocked the cupboard below.

'Nathaniel, old boy, why don't you stick to soft.' There was such desperation in Mr Scott's quiet voice, that Clementine felt more like someone having accidentally stumbled into a private funeral than a guest at a supper party.

Nathaniel sighed and put the bottle down. 'Well, Clementine, we've barely met and already you know my best kept secret: I've stopped drinking.' He sat back down at the table and drained his glass of cordial.

Mr Scott, having finished serving, joined them at the table. 'Yes, we all love sunshine,' he said, and relief rose from his voice like the steam from the food.

'Yet some people can't get enough cold and rain after living in a hot climate,' Clementine replied. She raised a forkful of curry to her lips and, shooting Nathaniel a glance under her eyelashes, she wondered if it might be a good idea, at this stage, to explain that normally she was no more boring than most women her age and class, it was just that tonight she was making an exception.

'Aah, but it can get quite cold in the mountains,' Mr Scott told her.

'Do you like the heat?' Clementine asked Nathaniel, as she was gripped again by some suicidal urge to keep a conversation going, however doomed.

'Oh yes,' he answered, and his fingers beat a silent tattoo against the edge of Mr Scott's dining table.

Clementine raised her eyes to his, holding his gaze for a moment. Suddenly he shook his head and smiled.

'In my opinion there's not a woman born who can resist chocolate.' Mr Scott beamed at her as he prepared to serve the chocolate mousse tart. 'Am I not right?'

Wrong! Clementine had eaten too much already, and anyway, she was one of those people who had had too much chocolate as soon as she saw it. Her stomach turned at the sight of the large pastry shell with its sticky dark-brown filling.

'Oh you're right,' she murmured, obediently, holding out her plate, 'Who can resist chocolate?'

'I won't have any thanks,' Nathaniel said. 'I'm not used to eating this much.'

Clementine looked down as a full quarter of the tart landed on her plate. 'And some cream,' Mr Scott said pleasurably. She looked on helplessly as Mr Scott poured on a generous helping of double cream.

'You must tell me about your work in Rwanda?' she turned to Nathaniel as she lifted a large forkful of food to her mouth. Her spirits sank further. Only she could be relied upon to bring up the suffering of a people at war with her mouth full of chocolate cake. she swallowed as quickly as possible, rinsing

109

down the rich sticky mess with a gulp of cordial.

'It must have been very harrowing.' The truth is, even when she was not pushing food into her mouth, she felt awkward around charitable causes. She was quite simply too big and healthy not to feel like a walking affront to the starving of the world.

While she waited for Nathaniel's reply she felt Mr Scott's eyes expectantly on her. She picked up another forkful of pudding, forcing herself to smile at Mr Scott. Turning back to Nathaniel she smuggled the food into her mouth, chewing with tiny movements of her jaw, as if that way, somehow, her appetite would seem less offensive.

'Yes, it was harrowing,' Nathaniel did not look at her as he answered, 'but in my business I'm afraid no news is bad news.'

'I feel so cheated,' Clementine said. 'I've felt cheated most of my life I suppose. There I was, toddling around my mother's knees, thinking life was full of smiling mummies and daddies and Christmas trees and women in fur coats chasing after strong and handsome men. Then look,' she spread out her large hands, 'just look what the world is really like. I don't know how anyone recovers from the shock of finding out.'

Nathaniel looked straight at her and then he laughed.

Confused by the sudden warmth in his eyes she said quickly, 'So where's your next trip going to be to, or don't you know yet?'

'I'm planning to stick around the UK for a while,' Nathaniel said.

Clementine nodded sagely. 'I know, there's quite enough death and destruction here to keep you going for some time.'

'There are more things in life to enjoy than death and destruction,' Nathaniel said. He was sitting back in the chair, one leg crossed over the other, relaxed enough if one did not look too close. Clementine longed to lean across the table and grab his hand, stop his well-shaped fingers from their incessant drumming. 'But seriously, you simply have to learn to look away.'

Clementine shovelled another large mouthful of chocolate into her mouth, wanting only to finish what was on her plate. She felt sick swallowing.

'I reckon having my fairy tales illustrated by photographs rather than drawings would be pretty interesting,' she said when she had finished swallowing. 'Not people dressed up like the characters, all velvet gowns and gold crowns, but real images: a young woman gazing down from a top-floor window; a man charging down the street in his car.' She thought of the busker outside Safeways. 'A down-and-out slumped in a shop entrance.' She smiled at Nathaniel. 'You say fairy tales have nothing to do with real life, but surely you have to ask yourself what curse turned a child like most others into a bundle of rags begging for pennies.'

'I think the photographs are a capital idea,' Mr Scott said and Clementine looked at Nathaniel for agreement.

'Could work,' was all he said. He stood up and began to clear the table.

What do you mean, 'Could work'? Clementine wanted to yell after his disappearing back. It was a very good idea. So good it had taken her completely by surprise. He had no right to sit there with his nervous hands and his green eyes and say, 'Could work.'

Standing up herself and picking up her empty plate, she told Mr Scott. 'That was just the most delicious pudding I've eaten for a long time.'

'Well then you must have some more.' Mr Scott beamed at her as he pushed another large slice of chocolate tart onto her plate. 'I don't know what I was doing not offering you seconds. You sit down too,' he said to Nathaniel who had returned to the dining-room. 'Clementine is having some more pudding.'

For the first time Clementine saw something resembling admiration in Nathaniel's eyes as he looked at her, and over what: her seemingly bottomless appetite? Resigned, she picked up her fork.

'Family values,' Jessica said to Clementine at the Chocolate House. They were enjoying the sunshine outside, as Mrs Challis had recently obtained permission to place three tables with chairs in the square.

'It's what Now is all about. It's taken me a while to realize.' She swallowed a great gulp of coffee, and slamming the cup down on the saucer, hauled a photo from her bag. 'This is it. This is where it's at.' She handed the photo to Clementine, who took it, expecting a picture of Michael. But if that was her friend's husband, it was a very bad likeness indeed. She peered down at the grey mass interrupted by a white line and some darker blobs.

'My womb,' Jessica declared.

Clementine dropped the photo and was left to crawl around the cobblestones to retrieve it. She handed it back to Jessica.

'Is someone there?'

'Do you mean, am I pregnant? No, not yet. But I will be.' Jessica beamed at her. 'Oh, Clementine, isn't it wonderful? I just feel my whole life coming together. I should have listened to Michael earlier. As you know he's wanted a family for years, but I was too into me. That's all changing. Life's about giving; projecting outwards.'

Mrs Challis clip-clopped her way across to their table. 'If it's plumbing you're talking about,' she said inexplicably, whipping a cloth from her apron pocket and rubbing vigorously at the table, 'Derek is your man. He's done a lovely job in my little bathroom it has to be said.'

Jessica looked alert, 'Clementine you've got a problem with your shower, haven't you?'

Clementine glared at her, but before she could protest, Mrs Challis continued. 'You just let me know when it would be convenient for Derek to pop round and I'll make sure he's there. He's very punctual, Derek.' Straightening up, her eyes turned steely. Clementine followed her gaze across the square to the closed-down sports shop opposite. There, the busker she had seen outside Safeways the other day was taking up position, unslinging the guitar from across his shoulder and throwing the old bowler hat on the ground at his feet.

'He's nothing but a beggar. Living rough by the looks of him.' Mrs Challis sucked her teeth and shook her head. 'I never thought we'd see his sort here in Aldringham.' She returned to her customers, switching her smile back on. 'More coffee ladies?'

'You do have a problem with your shower,' Jessica insisted when she had gone. 'You told me so yourself.'

Clementine leant closer to Jessica and hissed, 'But I don't want this Derek fixing it. I have a very bad feeling about him.'

'Oh, you have bad feelings about everything,' Jessica said impatiently.

Clementine sighed. This, of course, was true. 'But I really do believe he's a bad lot. These ghastly burglaries . . .'

'What ghastly burglaries?'

'Don't say you haven't read about them. There's been two really violent ones in the last few weeks. The first one, in which this old lady got beaten to a pulp, was perpetrated by a man looking very much like Derek Fletcher.'

'So have you told the police?'

Clementine shook her head. 'It seems so drastic. I keep thinking he could be the burglar, but I'm so used to being paranoid I can't quite believe I might be right. And poor little Abigail . . .'

113

'If you think this man has committed a crime, you must tell the police.'

'Well, that's the problem, I don't think that really. I just have a bad feeling about him, and he sort of fits the police description, but so do lots of people.' She thought for a moment. 'Maybe you're right though. Maybe I should just mention it to the police.'

It was not ten minutes before Derek himself arrived at the Chocolate House with Abigail and there was Mrs Challis, grabbing him by the arm and taking him across to Clementine.

'Here's your man, Mrs Hope.' Anyone would think she liked him. 'You'll do Mrs Hope's shower for her, won't you?'

Derek nodded. 'No problem,' he said. 'Eight o'clock tomorrow morning all right with you?'

Clementine wondered how many people had died from fear of being rude. 'Eight o'clock is a bit early,' she mumbled.

'I'll make it nine then shall I,' Derek said.

'No, no eight's all right,' Clementine said, resigned.

'The happiest, most fulfilled people on this earth are the ones with least sense of self,' Jessica said, not the least concerned, it seemed, that Clementine had just invited a possible criminal into her house.

'I know that,' Clementine said testily, 'of course I know that. But as hard as I try to forget, I always know I'm there somewhere.' She looked past Jessica and out across the square, squinting against the bright sunshine.

'Can you be in love with a man you barely know and seem to have little in common with?' she asked.

Jessica thought for a moment. 'Only if you're a fool,' was her answer.

Clementine picked up her bag. 'Well, there we go.'

Chapter Eight

Keep him calm, Clementine told herself as she smiled at Mr Scott across the small attic room. It was not a very successful smile, but it was the best she could manage at the time. Mr Scott was still sweating. By now his handkerchief was so wet he could have wrung it out.

'Jessica talks a lot of rubbish,' Clementine said, 'but I'm sure she was right when she said that happiness is all about forgetting oneself. I just suspect she has not managed to. I mean, if I've forgotten something, I don't keep talking about it.' She hugged her knees, rubbing her tired eyes against the soft cotton of her skirt. 'I thought love would make me forget myself, but it didn't.' She gave a little laugh. 'But you're different. You dedicated your life to others. It might be that you're the only truly good person I have ever known.' She looked intently at Mr Scott. 'Tell me, what does it feel like; forgetting about oneself, being good?'

'Oh, what would I know,' Mr Scott said testily. 'I went to Africa in spite of my wife's misgivings. I blighted her life for entirely selfish reasons. I think Nathaniel always suspected as much.'

Clementine was about to say something playful like, 'C'mon, you're being modest,' but she stopped herself. Mr Scott had sounded deadly serious.

'I was, still am, a deeply prejudiced man. Oh, I was

scrupulously fair in my dealings with people, whatever colour or background, but I knew the coldness that lay in my heart. To me, some people were definitely more equal than others. A starving child in a picture from a concentration camp brought me to tears. I was haunted by images of mothers seeing their children dragged away and killed. A mother in Africa, cradling her dying baby did not move me in the same way. There's no excuse for that, only bad reasons.'

'But surely everyone . . .' Clementine interrupted.

'I know what you're going to say. "It's too far away, too much to take in." I've heard all of that but I knew it was not the truth. The truth, stark and ugly, was that because these people suffering in a living hell were black and uneducated, I simply could not feel that process of identification which lies at the heart of true compassion. Deep down I did not believe that those poor mothers holding their dead babies felt the same agony as Ethel would, or my mother, or sister, or any of the women in my own circle. After that I asked myself questions that were too uncomfortable to dwell on. In the end I couldn't live with myself, so I packed up and left for Africa.'

'And you learnt to love the people?' Clementine said, brightening.

Mr Scott gave a little shrug. 'I learnt to weep for them.'

Clementine said nothing for a while, then she got up and walked across to the window. 'I think I should risk it and call for help. Ophelia might just hear.' She turned to Mr Scott. 'But what if he's still down there? You hear of burglars making themselves completely at home if they feel safe, even preparing little meals. Oh Mr Scott what is the best thing to do?'

*   *   *

116

Clementine had slept badly. Mostly she had not slept at all, but tossed and turned, arms all over the place and her shoulders growing larger and sharper, so that however she lay she was in her own way. What could she have been thinking of, practically inviting Derek Fletcher to inspect the contents of her home? At five o'clock she was up, tiptoeing downstairs to unplug the video recorder. She stood in the middle of the room with the machine cradled in her arms, wondering where to hide it. In the end she put it in the cupboard under the bookcase, moving some photo albums to make room. Next she hid the photograph of Aunt Elvira. That heavy silver frame would tempt anyone. She listened in the silence for sounds from next door. All was quiet. Nathaniel must still be asleep in his bedroom on the other side of the wall from Ophelia's. Clementine imagined him sprawled across a narrow single bed, clad in tasteful blue and white striped pyjamas. It did not look quite right, so she turned the stripes burgundy. She shook her head and there he was, naked, his skin moon pale.

She was too wideawake to go back to bed, so she made herself a cup of breakfast tea and sat down at her desk with a bunch of Aunt Elvira's notes. At eight o'clock the doorbell rang. Clementine knew it would be Derek, but she opened the door on the chain nevertheless. 'You can't be too careful these days,' she said as she let him in. 'Call me a silly old worrybean if you like, but I don't think one can take security in the home too seriously these days.'

'Nice mirror,' he said instead, pointing a black thumb at the large gilded-looking glass that hung on a heavy chain above the chest of drawers in the hall.

'Oh that old thing,' Clementine said dismissively. 'A copy I'm afraid.'

'You'll be interested to hear that Abby is in the family way,' Derek said as he followed Clementine's brisk steps towards the stairs.

Clementine turned around and smiled at him. 'Abigail's having a baby, how lovely.'

'Well I have to take what work I can now,' Derek said. 'Costly things, children.'

'Well I'm thinking of fitting a burglar alarm,' Clementine said, as she opened the door to the bathroom. 'Not that there's anything worth stealing in this place,' she laughed at the very thought.

'I don't know,' Derek said putting his tool-bag down on the floor. 'That tallboy out on the landing. Lovely piece. You'd be surprised what that would fetch at auction.'

Clementine blinked. 'Really. Oh well. I'll let you get on shall I?' She retired to the kitchen, picking up the mail from the front doormat on the way. Upstairs Derek was running the water in the shower. Thank goodness her mother was not there now, with her double row of pearls and that ring with the sapphire as large as a penny piece.

'I'll just stick my card through your neighbours' letter-boxes,' Derek said as he left. 'People just don't think plumber until it's too late, and then they scrabble around those Yellow Pages getting nothing but cowboys as likely as not.'

Clementine, squinting against the sunlight, waved at Toby Scott who was just coming out of his house. Derek, surprisingly nimble for someone as big and heavy, had got around to Mr Scott's gate in no time, and the next thing she heard was Mr Scott saying that, actually, he had a problem with his hot water. Before she could think of a reason to stop him, Derek had followed Mr Scott into the house. Clementine lingered in her front garden, weeding the two terracotta pots with azaleas, until, ten minutes later, Derek came out of the house. By now, she thought darkly, he would know exactly where Mr Scott kept his video recorder and he had most probably spotted the Georgian teaset as well. She decided to call the police.

An informer's lot was not an easy one, she felt, as she waited for a constable to answer the phone, but how could she live with herself if Mr Scott got burgled, or worse, and all along, she could have prevented it. 'He's probably as innocent as you or I,' she said to the WPC who took the call. 'Although, come to think of it, as far as you know I could be far from innocent. I suppose I could even be an accomplice planting false herrings, red herrings, I mean. No, you don't think so. Well, it's just that this man does rather fit the description of the suspect in the recent burglaries.'

She gave the policewoman Derek's full name and that was that. She put the phone down with a heavy heart. She might well have rendered poor Abigail's unborn child as good as fatherless, because what good is a father in prison, and it was still only nine o'clock in the morning. What could she do with the rest of the day? Run over a crippled old lady? She tried to cheer herself up by reminding herself that she had still not got a car. In the end, she spent the rest of the morning harmlessly enough preparing her afternoon lessons. She made herself coffee, although she really did not care much for that particular drink, preferring tea. It was the image of coffee she liked. Coffee was for sharp minds and tight schedules, tea was for comfort and putting your feet up. Clementine had a suspicion that tea drinkers, on the whole, did not set the world on fire. She found it hard to concentrate on her work, even with a second cup of milky coffee at her elbow. She kept listening out for sounds from next door; a voice, Nathaniel's voice, a guitar playing, even a slamming of a cupboard door, anything. Silence, she thought, the absence of a longed-for sound – a telephone not ringing was far more disruptive than any noise.

When the doorbell rang soon after lunch she expected it to be a collection or a pupil arriving early, but it was Nathaniel, leaning against the door-frame, his fingers crouched ready to drum impatiently against the wood.

'I've brought you some photographs,' he said, handing her a large envelope. 'Don't grab at it,' he snapped as she clasped her fingers round it. 'You'll wreck them.'

It was so unfair. She had only wanted to show enthusiasm. 'Sorry,' she mumbled, showing him inside with one hand while carrying the envelope, as daintily as she could, with the other.

'You remember you told me you were interested in having photographs to illustrate your fairy tales,' Nathaniel said as they sat down at the kitchen table. 'See what you think of these.'

There were three pictures, all black and white. 'That, of course, is where your damsel lives, always assuming you have a damsel.' Nathaniel pointed at the first picture, showing the old brewery at the top of Wagon Lane. 'See, it's even got a tower.' He looked straight into her eyes and her stomach lurched.

'Are you all right?' Nathaniel, the cause of the commotion, asked.

For a moment she debated whether to say, 'Yes, I'm fine thank you, apart from the fact that the proximity of you makes my stomach churn and my pulse race and my fingers tingle with the desire to touch your skin just where your neck meets your collar-bone.' She decided against it.

'I'm fine, thanks,' she nodded emphatically. 'And the photos are just perfect. Thank you.' As she spoke, she found herself moving closer to him across the table as if to catch his breath with hers, and embarrassed, she withdrew, getting up from the table altogether for good measure. 'Coffee?' she waved her hands in the direction of the kettle.

'Lovely.' He smiled that little half smile, the corners of his mouth turning down, and she wondered if he knew how attractive it was and if it was done to charm.

'This, of course, is our distressed damsel herself.'

Clementine switched on the kettle before coming back over to the table to look. Nathaniel pushed the photograph towards her and she looked down to see a woman pictured at an open window, a wistful look on her face, her long hair cascading down across her shoulders.

'But that's me,' she said.

'Well spotted!'

She pulled a face at him. 'When did you take it?'

'Oh, a couple of weeks ago. You don't mind do you?'

She shook her head. 'And who's that?' She picked up the last photograph and studied the picture of the life-sized cardboard male model in the window of the local branch of Next.

'Prince Charming, of course.'

'Oh no, no that's not him,' Clementine exclaimed.

'So who is?' Nathaniel smiled that half smile again and Clementine pressed her spine against the back of her chair so hard it felt as if it might leave her flesh and take its place amongst the spindles on the chair instead.

'Oh,' she exhaled. 'Oh I wouldn't know, but not a cardboard dummy anyway.'

'But isn't that the essence of Prince Charming . . .'

'Being a cardboard dummy?'

'No.' Nathaniel said with mock patience. 'But this man in the shop window is there because he represents an unobtainable ideal, physically perfect, impossibly suitable, but no-one knows what lies beneath. Advertising like fairy tales, does not delve deep.'

'Prince Charming is not unobtainable, that's the whole point.' The passion in Clementine's voice surprised even her, so she pruned it back into a nice level tone when she continued, 'And just read *The Little Mermaid* for example. The hero and his motives are anything but cardboard.'

'If I remember rightly,' Nathaniel said, lighting a cigarette, 'the poor deluded mermaid falls in love with his statue first; his perfect image. The real man did not match up to that image. He was as weak and as given to take the easy way out as the rest of us.'

Clementine beamed at him. 'So we're both right. That's nice.'

'Or you could say we were both wrong.' He did seem to have a need to pick people up all the time, Clementine thought.

'I never gave you your coffee,' she leapt up from the table.

'Too late,' Nathaniel stood up, looking around for somewhere to stub out his cigarette. 'I have to get on. So much to do, so little time.' Clementine grabbed a saucer from the plate rack and handed it to him. And he was fond of clichés.

'Sorry,' she said.

'Don't worry. I'll leave the pictures with you shall I? Think about what you want and show me the manuscript when it's finished.' He put one hand on her shoulder and gave her a peck on the cheek. 'I'll see myself out shall I?' She watched him leave, and when the door slammed shut behind him she felt as if she had just lost something important.

Chapter Nine

Clementine pushed open the window, and peering out into the night, she let out a timid yell. 'Help! Ophelia, anyone, help!'

She leant out further, waiting, but all she could hear was the wind catching in the dry maple leaves. She turned round, shaking her head.

'The times I've told Ophelia to sleep with her window open,' she muttered. She walked over to the door, pressing her ear right against it, listening for heavy footsteps coming up the stairs. There was only silence. She went back to the window and called out again a little louder this time. Still nothing happened.

'Oh well,' she shrugged her shoulders, sinking back down in her chair. 'It looks like we'll just have to sit tight and wait.'

Mr Scott was fast asleep. Clementine wiggled her toes and rubbed the tops of her arms in an effort to keep warm. She walked around the tiny room, following the path, made by the moonlight, in the dark oak floor. At least Mr Scott was calm in his sleep, although his breathing was a little shallow. She went back to her chair and sat down again, unable to rest. She was exhausted and yet as restless as a five-year-old in a traffic jam, her mind fidgeting and poking at every passing thought. And where was Nathaniel? She closed her eyes for a second, remembering his warm dry hands blindfolding her that night in her garden. 'It's only me,' he had said. What an idiot, creeping up on her like that, scaring her half to death.

Across the room Mr Scott coughed and stirred.

*   *   *

A mile or so along the canal footpath a cattle gate opened up into a small enclosed meadow. Tall hedges punctuated by beech trees surrounded the half acre or so of land, shielding it from the footpath and from the road running the other side. Most people walked right past with their dogs and children, even lovers seemed to prefer to stroll further down along the path, but Clementine would often walk through the gate, settling down in the long grass with a book or a magazine. Today she was meeting Jessica there for a picnic lunch. While she waited for Jessica to arrive she made herself comfortable, lying back on the tartan rug with the cool-box, a bundle of Aunt Elvira's notes, today's *Mail* and a rape alarm at her side. Sipping mineral water, she picked up the paper. She was reading an article on education, and she finished reading feeling that being childless was not such a bad thing after all.

As there was still no sign of Jessica, she picked up the bundle of notes, leafing through the foolscap pages. Overhead the birds were singing and her skin was warm from the sun. She rolled over on her back, looking up at the sky and the small, busy-looking cloud sailing across on a light breeze. She must have fallen asleep and when she opened her eyes again, she looked straight up at Nathaniel Scott.

'Nathaniel,' she murmured, still not quite awake, 'have I been asleep long?'

'Oh,' he looked at his watch, 'about a hundred years.'

'Was I snoring?'

Nathaniel squatted down on the grass by her side. 'No. I didn't hear you breathe at all.'

'Did you think I had died?' Clementine asked sitting up.

'It seemed a possibility. I was about to leave and then, if you were still here when I came back tomorrow, I would have thought it more than a sporting chance.' He picked up the rape alarm, turning it round in his hand, eyebrows raised.

'I'm waiting for Jessica.'

'Dangerous is she?' Nathaniel sat back on the grass.

Clementine smiled at him and found that she didn't know how to stop. 'I like this place, but it's secluded and you never can be sure of wolves.'

Nathaniel nodded gravely. 'Indeed no. Then again, I've been told that wolves, given the right circumstances, make very good husbands and fathers.'

Clementine patted the rug. 'You'd better sit on this; the grass is quite damp.' Nathaniel inched onto the rug. 'I know wolves are nice,' she said. 'It was a poor example, but I just like the word; wolf. And it sounds so much nicer than rapist or murderer or psychopath.' She wiggled her left foot in its tan moccasin. 'I suppose it's only a matter of time until they invent new names, the way they've done with dustmen and the hospital for the dying. "No, Madam, that was not a burglar what did your house over but one of our Redistribution Officers. And the old lady across the road, she wasn't murdered, oh no, not at all. She just had a little visit from a Dispatch Engineer."'

'God, England is beautiful,' Nathaniel exclaimed, and grabbing her hand, he pulled her up along with him, spinning her round by her shoulders until they faced the hillside that rose behind the road.

Clementine looked and admired because it was indeed a lovely sight, sunlit and poppy strewn, but inside she was sulking. He kept his hands on her shoulders and she could feel the warmth of his fingers through the thin cotton blouse. Why did Nathaniel never listen to her? Their conversations, she thought, were not really conversations as much as a series of monologues with an invisible friend.

'Nathaniel,' she said, preparing to have it out with him. 'Why . . .'

'Why?' he repeated, drawing her closer, his eyes fixed on hers.

'Why do you never listen to me?' There, she had said it, but with a voice softening faster than butter in a microwave.

'But I do,' he whispered, his mouth twitching into that little half smile.

Clementine closed her eyes and waited to be kissed.

She was still waiting. 'Oh there you are,' Jessica's voice boomed towards her. 'Sorry I'm late.'

Slowly, Clementine opened her eyes to find Nathaniel standing several feet away inspecting a blackthorn bush and Jessica striding towards her in a long flowing cotton dress. 'Jessica, hi.' Clementine tried to stiffen her voice into something resembling her normal tones. 'This is Nathaniel Scott, my next door neighbour. Nathaniel, this is my friend, Jessica.'

Nathaniel smiled and said hello, then he turned to Clementine. 'Bye, you,' he looked her straight in the eyes before kissing her, fleetingly, on the cheek.

'Is he the alcoholic?' Jessica said, settling herself on the rug right on the spot where Nathaniel had sat not many minutes before.

'He has a drink problem, if that's what you mean.'

'So he's the alcoholic.'

Clementine sighed and unwrapped a bottle of chilled Sancerre from its layers of newspaper. 'Wine?'

'No thanks,' Jessica shook her head. 'I want my eggs to be in tiptop condition for Michael's return.'

Clementine shuddered. 'Well have some of this.' She served up the bean and pasta salad on two china plates; the chipped rose-patterned ones. She passed a plate to Jessica. 'I think I might be in love with him,' she said.

'With the alcoholic? You don't know him.'

'I know I don't.' Feeling defensive all of a sudden she added, 'I can't see why that should be a problem though. In my experience it's when people get to know each other that the real difficulties set in.'

'Now you're being silly. You're infatuated, that's all. He is very attractive, I'll give you that. But we women have a lot to consider when choosing our man.'

Clementine winced. '"Our man." Don't use expressions like that please.'

Jessica looked a little taken aback, but she continued. 'What would he be like as a husband and father? Is he a good hunter gatherer? I have no problems with the morality of leaping into bed with someone, but you must always, at the back of your mind, have these questions in mind, because anyone you sleep with is the potential father of your child.'

'Lordy Lord, Jessica, I just said that I might be in love with the man. I haven't really thought any further.'

'Well, that's very typical of you. You worry yourself sick about all kinds of silly things and then you're completely reckless about others. Anyway,' Jessica held out her plate for some more salad, 'you'll be glad to hear that Derek Fletcher is still at large, so you haven't caused too much havoc there. You know Abby really should be careful with what she eats. She's eighty per cent chocolate gateaux and just twenty per cent baby, that girl, I'm sure of it. Still, she's having her moment in the sun. I've watched her. For the first time in her life, practically, her mother is taking an interest. She is the centre of attention and she is making the most of it. It's quite touching to see really. People talk about all these girls getting pregnant to get a council house, but I reckon, more often than not, that it's because it's the only time in their lives they feel important.'

'She deserves better than that Derek.'

Jessica finished a mouthful of salad. 'You don't know him either, you've cast him as the villain, just as you've cast this Nathaniel as the hero, but for all you know the reality could be the reverse.'

The sun was still shining, the birds were still singing, but inside Clementine, unease was beginning to seep through her sense of well-being.

'You don't believe in destiny; of two people simply being meant for each other then?'

Jessica shook her head. 'Certain gene combinations make people attracted to each other because they know they would produce good offspring, but otherwise not.'

Clementine ate the rest of her salad in silence, thinking that sense had done nothing for Jessica as a companion.

The roses in Clementine's garden smelt especially sweet that night, as if the heat of the day had distilled their scent into something altogether more potent. She wandered across the lawn, pausing now and then to bury her nose in the dew-drenched blooms. She was alone. Ophelia was away in Edinburgh helping a group of pupils set up an exhibition of sculpture. Clementine stopped to admire an especially lovely rose: white with a green and yellow centre, it shone like a Japanese lantern in the dusk.

Once she had dreamt of making people stop and gasp at the beauty of her music, but that was before reality had pushed a stake through the heart of fantasy. As she wandered on down the garden, she found herself asking how it was that she had wasted quite so much of her life. There were a few rare people in the world whose lives took flight, who made their moment on earth count as they soared above the rest of humanity. Clementine had been born without wings, leaving her scurrying hither and thither with an occasional longing glance at the heavens. Maybe, she thought, those other people had simply been elsewhere when the rest of us learnt the meaning of pie in the sky and that life was short and ugly.

She looked up at the evening sky and suddenly two warm dry hands were clasped over her eyes. 'Guess who?' he whispered.

'What a prat,' she whispered back, freeing herself and turning round to face him. 'How on earth did you get in?'

Nathaniel pointed to the tall fence that separated the top of Clementine's garden from next door.

'You didn't climb?'

'Shush,' he put his finger to her lips and then, slowly removing it, he bent down and kissed her.

Dear God, she prayed, forgetting all about blasphemy, don't let me drown him in saliva. But soon she was not thinking about anything at all.

Many minutes later Nathaniel let go of Clementine. 'I'm terribly sorry,' he said, 'but I seem to have the most enormous erection.'

Clementine took his hand, careful only to look at his face. She began to laugh, softly, happily.

'It's not meant to be amusing,' Nathaniel complained. He looked intently at her. After a moment he shook his head, as if he was trying to wake himself up from a deep sleep. 'I'll always remember you exactly how you are now, this moment.'

'Let's go inside,' asked a new bold Clementine, pulling him along towards the house and in through the French windows. 'Have you had supper?' She led him into the kitchen.

When he said he'd love a drink, she handed him a bottle of red wine and an opener, mindless of the fact that it was her duty to help him not to drink, caring only that he should be content in her company.

She sipped her wine, unable to take her eyes off him. She watched his throat as he swallowed, allowing her gaze to travel down his chest to his flat stomach, but no further.

'You're sure you don't want something to eat?'

He smiled and shook his head. 'I couldn't eat a thing. Here,' he took her hand and put it to his heart, 'feel how fast it's beating?'

She nodded. 'Mine too,' and she moved his hand to her breast. So this, she thought, is how it feels to be happy.

Chapter Ten

Clementine was weeping silently, her head pressed hard against the green wing chair. Whoever it was who said it was better to have loved and lost than never to have loved at all was an idiot. And so was she for having allowed light to pierce the mellow gloom of her existence, only for it to be extinguished, leaving her hating the darkness. She sniffed and wiped her nose with the back of her hand.

'Mr Scott,' she whispered. 'Toby, are you awake?'

* * *

'With my body, I thee worship.' Clementine looked down at Nathaniel's sleeping face as the first shafts of sunlight shone through the open curtains of her bedroom. He had fallen asleep in her arms and she had stayed awake watching over him. Her shoulder had begun to ache, but at first she had not wanted to move in case she disturbed him. When she could stand the pain no longer she had slipped her arm from beneath his chest and he had stirred and turned round to face her.

'I love you,' he said, quite loudly, quite clearly, and then he had gone straight back to sleep. Resting on her elbow she had stayed looking at him, at his pale profile barely discernible in the darkness, at the way his hair curled behind his ears, and at his square shoulders and his upper arms, soft in repose.

She could see from the alarm clock on the dressing-table that it was five o'clock. The room was filled with light, and any moment he would wake and find her lying there puffy-eyed and with bad breath. She edged out of the bed and tiptoed into the bathroom. As she brushed her teeth, she wondered what Sleeping Beauty's breath must have been like after a hundred years. That was just the kind of issue she should raise in her version of the story, she decided. She washed herself down with a flannel soaked in scented bath oil and, finally, she put some creme blusher on her cheeks and a tiny bit of raspberry-red lipstick on her lips. Slipping back into bed she reached out her hand and, her fingertips touching his, she went to sleep at last.

Nathaniel woke her with a kiss. Well, he would, wouldn't he, she thought contentedly, smiling before she had even opened her eyes. He kissed her again, and when he had finished kissing her he just lay there, resting on his elbow the way she had done earlier, studying her face in a thorough, considered way. Clementine squirmed under his scrutiny, wishing in an instant for perfect features and flawless unlined skin.

'I love you,' he said again. Clementine clasped him tight, mumbling words of endearment that embarrassed her even as she spoke.

'What's that my darling?' Nathaniel asked.

'Oh nothing. I'm just so in love with you I'm quite beside myself.' And she thought, This is what it must be like to be immortal: living only for the present and caring nothing for the past and nothing for the future.

Nathaniel sat up, looking at his watch. 'Fiddle-de-dee! Oh fiddle-de-dee. I'm meant to be in London by nine.'

He was out of bed and dressed in minutes, coming back to give her one last kiss before disappearing down the stairs and out onto the street.

You feel light when you are immortal, Clementine thought, even when you were nearly six feet, and you felt clever too, and powerful. Then she fell asleep.

When she woke she was her old mortal self, heavy with worry. This love, it would never work. How could it? They had nothing to say to each other and he was obviously intent on drinking himself to death. She got up, and as she showered and dressed, she tried to calm herself. Why be so pessimistic? The love of a good woman could change all that. Who was she kidding? Everyone knew that the only thing changed by the love of a good woman was the woman herself. No, it would all end in tears: hers. They would have a brief wonderful time together, Nathaniel Scott and she, and then she would be left to spend the rest of her days aching for the feel of his arms around her and his lips against hers, crying herself to sleep at night in a bed which would for ever bear the imprint of his body.

'Why are you washing your hands again?' Nathaniel came up behind her as she stood at the sink, giving the back of her neck a quick kiss.

'I've just taken the rubbish out.'

They were in the kitchen together and Ophelia was there too. Clementine busied around preparing supper, but every five seconds she had to pause and look at Nathaniel, and then she had to look away again because she understood all about melting now. It started with your heart expanding in a loose undisciplined manner, until it had taken over every nook and cranny of your chest. It did not stop there, but seeped through down to your stomach and up to your brain, finally reaching your eyes, where it clouded your vision, causing that commonly described melting gaze.

It all seemed to get on Ophelia's nerves. 'She does it all the time: washes her hands,' she said disloyally. 'Any minute now she'll start detoxing the door handles. That's how it began with the mother of a friend of mine and now she's an outpatient at a psychiatric clinic.'

Clementine stirred the mince in the frying-pan and pretended to smile.

Nathaniel came up to her and put his arm round her shoulders, giving her a kiss on the neck, just below her ear, and one on the cheek. 'You shouldn't worry about things like that,' he said. 'I tell you, if you were to die now, and we left you here in the nice warm kitchen, in two days you would be nothing but a heaving bloated mass of bacteria. It's a thought, isn't it?'

Clementine had to admit that it was. 'Most things are,' she added.

'I simply don't allow myself to worry,' Ophelia said. 'Very little matters very much. It's all about getting things in proportion.' Nathaniel nodded approvingly. Clementine allowed herself to slam the wooden spoon down on the piece of kitchen paper by the side of the cooker. It was not a very loud slam though, and no-one took any notice.

'You're absolutely right,' Nathaniel agreed with Ophelia. 'What you concentrate on grows. If you concentrate on the negative, that grows; if you concentrate on what's good and positive, that grows. I really believe that.' He picked up his glass of peach water and turned it round in his hand before putting it back down on the table with a little grimace of distaste. 'Are you sure I can't help with anything?' he asked Clementine.

'Absolutely not,' she smiled; 'you sit down and relax.'

Ophelia already was. 'You're not really an alcoholic?' she asked, curling up in her chair.

It was bad enough that Ophelia was able to curl up in such a tiny chair, it was even worse that she felt able

134

to ask Nathaniel a question that Clementine, his lover, still had not had the courage to ask. There had been so many times in the past weeks that she had wanted to, but it had never seemed the right time. Even when he lay naked in her arms, she had felt he might not yet trust her enough to answer such a question. And there was Ophelia, asking away; Ophelia who had spent no more than a few hours in his company, all told. Clementine added the chopped garlic and chillies to the mince with little bad-tempered flicks of the spoon.

'I've been waiting for Clementine to ask me that,' Nathaniel said. 'And the answer, I suppose, is yes, but in a fairly house-trained way. It was beginning to affect my work and my father is worried sick, so I decided to take a few weeks off and come down here to try and sort myself out.' He smiled and shrugged his shoulders. 'But I love drinking, so I'll probably start again.'

Clementine dropped the spoon in the pan. 'Oh no, oh no don't. Your liver will pack up and then that's it, you're finished.'

'Nag, nag, nag,' Nathaniel said, but he walked across the room and gave her a hug. 'We've all got to go some time,' he said.

'That is such a meaningless phrase in the circumstances,' Clementine snapped. 'I know we all have to go some time. Most people know this, but it's seldom used as a defence at a murder trial. "Well M'lord, it was unfortunate that my client should have taken it upon himself to strangle the victim, but do bear in mind, members of the jury, that we all have to go some time."'

'A lot of artists drink and a lot of them achieve their best work while they do it,' Ophelia said.

Clementine had to leave the room. Ophelia could sit there, curled up on her little chair and coo those weasel words that Nathaniel wanted to hear. It was easy for her because she did not love him. Clementine knew; she had been there herself.

'Darling!' Nathaniel called out after her. 'Is everything all right?'

'Yes, fine!' she called back from the sitting-room. 'Just getting something.' In fact, she was getting herself together. Nathaniel might well love her, but if he witnessed her hitting such a little creature as Ophelia, he could go off her. She stayed in the sitting-room, sulking, for ten minutes, then the need to be with him grew too strong and she went back to the kitchen, her steps firm, as if she had had a purpose in going off all along. She paused for a moment outside the kitchen door, taking a deep breath before bustling into the room, a cramped smile on her lips. Ophelia was busy opening a bottle of red wine.

'It's a great preventative of coronary disease.' She waved the cork at Clementine before her eyes were on Nathaniel. Clementine said nothing.

'Hello, my darling,' Nathaniel reached out for her, pulling her down on his lap. 'I love you,' he whispered as she perched on his knees.

Clementine was wondering whether she could achieve some kind of semi-levitation to make herself lighter, but now she turned and cupped his face in her hands. 'And I love you,' she whispered back with an intensity which surprised them both. After a few minutes she got back up and started to lay the table. Ophelia poured out the wine.

'Cheers,' she lifted her glass.

Nathaniel raised his in response. Clementine was about to protest, her hand ready to reach out and take the glass from him, but in the end she did nothing. She loved him, but it seemed she did not have the strength to love him well. She dished up the chilli and sat down herself, smiling at Nathaniel when he looked hangdog and fumbled for her hand under the table; it was the kind of thing you did when you loved selfishly. As she lit the candles she tried to think of something bright and cheerful to say. Nathaniel liked bright and cheerful; most men did far more than they liked the truth. Who could blame them?

'I do hope your father didn't show that Derek Fletcher round the whole house,' she said. Now that was not really very bright or cheerful. She tried again. 'He seems a good plumber. If he really is a plumber that is.'

'If he isn't a plumber,' Nathaniel said, 'why is he going round people's houses doing plumbing jobs?'

'Clementine thinks he's a dragon,' Ophelia said.

It was Clementine who opened the third bottle of wine, sunning herself in the adoring if unfocused glances from Nathaniel. All she cared about was his approval. Love, she decided, did not necessarily make you a better person.

After dinner she played the piano. She did not play well, she had had too much to drink for that, but to an audience who had drunk even more, she sounded good. When she had finished playing, Ophelia and Nathaniel both clapped. Cheered by her success, she proceeded to accompany herself singing 'Marble Halls'. She had a pretty enough voice, clear and soft, but she did not usually sing to anyone but herself.

'Isn't she amazing?' Nathaniel exclaimed when she had finished. 'Isn't your sister the most amazing woman who ever walked this earth?' He stood up and put out both hands to Clementine. 'Let's go to bed.'

Clementine got up from the piano and joined him. 'Good night.' She gave a little wave to Ophelia, who, it had to be said, looked rather silly sitting there with her superiority all in tatters.

The next morning Clementine went off early to shop. She wanted a particular piece of sheet music for Beatrice who was coming for her lesson later that day. She was preparing to do her usual detour around John Melchett's carpet shop when she looked up, stopped and stared. Every window in the shop was smashed, the jagged shards of glass glinting on the cobble-stones and red paint had been sprayed across the shop front and on what was left of the windows. Clementine stepped forward, careful to avoid the broken glass, and peered through the open door. She could see that the rugs too had been assaulted with the same red paint, sprayed on any old way in great gashes. A carpenter had begun to board up the windows, but as she edged closer she could just distinguish a small figure inside, seated on a rolled-up carpet, head in hands. The carpenter might just as well have cordoned off a ten-yard area around the shop she thought, the way everyone kept their distance, necks craned, as they walked past. It was as always, Clementine thought, misfortune being treated as a contagious disease.

'I don't even believe very much was stolen,' she said to Nathaniel that evening. 'It was simply destruction for the sake of it. A way for someone to pass the time. And like everyone else, I just walked on past, tutting as I went.'

'So what should you have done?' Nathaniel gave her shoulder a little squeeze. They had eaten and now they sat together on the sofa in the sitting-room, as contented, Clementine thought, as an alcoholic and a compulsive worrier could be.

'Gone inside and said how sorry I was. Offered to help clear up. Told him I had always preferred my Persian rugs with red paint sprayed on them. Anything rather than just walking on by. June Challis says it has to be the busker. She calls him a shifty-looking good-for-nothing vagrant and that's that as far as she's concerned. Peculiar woman. She's got a perfectly good criminal in her own family and yet she has to go and cast aspersions on a complete stranger. Anyway, if I was living rough, I would take the rugs to lie on, not paint them.'

'Whatever you say, darling,' Nathaniel gave her shoulder another little squeeze and Clementine thought, not for the first time, that it would be nice if he listened to her, really listened. If she were to be honest with herself, and sometimes one had to be, however disruptive and unpleasant that was, there were times when she felt that Nathaniel might as well spend his time sitting underground playing a lute, he lived so much in his own world.

Nathaniel turned her towards him. 'I adore you, my beautiful Clementine,' he said. And like so many times before, she looked into his eyes and wanted nothing more than to share that world, any world, with him. She supposed this to be love.

Chapter Eleven

Clementine had dozed off and in her sleep she dreamt she was lowering Mr Scott to the ground by her hair. She woke with a start, feeling stiff and cold and, stretching, got to her feet. She went up to the window, holding her watch to the faint light. It was almost two o'clock. She looked around the room. Maybe now she felt sure the intruder was gone, she could switch the light on, but she decided against it. She did not want to risk waking Mr Scott. She wondered what devastation was awaiting them downstairs. When they were finally rescued, she would insist that Mr Scott went straight to his room and waited for his doctor. His poor heart might not be able to take any more shocks. She looked at her watch again. Where was Nathaniel?

*　　*　　*

Jessica was pregnant. She and Michael had been on holiday in a friend's villa in Italy and soon after their return she had found out she was pregnant. She arrived at Clementine's house for lunch, all flushed cheeks and shiny hair, dressed in leggings and a tent-like white shirt.

'You look blooming,' Clementine said, feeling that was what she was expected to say. She was right.

Jessica beamed at her and said she had never felt better. 'I think I shall be pregnant for the rest of my life.' She edged into the kitchen chair, practising, Clementine thought.

'So how far gone are you now?'

'Nine weeks,' Jessica held up nine pretty fingers. 'So it must have happened before we went away.'

'Try doing that but leaving out your little finger not your thumb,' Clementine said. 'It's almost impossible. You just can't fold your little finger without the ring finger following suit.'

'Really,' Jessica mumbled. 'I can have the soup but no soft cheese or uncooked vegetables.'

'Of course not,' Clementine hid the weeping Camembert. She should have remembered about listeria. 'It's lentil soup, that's OK isn't it?'

Jessica said it was ideal. 'It's amazing how this little thing', she patted her stomach, 'has taken over. Poor Michael is feeling quite neglected.'

'I thought you were meant to neglect your husband after the baby was born,' Clementine said, but then she was jealous.

'Don't be silly. It's nothing you plan, it just happens. I love this baby more than I love anything in the world and that's all there is to it.'

'But you don't know it.'

Jessica didn't even bother to answer. Instead she asked, 'And how are things between you and Nathaniel? I'm dying to meet him properly.'

Clementine sighed. 'How do you know if you love someone?'

'You just do. Like with me and the baby. Or', she added, 'me and Mike, for that matter. Anyway, you shouldn't have to ask. You loved Gustaf didn't you?'

Clementine served the soup and sat down opposite Jessica. 'I'm not sure. Sometimes I think I did and sometimes I think I didn't. Anyway, it's all so different with Nathaniel. I tell you, just talking about him makes my heart beat faster. Being with him is like . . . well, like being with one of those fairies who flits around colouring the world with a magic wand, dab dab dab, making flowers explode into bloom and stars appear in the heavens.'

'Fairy?'

'Well, you know what I mean.'

'So why the questions? What does it matter anyway? You're having a lovely time together. Relax, enjoy it for what it is.'

'But what is it?' Clementine nagged. 'And what about if one day he asks me to marry him or live with him or something, how will I know that what I feel for him really is love? Love is supposed to be unselfish, but I'm not sure I would die for him, although it's possible I would die without him.'

'I would die for my baby,' Jessica said.

Was this statement helpful? Clementine was not sure. That was the problem, she was never sure of anything.

That evening, Beatrice was due to give her first recital at a charity concert organized by three local schools. Beatrice was excited and, to begin with, not a bit nervous. She had been having two lessons a week for the past couple of weeks, instead of her usual one, and Clementine was proud of her progress. Her technique had improved and her understanding of the music she played went far beyond what one would expect from someone of her age. She remained calm as the date of the concert approached. Clementine flapped. Beatrice told Clementine she had always dreamt of performing at a proper concert. Clementine remembered the time when she, herself, was nine and had slipped off the piano stool.

'Now, if you make a mistake, don't worry. The odds are that no-one in the audience will have noticed anyway,' she said for the third time on the morning of the recital itself. Then she added, 'And don't panic and think you're getting MS if your fingers go numb.'

For the first time Beatrice looked worried and Clementine dug her nails into her palms, despairing of herself. 'Of course, there's no reason, no reason at all why your fingers should go numb in the first place.'

'What's MS?' Beatrice asked.

'Nothing for you to worry about, that's for sure,' Clementine chirruped. 'Now run through your pieces in the order you're going to perform them and with the proper length breaks.'

'I'm getting a bra,' Beatrice said.

'Really. How nice.' Clementine smiled mechanically. Think if her careless words about making mistakes and fingers going numb had lodged in Beatrice's mind. Think if the child froze on stage. It would be Clementine's doing.

'I want a black one, but Mummy says they're for easy ladies. She says white gets grimy and that I should have a flesh-coloured one.'

Clementine thought she might well have dented Beatrice's confidence for life.

'I want black with red lace,' Beatrice concluded as her small hands struck the first notes of *The Well-Tempered Klavier*.

Clementine was taking Beatrice across to St Andrew's Church of England Primary School where the concert was being held. 'Now remember, tonight is meant to be enjoyed,' Clementine said, clasping the child's hand as they crossed the High Street. As they approached St Andrew's Church the bells struck six.

'Let's go for a walk,' Clementine suggested. 'We've got masses of time and it's such a lovely evening.' Beatrice nodded agreement and they wandered on down the street and onto the footpath, still hand in hand. The setting sun reached out through the branches of the trees to the water, turning it golden. A lone duck swam past and Clementine smiled at the contrast between its gliding serenity and the furious paddling of its legs. So human, she thought; the calm we show to the world, hiding the frantic paddling that keeps us afloat.

'Once upon a time I met a very handsome prince type person here,' she said as they passed the place where she had first seen Nathaniel.

'A real prince?' Beatrice asked.

'No,' Clementine had to admit, 'not in real life. But you know how we have two kinds of lives, the one that everybody sees and the other one. You know how to most people you are a very pretty talented little girl. That's real life. But you, of course, know that you are really the world's greatest pianist in disguise, the world's greatest pianist who, by the way, would not be seen dead in a flesh-coloured bra.'

Beatrice did not reply, she just clutched Clementine's hand a little tighter as they wandered on down along the canal. A kingfisher dived into the water, a flash of cobalt blue.

'Why do you think he's really a prince?' Beatrice wanted to know.

'I'm not really sure,' Clementine said, 'but sometimes you just know these things.'

'I presume', the child said with a little smile, 'that he doesn't wear a crown.'

'Few princes do, whether real or imagined. Of course what they do in private we don't know.'

'Are you going to marry him?'

Clementine stopped for a moment and looked out across the water. 'I don't think so,' she said, resuming her walk.

'Why?' Beatrice did a little skip as she asked.

'Oh, he'd never find a slipper big enough.'

'That's not a really good reason,' Beatrice said. Then her attention was caught by a figure slumped on the grass verge a few yards ahead, just where the path turned into a bend.

'Now that's not him, is it? I really hope it isn't, but my mum says there's no accounting for taste.'

'That's most certainly not him,' Clementine said. As they got closer, Clementine saw that the sleeping man was the busker.

'Maybe he's in disguise? Maybe he's really a prince too?' Beatrice hissed.

'It's possible,' Clementine said, aware that she must not pass on her own middle-class prejudices to a child, someone else's child at that. For all she knew, Beatrice's parents could be of the belief that princes often lurked beneath the rags of vagrants. Who was she to argue?

'Maybe if you kissed him he'd turn into one, a prince I mean.'

'That's frogs,' Clementine said, feeling on safer ground. 'Anyway, no woman should be so desperate for a prince that she would go around kissing complete strangers, be they frogs or not.' She looked at her watch. 'We should be getting over to St Andrew's.'

'Look!' Beatrice darted forward. 'He's bleeding.' Before Clementine could stop her, Beatrice had picked up a broken milk bottle from the ground a foot or so away from the sleeping man. 'He must have cut himself on this. Ouch!' She dropped the bottle and ran across to Clementine, holding up her own bleeding thumb for inspection.

'That was a very very silly thing to do,' Clementine said, feeling herself go pale with concern.

The sleeping man, his face half hidden by the hood of a sweatshirt top, stirred and mumbled in his sleep.

Clementine grabbed Beatrice by the wrist, pulling her along with her back up the path. 'You must not pick up things like that. Now, we must get that cut cleaned as soon as possible.'

'It's a tiny cut. I'll still be able to play.'

Clementine did not answer as she hurried along back onto the road. They arrived at the school all of a

145

fluster, rushing past teachers and friends and not even stopping to see if Beatrice's parents had arrived.

'Where's the loo, please?' Clementine called to a woman arranging some chairs in the back row of the assembly hall. The woman pointed to a door at the side of the podium at the front of the room.

'I should be behind the stage with the others,' Beatrice complained.

'This won't take a minute.' Clementine pushed open the lavatory door and dragged Beatrice inside, holding her thumb under the warm-water tap and rubbing it with liquid soap from a dispenser on the wall.

'Ouch, it hurts.' Beatrice pulled her hand away. Clementine grabbed it back and patted it dry before pulling a plaster from her bag and putting it across the tiny cut.

'You shouldn't feel this,' she said. 'Now out we go and face the audience.'

It was Beatrice's turn to play. Clementine stood by her left shoulder, ready to turn the pages of the music. The first few notes were a little uncertain, but soon she was playing as well as Clementine had ever heard her. The child was a natural performer. She could go anywhere . . . if she lived. Clementine swallowed hard. The thoughts she had tried to ward off returned, regrouped and reinforced. What if Beatrice had cut herself on exactly the same bit of jagged glass as the man? What if he had Aids? Even now, as she sat there playing like an angel, Beatrice could be on her way to becoming one. Clementine tried to pull herself together. Look on the bright side, she thought. Why should the poor man be infected? Because he might be a drug addict that's why. He had been lying there, prac- tically unconscious, and there were no signs of any bottles other than milk. Then again, there had been no syringes either. So maybe he was naturally tidy? How could she tell Beatrice's parents?

'Clementine,' Beatrice hissed.

146

It was too late. Clementine had missed her cue. Beatrice tried to turn the page herself and lost concentration, her fingers stumbling across an arpeggio. There was tittering from some children in the audience.

'Sorry,' Clementine said afterwards to Beatrice. 'I am so very, very sorry.'

Ophelia was wearing a tiny black skirt and a black jumper to match the look she was giving Clementine. 'You really buggered that child up, didn't you?' she said, as if Clementine had not just told her that very same thing. 'And don't sit there feeling sorry for yourself either.' Did Ophelia know everything? 'You go on about Nathaniel being an alcoholic but you're worse. You're addicted to worry and you're too weak and pathetic to do anything about it. And don't snivel, it's very unbecoming. There's a whole ocean out there, beautiful, exciting, important. It's your time to swim in it and what do you do?'

Clementine wiped her nose with a tissue from the box on the dresser and looked interested.

'You paddle around in the shallows, too scared to venture out into the cool glittering sea, dragging others down with you.'

Clementine was just about to say that, all things being equal, she was less likely to drag people down while in the shallows, but she decided not to.

'You're becoming a bore,' Ophelia continued. 'You have no time for anything interesting because you spend all your time fretting. What a waste!'

That was it, Clementine could take no more. 'I can be carefree,' she said. 'I can be interesting.'

Nathaniel was tired. His face looked pinched. As Clementine clasped her strong arms around his neck he winced. 'I'm sorry but I really am very tired.' He had spent the week on an assignment in the Hebrides, taking photographs of the effects of a major oil spill a year on. When Clementine laughed in a carefree, unworried sort of way, he gave her a little shove and complained. 'I don't think you understand how tired I am.'

'Well I'll perk you up,' giggled the carefree, interesting Clementine. 'I've got supper all organized.' She pulled him along with her towards the kitchen. 'I've been pretty busy myself learning some new music. I can't stand the thought of stagnating.'

Nathaniel stopped in the kitchen doorway. 'Look, darling, would you mind terribly if I passed on supper. I really couldn't eat a thing. I'll go across and say hi to Dad and then I'll just crash out.' He put his arm around her, pulling her towards him. 'You don't mind, do you?'

'Of course not,' Clementine said with a voice as brittle as a glass thread. 'You go off to bed and I'll see you tomorrow.'

He was gone and she was alone in the kitchen, blowing out the candles, covering the food and putting it in the fridge.

'Fuck you, Ophelia,' she said. 'Fuck you.'

Chapter Twelve

'I suppose that's what happens when you fall in love with a man because he's the spitting image of an underground-dwelling, lute-playing visually-challenged prince; you talk yourself into love and you talk yourself out of it. At least there's a kind of symmetry there. You start off stupid and you end up stupid.' Clementine would not have put it like that if Mr Scott had been listening, but he was asleep still, and Clementine was talking to herself.

*   *   *

Ophelia came home to find Clementine sitting alone in the dark kitchen. 'I'm not surprised,' she said, once Clementine had told her about Nathaniel not even bothering to stay for supper. 'I wasn't going to say anything, but Veronica told me a friend of hers was left a complete mess after having a relationship with him. She rearranged her whole life to suit him and apparently he treated her appallingly before breaking it off and disappearing abroad. It took her years to get back to normal.'

Clementine looked up at her with red-rimmed puffy eyes. 'But he's so lovely,' she muttered.

'You haven't been crying?' Ophelia said, exasperated. 'Honestly, I would take a good look at where this relationship is taking you before it's too late.' With those words she went upstairs to bed.

'Darling, wake up, darling.' Nathaniel was calling Clementine from the street outside her bedroom window. 'Clementine, come for a walk with me.'

Clementine was awake, but she had been staying in bed watching the sun's progress across the room. When she heard Nathaniel's voice she threw off her bedclothes and hurried across the room, opening the window.

'Hi, you,' she said with a voice that was so soft she hardly recognized it herself. She leant out, putting her arm across her chest to support her breasts, thinking that Rapunzel did not have this problem. No, that girl could just allow her hair to tumble down the wall seductively without having to worry about a pair of breasts following suit.

'Come for a walk with me,' Nathaniel smiled up at her, picking up a basket from the ground and holding it for her to see. 'I've brought breakfast.'

Clementine rushed into the bathroom and showered. She dressed in a pair of black jeans and a soft green sweater and she applied some mascara and lipstick before stepping back from the mirror and studying her face. She added some blusher to her cheeks and brushed on a second layer of mascara. Nathaniel kept telling her not to bother with make-up, so she had become increasingly artful in applying it. If she had a pound for every time a man fell in love with a woman with foundation-smooth skin and scarlet lips, only to tell her, once they were lovers, that he much preferred the natural look, she would be a rich woman. Well, she would have about ten pounds anyway. 'If I had looked the way you now say you want me to look the first few times we met, you would never have looked twice at me,' she had argued with Nathaniel. She gave her hair a quick brush and then she was off, running down the stairs and out onto the street into Nathaniel's waiting arms. She felt the warmth of his skin through his shirt and the heat of his cheek against hers, she also smelt the alcohol on his breath, but for the moment she made no comment.

'Where are we going?' she asked instead.

'Canal, if that's all right with you?'

'Of course,' Clementine, again forgetting her size and age, did a little skip. She looked up at the sky, feeling the sun on her face and blaming it for her blushes. Fanning herself with the palm of her hand, she said, 'Indian summer.'

Nathaniel let go of her hand and put his arm round her shoulders pulling her close. 'It is for us,' he said quietly.

The town was about to wake, as yet only the newsagents were open for business, but the metal grids across the windows of Harper's Hardware were being unlocked as they passed and crates were arriving for the fruit stall at the corner of the High Street and East Street. They turned off down towards the canal and Nathaniel said, 'I'm sorry about last night.'

Clementine smiled at him. 'That's all right.' But she wondered whether it was. After a moment, she said, 'At least I think so.' But by now Nathaniel's attention had been caught by a kestrel hovering overhead. You often saw kestrels right there by the churchyard where the road turned into a footpath. They were watching for the mice and voles that scurried around in amongst the blackthorn hedges. She looked up at Nathaniel and she could see from the little smile at the corner of his mouth that he knew he was being studied. He was a silent solitary kind of man, she thought, but his silence seemed more a result of there being too much on his mind than too little. So he took the easy way out and said nothing. At least that's how it seemed to her. What did she know? She observed him the way a dog observes its master, twitching and ready for his every move and mood, retreating mournfully to her basket when ignored or excluded but still with those big brown eyes intently fixed on the object of her worship. This, she suspected, was not the way to an open and equal relationship.

They reached the tiny meadow where, two months ago now, they had almost had their first kiss, and Nathaniel spread out his jacket on the grass for them to sit on. Unpacking the basket he looked up at her for a moment. 'I love you.'

'I love you too.' Clementine gave him a wide smile. These wide smiles were useful for spreading over doubts.

Nathaniel had brought along bacon sandwiches and hard-boiled eggs; croissants, wrapped up in foil to keep them warm; a grapefruit, halved and wrapped in cling film, and even some strawberries. Last, he unpacked a bottle of orange juice and one of champagne. Clementine gazed at him. He was so beautiful with the sun picking out auburn lights in his hair and flecks of gold in his green eyes.

'Oh Nathaniel, you shouldn't have . . .' She was about to be good. She was about to tell him that they must not have that champagne.

'I love you. Now don't be a bore.'

'A bore, *moi*? Don't assume.' She put out her hand and touched his cheek, sliding her finger down to his neck, feeling the rough spot underneath his chin where he had not seen to shave. 'I was going to say that you shouldn't have gone to so much trouble.' So now she was a liar as well.

Nathaniel took her hand and raised it to his lips, kissing each of her fingers in turn. 'You're right. I shouldn't assume. I just have to remember that you are constantly surprising and invariably enchanting.'

For then his approval seemed the only prize worth gaining and to keep it she would not only have sold her grandmother, had her grandmother been available,

152

but she would have given her away as a free gift attached to a cereal packet. He handed her a glass of Buck's Fizz and raised his own glass in a toast. She twinkled at him above the edge of hers.

'Have something to eat,' Nathaniel said.

Clementine's hand hovered above the blue and white tablecloth. She wondered what would be the most enchanting and least predictable choice of food. The obvious thing, at breakfast, was to start with the grapefruit. Her hand passed over the cling-film covered fruit, pausing above the punnet of strawberries. Strawberries would usually come last, but at breakfast? Croissant, bacon sandwich.

'Here,' Nathaniel said impatiently, unwrapping the grapefruit and putting it on two plates, 'why don't you start with that.'

'I'm going to be a godmother. A very good friend of mine, Jessica Hubbard, you met her once, has just got pregnant. I don't mean just, as in last night or something, but a few weeks ago. She's very pleased.' Clementine tried to swallow a spoonful of grapefruit without making that awful glugging sound.

'That's nice. Is it her first?' Nathaniel did not seem to have a problem. He was the neatest eater she knew.

She nodded. 'She always said she never wanted babies and now it's all she talks about.'

Nathaniel stretched out on the grass, resting on his elbows. 'I would love to have children, but, as I'm never home, I don't think it would be fair to them or their mother.' Did she imagine it, or did he look at her in a very pointed way. 'This is probably the longest I've been in England in ten years. So what about you, do you want children?'

Clementine finished her grapefruit, swallowing as carefully as if it had been pieces of glass waiting to break in her throat. There she went again, making that sound. She almost choked on the juice. When she had recovered she said, 'It just never happened. There

153

seemed to be no reason, no medical reason I mean. I kind of wanted children, but then again, I was quite relieved not to. I don't think I could have coped with the worry.'

'You just can't think like that. Most people who have children worry about them. They still have them.' The sun went behind a cloud just as suddenly as Nathaniel's approval turned into irritation. Clementine shivered and bit into her sandwich. It was delicious. Nathaniel emptied his glass and topped Clementine's up before refilling his own. 'And don't look at me like that.' He took her hand again. Then he kissed her.

Clementine did not wish to be crude. Crudeness made her uncomfortable, but almost two hours later she was dying to ask Nathaniel how it was that two adults could spend all that time with their tongues in each other's mouths, and think it the most wonderful thing in the world. She sat up straight and pulled her sweater down over her hips. Best not to ask.

'Walk?' Nathaniel got up, putting his hand out and helping her to her feet. He was good, Nathaniel, she thought, at sweeping you along with him, but she was far from convinced that his was a hand to hold in a storm. And a storm would come sooner or later, of that she was sure. She had managed on her own for the last couple of years. It had been peaceful. She'd had only herself to worry about and that was more than enough. But increasingly, thoughts and dreams of Nathaniel were insinuating themselves into her daily routines, taking over, and the elation that had come from simply being in love was beginning to take on shades of pain.

'All right?' he asked her with a smile.

'Lovely,' she smiled back. As they wandered further down the footpath the track became thick with mud and rotting leaves, and with every step the sweet autumn smell of decay rose in the air around them.

Decay, Clementine repeated in her thoughts and she

asked Nathaniel, 'Have you been drinking a lot lately?'

'A fair amount,' he answered.

'Couldn't you stop? For me?'

He thought about it for a moment. 'Probably not,' he said.

'Then, just as you've made me really love you, just as I've become really dependent on you, you'll die of liver failure. I don't think that's entirely fair.'

'Don't you really love me now?'

It was Clementine's turn to pause and think. 'I love you partly,' she explained. 'What I think I mean is, I love you selfishly and quite joyfully, for me, but I don't think I love you maturely and selflessly yet. For example, if you were to get ill now from your drinking, I would mind for me, because I would be deprived of you. I don't know if I would mind for you.'

'But you think that one day you would love me enough to mind for me?'

'Hmm,' Clementine nodded.

'I wish you would stop going on about my liver. A wise man once said, "A man is to a woman what a derelict house is to a property dealer: something you acquire with a view to improvement."'

'What wise man?'

'Me,' Nathaniel said, rather pleased with himself, Clementine noticed. He stopped dead in his track and took her in his arms and kissed her. 'I do love you,' he said.

'It's strange,' Clementine said, 'but if asked, about ninety nine point nine per cent of people would say that you can't be in love for ever, yet ninety nine point nine per cent of people falling in love believe that they will be the nought point one per cent who stay in love. Or would that be nought nought point one? It's like dying: we all know we're going to die and still we insist on running through our lives as if we can't wait to get to the end and start again. We know these things in our heads, but we don't feel them in our hearts. Ask anyone. Are you going to die? And they'll say, Yes, of course, in an airy disinterested way. We talk about a terminally ill person as "Dying," when we are actually saying, "So and so is dying more urgently than some of us." You have headlines in the papers with people exclaiming, "I was told I was going to die," or, "I thought I was dying." Well, did they think that they weren't?'

'This is very true, my darling,' Nathaniel said. Then he kissed her again, and she thought that talking was probably overrated anyway. Why should a relationship built on deep and meaningful conversation be more lasting than one built on deep and meaningful kissing? The answer, of course, would be that sooner or later you tire of kissing. Then again, it was Clementine's experience that people soon grew pretty tired of talking to each other as well.

When they reached the derelict boat-house they sat down to rest on the broken hull of an upside-down rowing-boat. 'I remember when this was all still operating,' Clementine said. 'You would pay whatever it was and then you could take a boat out for half an hour or an hour.'

'I would like to row you down the canal,' Nathaniel said.

'But the boat's got holes in it,' Clementine said. She scrambled to her feet, balancing with one foot on either side of the keel.

'Stay there,' Nathaniel ordered, whipping out a small camera from the pocket of his jacket. He walked backwards as far as the other side of the path and then he began taking pictures. Clementine posed for the camera doing what women do when they are embarrassed by a lens being pointed at them: she twirled and she pouted and she played with her hair. She was about to slip down off the boat when she noticed a man stumbling out from the boat-house towards them. After a moment she recognized the busker in his black-hooded sweatshirt. Suddenly he stiffened and then his whole body began to twitch as if an electric current was being conducted through his thin frame. Clementine stared; scared, fascinated and disgusted all at once. Then she slid down from the boat, yelling for Nathaniel to help. The man collapsed to the ground, twitching still, and for a moment Clementine just stood there, wondering what she might catch if she went any closer. His back arched in a massive convulsion and Clementine darted forward, falling to her knees at his side. His hood had slipped off his head and Clementine found herself looking at him properly for the first time and finding nothing but a boy, a fair-haired boy with a dirty face.

Clementine called out again for Nathaniel to help. The boy was choking, gasping for breath as his skin turned from grey to skimmed-milk white. Clementine hesitated for a second, then she prised his lips apart and forced her fingers into his mouth, groping around for his tongue to clear the back of his throat. She tried to remember what she had heard about people having fits. Clear the airways; that was done now. Lie him on his side; that was it. She turned around, looking for Nathaniel. He was there, right behind her, taking pictures.

'Call an ambulance!' she yelled. 'For heaven's sake get some help.'

The boy had stopped twitching. He lay in the grass and for all Clementine knew he could be dead. Nathaniel knelt down, and changing lenses, fired off another few shots. Finally, he did get to his feet, screwing the lens cap back on the camera.

'I'll go to the call box at the top of the road.' She watched him disappear, running, up the path back towards the road. Now what? She could have been part of a government campaign – The Woman Who Did Not Go Along To Her Local First Aid Class – she was so little use. She picked up the boy's hand, gingerly, as if it might snap from the wrist, and held it in hers. His chest moved up and down steadily; at least his breathing seemed normal.

'Wake up,' she whispered as if she was afraid of disturbing him. 'Please wake up.'

'He still hasn't come round?' Nathaniel dropped to his knees beside them. 'The ambulance is on its way.' He shook his head. 'He's just a child.'

Clementine turned and looked Nathaniel straight in the face. 'Yes, you bastard, he is just a child. A dead child for all you care.'

Chapter Thirteen

'I shouldn't have listened to Ophelia,' Clementine said. Mr Scott snorted in his sleep. 'I tell you,' Clementine carried on, 'that girl is more Iago than Ophelia. I was angry and disappointed when he walked out that evening and I listened to her. Then there was that terrible day on the footpath. I can't blame him for hating me now.' Her shoulders heaved in a deep sigh and she shook her head. 'Stupid, stupid, stupid me, wasting time, wasting happiness as if there was enough of it around to throw away.'

*   *   *

Now she knew what it was like to really miss someone. She felt hollow, as if there was this big empty space where her heart and stomach should have been. There were mornings when she woke with her jaw aching from all the crying she had done in her sleep and others when she woke like a fool, with a smile on her lips, because she had dreamt that she was with him. Once, during a lesson, she closed her eyes and she could have sworn she felt Nathaniel's lips on hers. She must have been smiling then, too, because when she opened her eyes again, Mrs Pryce, who had made more of a mess than usual of her arpeggios, stared back uncomprehendingly. The leaves were turning, but there did not seem to be much colour around. When Ophelia told her how lovely the late roses in the garden smelt she bent her head obediently to the flowers, but to her the scent seemed thin, diluted. She went to sleep hugging the pillow which still smelt of him and spoke to him from the safety of her dreams.

By the time the ambulance had arrived that afternoon on the footpath, the boy was already conscious, sitting up against the upturned hull of the battered old boat. Clementine had watched the colour return to his cheeks and she had noticed that he had barely started to shave. His chin was covered in soft fair bristles, a shade darker than the fair hair on his head.

'He doesn't seem to have a home,' Clementine told the driver as he closed the door of the ambulance.

'There's a lot of them that don't,' he answered. And that had been that. The ambulance had driven back up the footpath without so much as a blue light flashing. At least the boy was all right, for now.

'He's going to be fine,' Nathaniel had said, putting his arm around her shoulders. She gave a little shrug so that his arm slipped down off her shoulders.

'You think you have a view of these people, and then you realize that there aren't even any "these people", just people, and that your sympathies are nothing more and nothing less than a matter of proximity. Well, for most of us it's like that. Then there are some people who can't stand the responsibilities that come with closeness, so they put up a bloody lens between themselves and the world and get away with doing nothing. Well, I'm sorry, but I don't think that's the kind of person I can love.'

'Well, you can fuck right off,' Nathaniel said, marching off down the path without a backwards glance.

That afternoon he had come to the house to see her. 'Tell him to go away,' Clementine said and she had stood on the landing as Ophelia opened the door and told him her sister was out, telling him in a way that made it clear that she was not out at all, but simply unwilling to see him. Clementine had listened to his voice, unable to distinguish any words or the tone they were spoken in and she had told herself that she hated and despised him. She had to be quite persuasive. 'I hate you and despise you. I really do hate and despise you,' she mumbled over and over to herself, and yet her feet were bringing her closer to the stairs with every word. The door slammed and Ophelia called out, 'The bastard's gone!'

Clementine had hurried to her bedroom window and watched him disappear out into the street. He walked like a boy, his hands thrust deep into the pockets of his tweed jacket, his shoulders a little hunched as if he was avoiding a clip round the ears. She raised her hand to the glass and traced the way his dark hair curled into the nape of his neck.

'Nathaniel,' she whispered. Nothing else, just 'Nathaniel.'

She waited for him to return, but he had disappeared. 'Oh, London or Scotland, something like that.' Ophelia shrugged her shoulders. 'I can't remember what the old boy said. Anyway, what's it to you?' They sat curled up on the hearthrug, roasting chestnuts and drinking hot chocolate with tiny marshmallows sprinkled on top of the whipped cream. Clementine stretched her legs out, warming her toes by the fire and pondering on the possibility of starting a catering firm dealing exclusively in food for the broken-hearted: pasta in creamy gorgonzola sauce, chocolate fudge cake with soft milk-chocolate icing, jam doughnuts . . .

'You did the right thing,' Ophelia nodded so emphatically that the whipped cream spilt over the edge of her large pottery mug. 'You should hear what Veronica has to say about him.'

Should I? Clementine wondered. It was a question

161

people asked themselves all too seldom when told they 'should hear' something. Should-hears and should-knows were seldom tales of virtue. They were not, as a rule, passed on with charity in mind. Did she really want Nathaniel to be torn into by a should-know? Ophelia was looking at her. Clementine wriggled on the hearthrug. Now Ophelia was smiling, a smug, I know you better than you do yourself, little smile.

'You're still in love with him aren't you?'

Clementine sat up straight, clasping her mug. 'No, certainly not.'

'I just think you did the right thing. He's almost forty and apparently he's never had a relationship that's lasted more than a year or two. At your age you are bound to be looking for commitment. You would have to have asked yourself whether Nathaniel Scott is able to give you that. And then there's the drinking.' Clementine opened her mouth to speak. 'And don't delude yourself that it would all be different with you,' Ophelia went on, 'that you'll be the one to change him.'

This was another of those things we know but don't always feel. Any fool who's been watching films and reading books in the last sixty years would know that thinking *you'll* be different sets you on the road to ruin. Stand by your man and you'll end up flat on your face.

'His mother went mad out in Africa, did you know that? She killed herself when Nathaniel was fifteen. I know you can't blame him for that, but it's left its scars and it might well have damaged him for life. Veronica says he didn't speak for a month, not one word, and then, apparently, he picked up a camera and walked around with it in front of his face, refusing to look at anything or anyone other than through the eye of a lens.'

'But that's awful!' Clementine exclaimed. She put her mug down on the floor beside her, clutching her knees, wanting only to rush out and find him and take him in her arms.

'And don't feel sorry for him.' Clementine started guiltily. 'All kinds of people have traumatic experiences like that, without it turning them callous and hard-hearted. Did you know that, thanks to our hero, Toby Scott has a scar running down from his armpit to his hip?'

Clementine shook her head. How did Ophelia know?

'Well, he does. Veronica told me all about that too. The two of them, that's Toby and Nathaniel, were out in the bush together when this hippo charged. What did Nathaniel do? Shoot some really nice pickies for the family album, that's what. He did help eventually, but not until it was almost too late.'

'How does this Veronica know so much?'

'Oh, she's a really old friend.'

'Ah,' Clementine nodded, 'that explains it.'

'Come on,' Ophelia put her hand out and gave Clementine's shoulder a gentle shake. 'Of course there are extenuating circumstances . . .'

'He's not on trial,' Clementine sobbed.

'No, of course not. All I'm saying is, for whatever reasons, he seems to me to be the worst possible person for you to be with, let alone love. I really think he would end up destroying you. And Clementine,' Ophelia gave her another gentle little shake, 'I love you too much to sit by and let that happen.'

Nathaniel returned from his trip, only to leave town again the next morning. Mr Scott told Clementine one morning when they were both collecting their milk. 'He's gone off up north again. Something for the *National Geographic.*' Mr Scott had sounded friendly in his normal, formal way, but he had kept looking at her, as if he was searching her face for an explanation.

'When are you expecting him back next?' she had asked.

'Oh, not for a couple of weeks. And after that he's going straight to London.' Mr Scott smiled. 'You must come and have supper with me one evening, I would be glad of some company.'

He could have tried to see her one more time. Then again, if she knew something about Nathaniel it was that he did not beg. And it was easier that way, Clementine decided, easier, too, knowing that he was no longer just on the other side of a wall. It was over. As she said to Ophelia, 'It was fun while it lasted, but you're right, there was never any future in it.' She said this in a carefree, upbeat kind of way and then she rushed upstairs to her bed and lay there crying for an hour until the doorbell rang, heralding the arrival of Beatrice for her lesson.

'You've been crying,' Beatrice said.

Clementine blew her nose and dabbed at her swollen eyes. 'Yes, yes, I'm afraid I have.'

'Why?' Beatrice asked. It was a reasonable enough question, but that did not make it any easier to answer. She could say, 'I'm crying because I told a man to go away and not bother me again and now he has.' But it made no sense, so in a way it was no answer. She could say, 'I'm crying because I've decided I'd rather be hurt now than later.'

She sighed and opened the lid of the piano. 'I hurt my finger in the door,' she said.

In the days that followed she concentrated on her work. At least she worked. Her concentration was all over the place and all over the place was Nathaniel. He appeared in the music she played and she found him in the stories she was writing from Aunt Elvira's notes and her own memory. The more she immersed herself in the fairy tales, the more she thought of how transformation was at the heart of each and every one of them. The weak became strong; the ugly, beautiful; the

164

poor, rich; the cowards, brave; people changed. Their lives were turned round. These stories, she thought, were really just old-fashioned self-help manuals. of the you-can-do-anything-you-set-your-mind-to variety; drastic ones, maybe, giving drastic but not always practical advice: so you don't like your work as a kitchen hand, well, stay cool, stay sweet, find a fairy and go to a party. Or, more down to earth: you fancy this really beautiful girl, but she won't even look at you because, not putting too fine a point on it, you're as ugly as a sin. Now, don't worry. Engineer a situation where you have to spend a lot of time together. Show her your gentle, caring, romantic side and before you know it, to her you'll appear a beautiful prince. People can change; these stories said, love conquers all; no wonder fairy tales were synonymous with un-obtainable dreams.

Chapter Fourteen

The house was still. There was no creaking of floor-boards, no door left ajar to moan and squeak in a draught, even the heating pipes were silent.

'You understand, don't you?' Clementine whispered to Mr Scott. 'It was the waiting I couldn't bear; waiting for things to go wrong, waiting for him to grow tired of me, to go off. You might not have realized this, but I'm not the strongest of people. It's ridiculous, I know. All those pinched, frightened, inhibited little emotions rattling around this great big body. But still, what happened was all for the best. We would have ended up destroying each other.'

The moon was hidden behind a night-sky cloud; she could barely distinguish Mr Scott, slumped in the chair by the window. His breathing was so quiet. She listened for it, and after a moment, she got up and walked across to him. 'Mr Scott,' she spoke softly not wanting to startle him. She put her hand on his shoulder. 'Mr Scott.'

His head flopped forward and, with an anguished yelp, Clementine fell to her knees.

It had happened. The catastrophe she had waited for with the faithfulness of Miss Havisham waiting for her errant groom, had finally arrived. But it was she, Clementine, who had brought it about. She had got poor Mr Scott up to the attic and then she had locked them in, and now he was dead, most probably from a heart attack; a heart attack induced by fear, hers, and the absence of his medication. And then what had she done? She had sat there prattling and she had gone on prattling as he sat there, dead. Still kneeling next to Mr Scott's body, she buried her head in her hands and wept, and it went through her mind that all the tears she had ever wept before had been impostors, now she knew the real thing.

She yelled out of the window for help, but, just as before, no-one heard, or if they did, they did not care enough to answer. She tried to pray. She prayed for Mr Scott's immortal soul and she prayed for forgiveness. Her pleas were not impressive. 'Sorry, sorry, I'm so very very sorry.' God had answered her.

'What is the point of always being sorry after the event!' he boomed. 'When will you learn? Toby Scott was a good man. A particular favourite of mine, and you, useless self-centred creature that you are, are to blame.'

Clementine was not surprised at His sternness. She had never really gone along with the fashionable habit of keeping heaven while abolishing hell. She had never been too sure about this all-loving, all-forgiving God. No, Clementine's God was harsh and vengeful. He eavesdropped on your thoughts, especially the wicked ones, and His sense of humour veered towards the spiteful.

'You've pretended to be concerned for others, but you've not been able to see beyond your own pitiful mind.' Boom Boom Boom! On He went in Clementine's ear. 'And now you're sitting there with poor dead Mr Scott, pretending it's the voice of God speaking to you, as if He would bother. This is common sense speaking, dummy! No wonder you don't recognize the voice.'

Clementine sat in the wing chair, her head buried

in her hands. As time ticked by and the waiting became increasingly unbearable, she played a little game with herself. None of this had happened. She was in her own lovely little house, just waking up from a sleep in her own chair by the fire. Everything was lovely and soon it would be time for a glass of wine and a video or a nice television sitcom. Peekaboo! She opened her eyes and there he was: Mr Scott, dead.

Poor Nathaniel. The shock. 'Yes, it's me, Clementine, up here. And your father? Oh he's here too, only he's, how shall I put it, well dead.'

And what state was the house in? How much was taken or destroyed? Poor, poor Nathaniel.

At five minutes past three she thought she heard the front door snap shut. A few minutes later, minutes passing as slowly as beasts of burden up a mountain track, she heard footsteps on the landing below. Not caring any more who it was down there, she got to her feet and ran across to the door, hammering her fists against it, calling for help.

'Nathaniel, is that you? Up here. Please hurry!'

She heard footsteps running up the stairs. 'Clementine!' He rattled the door. 'Clementine, where is my father? What's going on?'

She pressed her forehead against the door and whispered, 'We're locked in.'

'Why are you whispering. Clementine, what is going on? Is my father with you, or not?'

'Nathaniel, please, just help me get this door open.'

'Have you got a sheet of paper? And I can't see any light in there. Why are you sitting around in darkness?'

Now was not the time to explain that the little attic study was in darkness because, first, they had been hiding from the burglar, and after that, she could not bear the thought of a bright light shining on his father's corpse. 'I've got the paper,' she said, grabbing a foolscap sheet from the desk. 'Shall I push it under the door with the key on?'

'Absolutely right,' Nathaniel said. 'It worked last time. How Toby could manage to get locked in a second time defeats me,' Clementine heard him mutter as he bent down to retrieve the key. 'Don't,' she wanted to say, 'he's dead, so don't say anything more because you'll hate yourself.'

She heard the key being inserted in the lock and long minutes later the door opened and she was facing Nathaniel. 'Clementine, you look dreadful.'

'Why are you so late?' she sobbed. 'Why are you so late?'

'Late for what?' He strode past her into the room. 'Toby? Dad?'

Clementine hid her face in her hands.

'Dad. Oh God. Oh my God, Clementine, he's dead.' She felt his hand grab her arm. 'Clementine, for God's sake, my father is dead.'

*   *   *

Later that morning Clementine and Nathaniel sat facing each other across Clementine's kitchen table. Clementine was wearing her old white towelling robe with make-up smears on the collar. She had had a shower but she had not slept. Nathaniel sat hunched in the chair, legs crossed, his arms hugging his chest, his hands clutching his elbows. He had not shaved and his hair was all fuzzed up and sticking out at the back. His face seemed smaller, narrower than she remembered it and his eyes were filled with hurt and confusion.

'There never was an intruder,' he said.

Clementine hung her head, looking down at her own hands that lay slack in her lap. 'I know. I know that now. The police told me.'

'A rook,' Nathaniel said. 'A young rook tumbling down the chimney.'

She dared to look up at him, hoping to recognize a friend but finding a stranger. Slowly tears filled her eyes, spilling down her cheeks and she looked away, rubbing her face furiously with her hand. There could be no refuge in weeping. Whatever he dished out at her she had to take like a man, or at least like a large thirty-six-year-old woman. Buck up! she told herself desperately, but before she knew it she was on her knees before him, dripping tears all over his left hand and the sleeve of his sweater.

'Sorry, sorry, sorry. Please, Nathaniel, I'm so sorry.'

'Tell that to my father,' Nathaniel said. Then, as she gave a little cry of pain, it was his turn to be sorry. 'Forgive me. And please get up off the floor.' Clementine was sniffing and mumbling something grateful when he went on, 'But for heaven's sake, Clementine, what did you think you were doing? Going on about intruders. Getting him all worked up. You knew he had a weak heart didn't you? I just don't understand? And why did you have to lock the bloody door?' Clementine, back in her chair, turned a tear-stained face to him.

'No, don't tell me,' Nathaniel carried on, 'you were trying to keep the intruder, this killer rook, out.' His words, angry, contemptuous, rained down on her and she sat there knowing she deserved nothing else.

She raised her eyes to his. 'I thought that I was protecting him. And I did believe there was someone in the house. I even thought I knew who it was. If it had been Derek Fletcher and we had recognized him face to face, he might have felt he had to kill us. Or something.'

Nathaniel gave a short laugh. 'Oh yes, the plumber. The police told me you had called in to report him as a possible suspect in some local burglaries.'

'It knocked all these china things off the mantelpiece,' she mumbled. 'The rook. The police told me. It flew around, all over the place, knocking things off things. I didn't know the lock jammed.'

'Well, it did, and my father is dead.'

'I'm sorry,' Clementine wailed. 'I'm so terribly sorry.'

Nathaniel shot to his feet. 'Will you stop saying that. I'm not some Catholic priest who can give you ten Hail Marys and forgiveness. What is the point of saying sorry? No-one is suggesting you're not, but it doesn't actually help anything.'

Clementine was about to say that she had spent the last couple of hours wishing that she was dead, but she realized that would fall into much the same category of unhelpful statements as, 'Sorry.' She thought she might say, 'At least he didn't suffer'. But what did she know? She had been with him in the same room, but she had been busy burbling on, not even noticing that he was dead. What did she know about his suffering? In the end she said simply, 'I know what happened is my fault and I know there's nothing I can say or do to put it right.' It was a start. She so seldom said precisely what she meant.

'I wasn't all that close to him,' Nathaniel said, looking across at her with those pain-filled eyes. 'In a way that makes it worse. For a long time I blamed him for my mother's death. It was unfair, I know.' He gave her a joyless little smile. 'And now I'm blaming you for his death.'

'You have every right to.'

He shrugged his shoulders. 'Maybe. He was a good man, but he was a man who saw the wider picture to such an extent that, for a long time, he lost his view of detail. Detail being his wife and son, mainly.' He scrambled round his trouser pocket for his cigarettes and, picking one out and lighting it, he threw the packet down in front of him on the table.

'What about your mother?' Clementine asked.

Nathaniel's expression softened. 'I loved her. But she was never very strong, mentally or physically. She tried so hard, I remember that. He never seemed to notice. She'd tell him about something she had achieved, some clever or courageous thing, looking at him with these large eyes, pleading for praise. She never got very much. My father was a your-reward-is-in-heaven type man and, bit by bit, my mother seemed to give up. She grew silent and she didn't seem to care much about anything. When her best friend died from cerebral malaria she hardly reacted. Then, some months later, just before she killed herself, we were sitting having coffee in the drawing-room when the school cook came tearing in with a sack of garbage. He shouted something about having been falsely accused of waste and then he tipped the whole bag on the floor. The stuff went everywhere, bits of rotting vegetables, chicken bones, you name it. I'll never forget, it was like a scene from an old silent movie; my mother getting to her feet, hands raised to her face, sinking back onto the chair, ashen-faced. She had displayed next to no emotion when told of her friend's death; she seemed oblivious to the poverty and suffering around her; and then', he gave a joyless laugh, 'all that horror because someone tipped some garbage on her floor.'

He got up and picked up the ashtray, bringing it across to the sink. She watched him emptying it into the bin before rinsing it and putting it upside-down on the draining-board to dry, then she hid her head in her hands; glimpsing the ordinary made the nightmare even more terrifying.

When she looked up again he was gone from the kitchen and she hurried after him into the hall. 'Please,' she whispered, 'I know I can never put right what happened, but if there's anything, anything at all I can do you must let me know.'

'I will.' Suddenly he smiled; a sad, friendly little smile. 'Take care.' His hand moved, almost involuntarily it seemed, up to her cheek and for a moment it rested there, warm and dry against her skin.

Then, with a brisk 'Goodbye,' he opened the door and walked outside.

She watched him disappear into his father's house and then she closed the door, and without locking it, wandered upstairs to her room and lay down on her bed. It was eleven o'clock and she had spent a busy old night bringing catastrophe on her fellow men.

Chapter Fifteen

'I'm sorry,' Clementine whispered to Nathaniel as she leant across the hospital bed, 'but I never was as strong as I look. No muscles.' She stroked his pale forehead with her left index finger, careful not to touch the bruised swelling above his left eye. Nathaniel did not stir from his drug-induced sleep.

'I'm being released tomorrow, already,' she said pulling the grey vinyl chair closer. 'I have to come back every other day for the next week to change the compresses,' she waved her burnt right hand at him, 'but otherwise I'm not too bad. I've got a bit of a cough, of course, but that's to be expected.' She smiled at him. 'What a way to spend Christmas Day eh?' She said nothing for a while, content simply to be near him. A nurse put her head round the curtains.

'You're not supposed to have them drawn you know,' she said, but she left without pulling them back.

'Oh Nathaniel,' she whispered, 'have I gone some little way towards atoning for what I did to your father? I hope so. You know, for weeks I just wanted to die. I kept buying all these painkillers and sleeping pills. It really did seem a good idea: dying. I tell you, I was so close one day. It would have upset my mother and my pupils would have had to find a new teacher, but otherwise no-one would have been any worse off really. Strangely enough, it was realizing how point-less my life was that made me determined to stay alive. I woke up one morning and the sun was shining. The street, our little street, looked so cheerful. I stood there by the window and I asked myself, have I learnt nothing? I was still ruled by fear, this time of living with the consequences of my actions. I had been given life and all I had managed to do with it was help someone else to lose theirs. I had to try to do better than that before I left.' She smiled again and shook her head. I had to try to do better than that before I left this world.

*　　*　　*

'Black for sorrow, red for fear, pink for folly, white for oblivion.' Clementine sat at the kitchen table, a week to the day after Mr Scott's death, counting out pills. She had lots, some sleeping tablets, but mainly painkillers. The problem with those, she thought, staring at the small pile in front of her, is that if one's not careful, they kill not just the pain but the sufferer too.

'Good,' she said loudly as if there was someone around to impress. 'Good,' she said again. She picked up the largest of the empty bottles and dropped the pills, one by one, inside it. 'Little friends,' she smiled at them through the brown plastic container.

'There you are,' Ophelia made her jump. 'I'm about to go over to Nathaniel's. I thought he could do with some company. You know the funeral is tomorrow?'

'Yup,' Clementine nodded.

'Will you be going?'

'Nope,' Clementine began to nod again before remembering that a nod was for yes and a shake was for no. She shook her head. 'Nope,' she said again.

'You're probably right,' Ophelia said. 'Will you be OK on your own?'

'Of course I will,' Clementine snapped. 'It's not my father who's died.' Finicky with the truth as always, she added, 'Not recently, anyway.'

Ophelia left and Clementine stayed seated at the table.

Two hours later she raised her head and said out loud, 'Now how bad can this be? Take stock. You're alive, you're healthy,' she paused, as far as she knew she was, although there was that bony lump on her foot . . . anyway, she was youngish and . . . and she had just caused a death, the death of a dear old man of whom she had been fond, all because of her idiotic compulsive worrying. But look on the bright side, she straightened up in her chair. It's a first offence. Up until then she had not done too much actual harm. She flopped down. Nor, she thought, have I, in all my thirty-six years, done anything of any value either. But it was my pet, my dragon, the dragon of my mind, who laid waste a life.

'You haven't been sitting there all evening?' Ophelia was standing in the kitchen doorway, feet apart, her arms crossed over her chest.

Clementine raised a tear-swelled face to her. 'So what if I have?'

Ophelia shrugged her shoulders. 'Guilt won't change anything, you know.'

'Now it's interesting how people always say that. Well, I reckon it's worth a try. Maybe if I yell *mea culpa*, *mea culpa*, at the heavens often enough and loudly enough, God will get bored and let me go back and change it all.'

'I think you should go to bed,' Ophelia said. 'I certainly am.'

'How was Nathaniel?' Clementine mumbled this, as if somehow she had no right to ask.

'Oh, not too bad, all things considering.' Ophelia paused in the doorway. 'He's actually very interesting once you get talking to him. Very aware. You

176

know, I think you've misjudged him.'

Clementine groaned and went back to doing what she did best: wailing with her head in her hands.

On the last morning of November Clementine woke up to find the sun shining. She walked over to the window and looked out across the street. It was ten o'clock; she had made it her habit over the past few weeks to rise late, and the pavements were bustling with shoppers looking up at the sunny sky with the cautious delight of a child having its first taste of ice-cream. She felt the warmth of the sun through the glass and enjoyed it. She noticed the tiny Christmas tree on the first-floor balcony of the house across the street. Maybe, just maybe, she was glad to be alive. Alive and poor. After Mr Scott died she had cancelled all her lessons, asking her pupils to bear with her until further notice. Now she realized she missed them, well most of them; she could still do without Mrs Pryce. As soon as she had dressed she got her address book and began calling round, apologizing, arranging new lessons. For the first time in weeks she read the paper over breakfast, but not once did she tut-tut. Tutting led to more worry and worry led to fear and fear, her fear, second-hand fear, was what had killed Mr Scott. It was all so perfectly clear; she just had to stop being frightened. She finished her tea and toast and looked around for things not to be frightened of. The kitchen was not a challenge, so she decided to look further afield. She caught her reflection in the hall mirror as she passed and that, already, was a little scary, there was no doubt about that. It was not just the dark circles under her eyes – the kind that looked so fetching when applied by a make-up artist on Michelle Pffeifer and so unfetching when just there on Clementine – but the bags too. One bag under her left eye and two under the right, the side she slept on. Dimly she remembered her stepmother Grace saying

177

you could tell by a woman's face which side she slept on. Grace herself, apparently, slept on her back. And Clementine's hair seemed to have got curlier, wilder looking, springing from her scalp as if it couldn't wait to get away. And what was she doing wearing a sprigged cotton frock in the middle of winter, even if it was teamed with thick black tights? No matter. She grabbed her navy duffle-coat and strode out into the sunshine. Christmas shoppers were arriving from the smaller towns and nearby villages, and in the square a Father Christmas wandered around accosting little children in a manner which would have earned anyone not wearing a long red coat a severe talking to. She bought Ophelia a short black sweater and for her mother she chose a leather appointment diary with a small gold biro to go with it. She did not get anything for Grace that morning; she was feeling bold, not forgiving.

She was putting the key in her front door lock when Nathaniel stepped out from next door. 'I thought you were away,' she said.

'Well, obviously I'm not,' he answered. His expression softened. 'How have you been?'

She was staring at him, not really answering. She had not seen him in over three weeks and she was struck anew how beautiful he was, how very like that prince underground. 'I've been well,' she lied.

'That's good.' Nathaniel transferred his weight from his left foot to his right and then back again.

'I've decided not to waste any more of my life being frightened,' Clementine told him. 'I've decided to be bold.' Oh dear Lord, she thought, the moment the words had left her lips, how could I? Just the other day I helped his father to his death and here I am talking about not wasting my life.

'That's great,' Nathaniel said in a voice better suited to a sentence like: 'Lovely day,' or 'Is that the time already.'

'What I mean is, that's the way to be of use; to be bold and fearless.'

'If you are, yes.'

Clementine had always wished to be smaller, but not, she thought, this small, 'Well, bye then.' Even her voice was a tiny squeak.

'Bye,' Nathaniel said airily, shutting his gate behind him and striding on down the street.

Once, when she was seven, Timothy had offered to extract an already wobbly tooth from her mouth, so that she could cash in the ten pence from the tooth fairy. He had tied one end of a piece of string round the tooth and the other round the nursery door handle. When the string was nice and taut he had slammed the door closed and Clementine's tooth, the wrong tooth, had been extracted from her bleeding gums. Nathaniel walking down the street had one end of a rope tied round his waist, the other end was round Clementine's heart, and with every step he took her heart was tugged, until, as he disappeared round the corner, it felt as if it was being torn right out of her chest.

She dragged herself inside, chucking her bags of shopping on the floor. In the kitchen she made herself a cup of tea and brought it, together with a packet of chocolate-covered digestives, into the sitting-room. She sank down on the sofa and opened the packet of biscuits, only to discover that they were plain chocolate rather than milk.

Ophelia arrived home for her lunch break. 'What's the matter with you now?' she asked Clementine.

Clementine was spoilt for choice. She could either say, 'I'm really upset because I've lost my love,' or, 'I'm really upset because I was looking forward to a nice milk chocolate biscuit, only to find that they aren't milk chocolate at all, but plain.'

'Oh, nothing,' she said, moving across to her desk, the mug of tea in her hand.

She worked on her fairy tales for a couple of hours,

but she was restless, fidgety, her mind scampering about all over the place like an ill-disciplined puppy. Suddenly she leapt from her chair and hurried outside with her bag and coat. She ran all the way to the hairdressers at the corner of the High Street and East Street. 'Have you got someone who can cut my hair right now?' she asked.

The girl in the reception glanced at the appointments written in the notebook in front of her and then she turned round and called, 'Theresa, can you do this lady here?' Theresa said she could.

'It's really lovely,' she said a few minutes later as she ran her fingers through Clementine's newly washed hair. 'Are you sure you want it all off?'

'Sure,' Clementine nodded. 'Actually,' she glanced around the room before continuing in hushed tones, 'I'm taking part in one of those television make-overs, but the producer's car broke down, so the others are all stranded at the Little Chef at exit six of the motorway.'

'A make-over.' Clementine saw Theresa's eyes widen in the mirror. 'I've always wanted to do one of those. You're sure it's all right to start?' Clementine nodded. 'So what are they making you into then? What style?'

'Someone with very short hair,' Clementine said, bored already with the conversation she had started.

The job done, Theresa stepped back and admired the effect. 'I hope you're pleased. You know nine out of ten times when a woman comes into the salon and asks for all her hair to be chopped off it's boyfriend trouble. It's sad. Hairspray? So it makes a really nice change to do it for a make-over.'

At least her hair looked quite pretty, all soft wispy curls framing her face. Her eyes looked huge. It made a nice change, she thought, from huge feet and huge hands.

'Bloody hell,' Ophelia said when she came home that afternoon and saw Clementine.

'Do you like it?' Clementine asked, opening her eyes wide in case Ophelia had not noticed the improvement.

'It's different.'

'This is true,' Clementine said patiently. 'It was very long and now it's very short. But do you like it?'

'Do you want me to be honest?' Ophelia said.

Clementine looked thoughtfully at her. 'No,' she said finally, and she wondered, not for the first time, why, when someone said they were going to be honest, you always knew you were not going to like what would follow.

'All right then,' Ophelia said. 'By the way, I'm not in for supper. I'm seeing a movie with Nathaniel. He's just come back so I thought he could do with some company.'

Clementine spent most of the evening, in between preparing for lessons, trying to find things to like about Ophelia. She went to bed exhausted but none the wiser.

The next morning, the first of December, Clementine sat at the kitchen table cutting out little squares of paper and writing on them. She finished when she had twenty-four, five of them blank. Next, she brought down her Swedish Advent calendar from the linen cupboard on the landing. It was made of cloth and had a little pocket for each day leading up to Christmas. Her mother-in-law had bought it many years ago and told her to hang it on the wall for Gustaf to fill with tiny gifts. So Clementine had hung it on the wall by the side of the cooker in her kitchen. It was just that Gustaf never put anything in it. He always said he was going to, every run-up to Christmas, but he never did. She had not seen it as a problem, but simply as another one of those little disappointments that made for conversation between married women. She could not remember having brought the calendar from Sweden, but it had been there, at the bottom of one of the

packing-cases and here she was, putting it to good use,
mixing the pieces of paper up and putting one in each
pocket. When that was done she hung the calendar up
on the wall above the table.

'What's that for?' Ophelia asked.

'Aversion therapy. I aim to be fearless by Christmas.'

'You're joking?'

'Only a little bit,' Clementine said, reaching into the
pocket with a one embroidered on it.

Chapter Sixteen

'I didn't have a Christmas tree this year, I had a many-headed dragon. It sat there by the French windows, gloating, and now and then it would stretch and unfurl, rising to its full huge height, its many hideous heads lolling on its scaled neck. For years it had fed on my fears, sapping my lifeblood and then it had gobbled up your father. It had to go. I had to destroy it, one ugly head at a time: the little grinning gargoyle heads, the large fire-breathing ones, they all had to go.' Clementine put out her hand to touch Nathaniel's which rested on the white hospital sheet. She winced as her burnt wrist hit against the metal side of the bed, but the feel of his skin against the tip of her finger made her smile.

'Queen's speech everyone,' someone announced and she heard brisk footsteps pass the other side of the orange curtains. They stopped and returned. The curtains were pulled back.

'That's better,' the nurse smiled. She glanced at the chart attached to the headboard and, perching on the side of the bed, she measured Nathaniel's pulse.

'You chat on,' she said to Clementine as she left, 'you won't be disturbing him.'

'Are you sure he's not in a coma?'

'A coma? Whatever gave you that idea?'

'The fact that he's lying absolutely still not moving

the smallest muscle. The way he doesn't react at all to being spoken to.' Clementine heard her voice rise to a complaint.

'He's asleep,' the nurse said. 'There's a hot-drinks machine in the corridor if you want something.'

Clementine watched her uniformed back disappear down the ward and then she turned back to Nathaniel. The soft sound of his even breaths, the sight of him, bandaged though he was, that was happiness enough.

*   *   *

'Stride into public lavatories as if no care in the world,' Clementine muttered to herself in shorthand, as she turned down towards the High Street. She caught the low-built red-brick building in her sights and marched on. 'Through the doors, do not turn away at first whiff of the air.'

At the sight of the surprised-looking middle-aged man at the urinal she turned on her heel and fled. There was nothing in her task about going into the gents. She spent half an hour choosing Christmas decorations at Oldhams before she felt able to return. This time she went through the right door.

'Sit down with nothing but a cursory glance at the seat, allow hem of trousers to touch floor,' she instructed herself. 'Flush using whole hand not just tip of middle finger and leave cubicle not minding being squashed between the door and the lavatory bowl.' She was out in the wash area, staring at a cracked basin with two long black hairs sticking to its side. 'Turn on taps with hands, not elbows. Turn off taps using the self-same hands. Blow-dry hands regardless of newspaper article headed THE GERM FACTORY – THE TRUTH ABOUT THOSE HAND DRYERS. Leave public facility by grasping the door handle firmly although you know the person before you most probably didn't wash her hands at all before leaving.'

Back on the pavement she stopped for a moment, feeling good. One head down, 'Swish,' she cut the cool December air with an imaginary sword. It was a foolish little head, but a head nevertheless. She glanced at her watch, eleven o'clock, it was time to go back home; her pupil, a retired bank manager who had recently progressed to grade four, was arriving at twelve.

'Having all my hair cut off; it's like an amputation,' she complained to Ophelia over Sunday brunch a couple of days later. 'I keep brushing my neck, look.' She turned her head so that Ophelia could see the red scratch marks made by the nylon bristles.

'I thought you refused to eat sausages,' Ophelia replied, helping herself to three from the dish in front of her and adding them to the eggs and bacon already on her plate.

'Not any more. These days I'm the sort of woman who takes eating the hairy end bit of pig's ears in my stride.' She stabbed a sausage with her fork and lifted it to her mouth, biting the tip off and chewing with evident relish. Once they had finished eating, Ophelia slipped out from her chair and wandered off towards the door when Clementine called after her, 'What about the washing-up?'

Ophelia half turned her head. 'I'm meeting a few people from college, so do you mind?' She was already out of the door.

'Yes,' Clementine called after her, clutching the scrap of paper with that day's task. 'Yes, I do mind.'

Ophelia poked her face round the door, a hurt face. 'What do you mean?'

'I mean,' Clementine said standing up, 'that I've got things to do today and I would appreciate it if you pulled your weight, slight as that weight is, and did the washing-up.'

'This is not like you,' Ophelia said, her slender arms up to the elbows in Fairy liquid bubbles, 'being petty like this. I'm going to be late.'

'You should have thought of that earlier. There was no need for you to have a third helping.'

Ophelia's aggrieved gaze fell on the slip of paper on the worktop next to her. Picking it up with her soapy fingers she read, 'Stand up to Ophelia. Tell her to do the washing-up.' She spun round. 'Is that the sort of things you've put in that bloody calendar?'

Clementine nodded vigorously. 'Yes, absolutely.'

'Well,' Ophelia placed the sausage dish upside-down on the draining-board to dry, 'that's pathetic.' Clementine, who was sorting out the drawers of the dresser, throwing out old receipts and candle ends, the half-eaten Mars bar and the empty soap boxes, raised her head and contemplated the rivulets of water running down the black metal sides of the dish, along the grooves of the sink and back into the washing-up bowl.

'From little trickles great rivers grow,' she said, adding, 'take care of the small fears and the big ones will take care of themselves,' for good measure. She turned back to the drawer. 'Anyway, there are other tasks and some blank notes as well, leaving room for the unexpected.'

'Don't you think you are taking this idea of yours a little too seriously?' Ophelia slammed a wooden spoon down on the side.

'You can never be too serious when it comes to drag-ons,' Clementine replied. She sounded so confident right then, she herself was impressed, but it only lasted until Ophelia had clattered bad-temperedly out of the room, leaving her perched precariously on her heap of shattered dreams. If she looked out from the kitchen window, across the garden wall, she could glimpse the back of the house next door. Once upon a time it was her lover who slept in the small back room facing both their gardens, the door had been opened by Mr Scott, her friend, and she had been quite a good woman.

186

She carried on chopping at the weasely bloodsucking little dragon heads. She booked a trip to Tanzania, for one.

'That's not what I call hardship,' Jessica objected, helping herself to Clementine's portion of chocolate cake while simultaneously signing to Mrs Challis to bring her another cup of herbal tea. 'Most people would give their eye-teeth to go on safari.'

'Not if they hated travelling on their own; had no interest in looking at wild animals which can be viewed perfectly well through David Attenborough; an exaggerated, ill-founded but serious fear of catching Aids, Malaria and Hepatitis; and a feeling that a trip to Oslo is an adventure, no.'

'So when are you going?'

'June.'

'You'll have changed your mind by then.'

Clementine looked sternly at her. 'I might be many things, most of them unimpressive,' she said, 'but I'm not a cheat.'

She called the decorator, Mr Cook, who had painted the kitchen, and asked him back. 'I meant to tell you at the time,' she twittered, 'but I didn't want to upset you. But this colour', she gesticulated at the bright kitchen wall, 'is not really what I asked for. What I wanted was soft grey-toned blue, and what you actually put on the wall is a bright baby blue. It's pretty, but it's not what I asked for.' She took a step back, preparing for a fight.

Mr Cook sighed. 'Okey-dokey. You have a look at the colour chart and we'll try again.' Sometimes the heads came off with nothing more than a puff of air.

On the second Sunday of Advent, Clementine returned home with a black eye.

'How did that happen?' Ophelia asked.

'That's precisely what Annabelle Harris asked when I saw her outside Boots. You remember Annabelle?'

Ophelia assumed a look of infinite patience. 'And what did you say to Annabelle?'

Clementine brought some ice out of the freezer and wrapped it in a tea towel before placing it against her throbbing right eye.

'Well,' she said, slopping down on the chair nearest to her, 'it was like this. I was walking past the Prince of Wales, that's the pub on East Street by the way, not the man.'

'I gathered that.'

'Anyway, these yobs came out of the pub and one of them was eating a packet of crisps,' she paused for a second. 'That should be eating *from* a packet of crisps shouldn't it? Or it sounds as if he was actually munching on the packet which, of course, he . . . anyway, when he had finished eating, he crumpled up the empty packet and chucked it on the ground, just like that, with everyone watching. In the good old days, if you were littering, you at least had the grace to keep the rubbish hidden in your fist before dropping it accidentally on purpose and walking on, fast, as if you had no idea something had fallen out of your hand. Still, I was about to walk on with the briefest of tuts, when his mate chucked this empty cigarette packet right at the feet of an old lady passing by. They didn't care, not about anything most probably. It made me so angry. I thought, I'll do it. I'll tell them to pick up their beastly litter.' She paused before Ophelia's cold glance. 'It seemed a good idea. I had a blank day today. I mean, I had a blank note in my calendar, so I thought this could be my task for the day. They didn't look that nasty,' her voice petered out.

'So you went up to the group of nice young men and asked them politely if they would mind clearing up their mess and they turned around and gave you a black eye, is that it?'

Clementine hung her head. 'That's about the size of it, yes.'

'You're an idiot,' Ophelia said. 'They might have really hurt you.'

On Monday the twelfth she pulled out a piece of paper and read . . . Clementine blinked and looked again. The note still read: *Hire out 'Erik the Viking Love God' from the video section of the petrol station on the bypass.* On the third reading she saw that, although Ophelia's imitation of her handwriting was good, it was by no means perfect. She chucked the piece of paper in the bin and sat down to think of a proper task for that day.

On Wednesday the fourteenth the note said: *Take a walk around town late at night*, and in brackets underneath it said, *And I mean late.*

Who walked around Aldringham at night long after the pubs had closed? The last showing at the cinema had long since ended and the few restaurants had closed their doors hours earlier. There were no clubs in the town and no late buses. It was a cold night, but still. All around her multicoloured lights twinkled from the trees lining the shop fronts, but the lights faded as she neared the end of the street. Starlight would have been nice, she thought, as she left the High Street for the darker South Street; starlight reflected in the canal. She remembered Nathaniel telling her how once he had seen the light of one bright star reflected in an African river. 'The sun or the moon,' he had said, 'that you see all the time, but starlight . . . have you ever seen starlight reflected in the water?' They had been sitting on her sofa in the sitting-room, close together, her head on his shoulder. The memory made her smile and for a moment she forgot to be afraid of the dark streets, streets deserted by everyone other than Clementine and the murdering rapist who was most probably stalking her footsteps that very minute. She stopped and listened: nothing. She walked on. She did not really mind dying, she would just prefer the manner of her death to be nice and quiet, a death in the school of Mrs Granquist. There was no chapter on graceful dying in that valuable book, Clementine had checked, but if she knew anything, she knew the kind of death of which Mrs Granquist would approve: clean nails, polished shoes and neatly styled hair. A few whispered words, nothing too sentimental; a sigh, nothing ostentatious; a weak smile would be nice and then, exit.

She turned down Wagon Lane and at the top of Canal Street, a few steps from the church, she hesitated. An owl hooted in the large yew tree, otherwise there was silence. The silence made her anxious. So what do you want, she asked herself? Footsteps following you. The sound of knives being sharpened? No, of course not. So silence was good. Straightening her shoulders she walked on, past the church yard and on to the footpath, the moon lighting her steps. Looking up at the night sky she saw a lone star, but she did not expect to see its reflection in the water.

Moments later she heard a twig snap in the wooded area by the old boat shed. She paused before walking on again. No more overwrought reactions from her; no more giving in to fear. She thought she could definitely distinguish soft footsteps on the soft soggy ground, but she forced herself to walk on in the direction she was going. All in all, she thought, there was a much better chance of it not being a killer rapist wandering around at the edge of the path than there being one. She, Clementine, had to get used to listening to the voice of probability and sense so long silenced in her.

'Have you got a fag?'

Clementine stopped and turned round, surprised rather than frightened at the sight of a pointy-headed figure appearing from behind the old boat shed. As he got closer she recognized the young boy she had helped the other day; the boy who, through no fault of his, had caused the break-up between her and Nathaniel. He wore a Father Christmas hat pulled right down over his blond head and his breath smelt of beer.

'I don't smoke. Sorry.' Clementine shook her head.

To her surprise the boy laughed. 'Why are you sorry, you should be happy.' His voice was light and, right now, a little slurred. 'Smoking kills.'

So it did. So did a lot of things. Maybe walking with a stranger along a deserted footpath did. Still, she waited for the boy to catch up.

'Is that where you live, in the boat shed? I remember seeing you there back in the autumn, you weren't very well.' The boy nodded, shivering in the cold night air.

'It's barely got a roof!'

Again the boy laughed, the over-loud laugh of an embarrassed child. 'It's somewhere to be, isn't it?' As they passed a row of naked beech trees a crow took flight from amongst its branches, squawking indignantly.

'How old are you?'

'Seventeen.' The boy kicked at a stone as if to confirm his lack of years.

'But that's terrible. Where are your parents?' As she asked her questions she understood how people became 'bleeding hearts, lefties, trendies, campaigners.' They just looked into the eyes of another human being, lost and frightened, and saw a soul not all that different from their own.

In the distance the owl hooted, otherwise the world was silent, wrapped in cold mist. 'I'm normally a bit of a Fascist,' Clementine said, 'but I don't suppose you live the way you do out of choice.'

The boy shrugged his shoulders.

'So what happened?' Clementine insisted.

It was the usual story, or at least a story Clementine had read many times in the papers, her eyes flicking over the words, her heart closed. A little boy growing up quite happily with his mother and father, going to school, playing football, joining the Cubs. Then his father died and after a while his mother married again.

191

To begin with things went quite well, but the little boy grew into a teenager, and his arms and legs grew faster than any other part of him so that he tripped over things and dropped things. His voice became a gravelly grunt and he never stopped eating. He was always in the way, taking up a lot of space. His mother became pregnant, and by the time the new child was born no-one seemed to have much use for the old one. One day his stepfather hit him across the face for worrying his mother and waking the baby when he came home late. After that he was hit quite often and one day he had enough and ran away. He had returned after a week to be met by his stepfather telling him he need not bother to come back until he had learnt some manners. His mother, looking drawn and anxious, had stood in the doorway behind her husband, the new child in her arms.

'I didn't want to cause her any more hassle,' said the boy, whose name was David, 'so I stayed away this time.' Again he shrugged his shoulders which were skinny but surprisingly wide. 'Anyway, I don't want to be where I'm not wanted.'

Clementine had stopped on the path, not wanting to walk too far from the comforting lights of town. 'What about a foster home?'

'Too old.'

'Council flat?'

'Too young.'

'Job?'

'No address.'

'Doesn't anyone have responsibility?'

The boy had continued to walk, but now he too stopped. 'My mum and stepdad. They told the social services they'd have me back.'

'So go back. It can't be that bad.'

The boy gave a short laugh. 'Can't it?' He started walking again. 'Bye,' he called over his shoulder and soon he was gone into the darkness leaving Clementine alone on the path.

Chapter Seventeen

'I walked back through town that night quite unafraid. It was the strangest of feelings and it didn't last, but while it did it was good.' Clementine smiled down at Nathaniel who slept on so quietly that Clementine had to put her ear right down to his lips just to reassure herself he was breathing.

'I looked around me because, for once, I wasn't looking inwards at myself, and I noticed things: a pretty colour on a house wall, a Christmas tree glimpsed through the crack in a pair of curtains, the shape of the trees against the night sky; little things like that.'

She gazed down at Nathaniel, leaning closer, allowing her hand to rest on the sheet next to his.

*   *   *

Jessica thought that Clementine was an idiot for walking round the town at night. She sat at the Chocolate House dressed in a navy corduroy smock which at long last she filled with her growing stomach. 'Why do you always have to be so extreme?' she asked, not, Clementine admitted, unreasonably.

'I think you have to be to arrive in the middle. It's a question of adjustment. I've been living a life confined by petty fears. Now I'm trying to be magnificently bold in order to finally arrive somewhere in the region of normal and sensible.'

'You're not magnificently bold, you're magnificently stupid.'

Clementine ignored her. 'Do you think that Mrs Challis knows that I reported Derek to the police?' she whispered instead. 'She seems friendly enough.'

'Don't worry about it,' Jessica said. 'Worrying about the past is just another way of refusing to face up to the future and, as I said to Baby the other day, the future is where it's at.'

Clementine thought about it. It sounded good, but would it hold up in court. 'What about conscience? Having a conscience makes you worry about past sins.'

'Your conscience should stop you committing a sin. A conscience is about prevention and reparation. If you've done something wrong try to put it right, but if you can't you have to let go. Resolve to do better next time, but let go. Sitting around feeling guilty won't help anything.'

'But how can I make things up to Mr Scott or Nathaniel. Mr Scott is irretrievably dead and Nathaniel doesn't seem to want to have anything to do with me.'

'Then you have to respect that and leave him alone.'

'But I think I love him.'

'Well,' Jessica scraped the last bit of chocolate fudge filling from her plate and licked the fork, 'that's your misfortune.'

Clementine's face brightened for a moment. 'You mean my punishment?'

'No,' Jessica sounded patient, 'it's your tough titty.'

'Ah,' Clementine stabbed at the cake on the plate in front of her. She looked up. 'Should I ask Derek Fletcher to mend the leaking tap in my kitchen sink? I know that doesn't sound much in the way of reparation, but it's a way of saying sorry, especially if I call him out at the weekend so he can charge me double.'

'Money is no solution.'

'No, no I don't suppose it is.' She gazed out of the window at the large wreaths tied with red ribbon that hung above the door of every shop in the square. 'I love Christmas decorations,' she said with a sudden smile, but her smile faded as she spotted Nathaniel and Ophelia coming out of the bookshop opposite, walking so close to each other that her shoulder touched his arm. Clementine could not stop looking at them, so she saw when Ophelia laughed up at Nathaniel and slipped her arm under his.

'To think,' Jessica said, 'Baby's first Christmas.'

'Don't be an idiot,' Clementine snapped, regretting it instantly. Dumbly, she pointed out over the square at Ophelia and Nathaniel.

'Now you say you love him,' Jessica said, 'but I was under the impression that you hated and despised him.'

'Well, I love him. And quite frankly I find Ophelia's behaviour most peculiar. She too hated and despised him without the mitigating feeling of love and there she is walking down the street, arm in arm with him, looking like she's in love. It wasn't long ago that she didn't have a good word to say about him and I listened to her.'

'You should have stuck up for him. If you let yourself be swayed that easily by other people's opinions then your love isn't worth much, is it?' Clementine hated it when Jessica spoke sense. She never expected it and it disconcerted her. It was much easier when people behaved true to your prejudices.

'It's too late now, anyway,' she said. 'He's obviously keen on her.'

'So fight for him. Anyway, isn't Ophelia meant to be getting married?'

'Not to William by the looks of things. And what weapons do I have to fight with? Ophelia is younger, smaller, calmer, saner. She's a successful sculptress.

What do I have to offer other than that I killed his father? Now there are men, no doubt, who might find that the finest quality of all in a woman, but I don't think Nathaniel is one of them.'

Clementine had just closed the door on her last pupil of the day when Ophelia arrived home, pink-cheeked and smelling of cold. She waited until they were sitting down at the kitchen table with a cup of tea before asking, 'Are you and Nathaniel together?' With a little laugh meant to underline the absurdity of the question, she added, 'I'm sure you're not. Silly question. I really only asked because I saw you and . . .'

'Yes, we are. Nothing is settled, but we are seeing each other. And you know Clementine, you were completely wrong about him. He's nothing like the cold uncaring bastard you made him out to be.'

Clementine could feel her cheeks redden. 'Well I never,' she stuttered. 'I'm lost for words.' She paused before adding, 'Obviously I'm not entirely lost for words because I'm speaking even now.'

Ophelia did not seem to be listening. 'I think your problem was that you never really bothered to look for the real man beneath the surface.'

This was true. Clementine could not deny it. And she thought of Jessica saying that if she had really loved him she would not have allowed herself to be swayed by the opinion of others.

'Do *you* really love him?' she asked Ophelia.

Ophelia shrugged her shoulders. 'As I keep saying, what's love?'

'That's what I kept asking myself.' Clementine looked intently at Ophelia. 'What I do know is that I ache for him. I know that a life without the hope of him will be unbearably bleak. I know I don't want you to be with him.' The last bit she mumbled.

Ophelia's chin dropped and her eyes opened wide.

'I'm really surprised to hear you say that. I thought you would be happy for us.'

Clementine looked away, embarrassed. For a while neither of them spoke, then Clementine asked, 'What about William?'

'Oh, I've written to him. Mum is extremely pissed off, but otherwise it's cool.' She stretched and yawned in her chair before getting to her feet.

'I'm going to have a nice hot soak before supper.'

'Are you in tonight?' Clementine crossed one leg over the other in what she hoped was a nonchalant manner.

'No, I'm going out with Nathaniel.' Ophelia paused in the doorway. 'These things happen Clementine. You have to accept that.'

And what a comfort that was. Clementine wandered into the sitting-room and sat down at the piano and played Liszt until her fingers ached.

The plump sales assistant in Pandora's Box wore a gold and peacock-blue scarf tied round her neck and a mock-motherly expression on her face. She offered Clementine a mince pie and a glass of red wine and confided that she knew just the thing for Clementine. 'I can see it on you.' She bustled off to return with an electric-blue silk jacket with black sequins on the collar and the lapels and a straight black skirt to match.

Clementine shook her head. 'No, no I don't think so. Something a bit plainer, younger looking maybe.'

Undaunted the assistant, Mrs Champney, according to the small badge pinned to the chest of her fuchsia jacket, disappeared again. It was Mrs Champney's misfortune, Clementine thought, to be serving Clementine on a day, the eighteenth of December, when the note in the calendar had read: *Go into a clothes shop and try on anything you wish, but do not, under any circumstances, buy even a scarf unless you love it, however enthusiastic and persuasive the assistant. Be brutal!*

'Now I just know you'll love this,' Mrs Champney had returned bearing a pair of shiny leopard-skin leggings and a black knitted tunic.

'No, no I'm afraid that's not me at all.' Clementine drained the wine. Mrs Champney did not offer to refill it. Clementine put her hand out for another mince pie.

'What about this?' Mrs Champney, her smile a little stretched looking, held up a bright green silk blouse with a pussy-cat bow around the collar.

'It's a lovely colour, but no, not bows. I'm too large,' she added. It was impossible not to try to soften the blow just a little bit.

'This?' A red and green silk dirndl skirt was proffered. 'No? Maybe this?'

Regretfully Clementine shook her head at the sight of the black and white dogs' tooth patterned suit. With visible effort, Mrs Champney smiled. 'I'll tell you what is very popular with our younger customers at the moment.' She pulled a tray out from a drawer and placed it on the counter in front of Clementine. On the black velvet lay an array of buckles in the shape of animals and insects; frogs, bees, horses heads, all to be fitted to a choice of different coloured belts. 'You see,' said Mrs Champney getting her second wind, 'you'll have a belt to go with every outfit for not much more than the price you would ordinarily pay for one. Very handy for travel too. It's always the buckles that take up space don't you find?'

It pained Clementine to tell her, it really did, but there was no turning back. 'I'm sorry, but I'm not overly fond of animals on clothing. Like those sweatshirts with skating hedgehogs, I can't help feeling they're best left to short people, preferably below the age of eight.' She smiled as nicely as she could. 'I don't think there's anything for me at the moment, but thank you so much for your help.' With those words she was gone, carried along by embarrassment as if it was a fair wind. Outside on the street she felt much better. Another spiteful little dragon head had bitten the dust.

She walked up to the square and on to The Flying Carpet, stepping inside. Just like the last time, John Melchett appeared from behind the rug which hung like a tent flap across the opening to the back of his shop, summoned by the tinkling bells of the chime. The shop was less crowded with rugs, but there was no trace of the vandals' night-time visit.

Clementine came straight to the point, which in itself was remarkable. 'Some time ago I came in and looked at your rugs, your lovely rugs,' she added, 'and you kindly put one by for me. Unfortunately it was way out of my price range, which I should have told you at the time. However, I would adore to buy a rug from you, so do you have something which you think is beautiful but could still be regarded as affordable.' She stopped and drew breath.

John Melchett's expression cleared and he beamed a smile at her. 'Mrs Simpson, I remember.' Clementine thought of correcting him and explaining that she had given a false name as well, but, deciding that one could take honesty and courage too far, she contented herself with a smile.

'Oh yes,' the little man rubbed his hands together. 'I remember our meeting well. I so enjoyed our chat, although I had a hunch you weren't going to come back for the rug. It's still here.'

'I'm so pleased it wasn't destroyed in the break-in.'

John Melchett shuddered. 'No, thank God. But don't let's talk about it.' He stopped on his way to the corner where the rug that was the colour of a desert sunrise, lay. 'It still hurts.'

'I'm sorry. I wish I had come over to see you.' Clementine followed him across to where the large rug lay spread out on the oak floorboards.

He turned with another of his quick smiles. 'Oh,

don't give it another thought. I know how it is. Misfortune is a social gaffe that many find hard to forgive.' He did a little bow in Clementine's direction. 'Present company obviously excluded.' He looked around the shop. 'Now for something beautiful but inexpensive. Where is it for?'

'My sitting-room. I would like it at the side of my grand piano. It's a black lacquered one, so clear jewel colours would be marvellous.'

Half an hour later Clementine carried home her purchase, a small embroidered rug from Pakistan in clearest blue and red and green on a pale gold background. Small as the rug was, it still obscured her vision as she carried it and she did not see Nathaniel until she was practically standing on his toes. As he said 'Ouch,' she realized she actually was.

'Sorry,' she muttered, her heart dancing its familiar jig around her chest. They were standing a few yards from her gate and she edged towards it, peering past the rolled-up rug at him.

'Let me,' Nathaniel took it from her. 'You go ahead and open the door.' He followed her inside. 'Where would you like it?'

'Sitting-room,' Clementine answered, gazing at his face, taking it in in great greedy eyefuls.

'It's very pretty,' he said having rolled it out on the floor by the piano. 'You've cut your hair.'

Clementine's hand flew to her neck. 'Goodness gracious me, so I have.'

He laughed and making him laugh made her so happy that she laughed right back. 'It suits you.' He put out his hand, touching the wispy ends of her hair where it curled under her ear. She stood absolutely still, so as not to frighten the magic away. It did not work. He withdrew his hand and moved towards the door.

'Have a cup of tea,' she offered quickly. 'It's that sort of time.'

'I suppose it is too early for a drink?' He frowned at his watch as if he blamed it for the time.

Clementine said nothing, aware of every step he took as he followed her into the kitchen. If she closed her eyes for a second she could almost feel his lips on hers and she thought she would gladly have given ten years of her life for a moment of what she had thrown away so carelessly. Some people believed that the universe was ruled by forces of good and evil, but Clementine knew better; it was irony that was the driving force.

'You look very well.' She handed him the mug of tea and sat down opposite him at the table.

He grasped the mug gingerly as if it might do him harm. 'That's probably because I've given up not drinking.' He pointed to the wall. 'So that's the calendar. Ophelia told me about it.'

Clementine turned pink. 'Ophelia is a blabber-mouth.'

'She also tells me that you went walkabout the other night. Bloody stupid if you ask me.'

Clementine sighed. She was getting tired of explaining. 'It's one of those phrases again, "if you ask me," when you know jolly well that's the last thing the other person wants to do.'

'Witter witter,' Nathaniel said, just the way he used to. Clementine attempted a long hard stare, but failed miserably as it turned into a melting gaze. His eyes look strained, she thought, and the little frown line above his nose seemed deeper than she remembered.

'All right then, it's aversion therapy,' she said, the way she had told Ophelia. 'You know how people who are terrified of contamination are made to wash their hands in the loo or sit on top of a nuclear power station and people who are frightened of spiders are given a tarantula to keep as a pet. Well, this is the same kind of thing. If I force myself to confront something I'm scared of, however small and silly it might seem to other people, each and every day, maybe the day will come when I'm not frightened. And maybe I will then be able to live a worthwhile life. I'm on day eighteen and I think it's beginning to work.'

'So what's next on the list? Riding through the town naked, wrapped only in your hair.' He looked thoughtfully at her, his head a little to one side, and then he smiled. 'It might have worked, but now I'm not so sure.'

'I thought of it, but it would be exhibitionism not fearlessness; there's a fine line.' She smiled back at him. Maybe, she thought, all was not lost. Maybe, however undeserved, she was to be granted a second chance.

'So when's that little sister of yours back?' Nathaniel asked.

The light in Clementine's heart did not die instantly, it faded slowly. She got up from the table unable to sit still with all that hurt inside her. 'Soon. Soon soon soon.'

'Are you all right?'

'Sure sure sure.'

'You keep repeating yourself.'

'Do I?' She sat down again. 'Do I really?'

'Look Clementine, if you're thinking about my father, don't. At least, don't blame yourself any more. You know what his GP said; with his heart condition he could have died at any time. I was very hard on you after it happened and I'm sorry about that, but you really must stop torturing yourself like this.'

And what do you know? How could he fail to see all that love and lust welling out of her? How could he sit there and look at her and talk to her and not notice? The front door opened and was slammed shut. 'That's Ophelia,' she said, getting up once more. 'I'll leave you to it.'

She lay on her bed, all cried out, listening for their

voices coming from downstairs. Finally she fell asleep and when she woke again the house was quiet. On the kitchen table lay a note from Ophelia. 'Gone next door. Don't wait up.'

With a howl of anguish Clementine crumpled the note and threw it on the floor, then she grabbed her coat and scarf and ran outside into the night.

Chapter Eighteen

'I tell you, it nearly sent me crazy seeing you like that again, only to realize that you were spending the night with Ophelia. I certainly didn't need a calendar to make me go running through the town that night. Still, it was a good thing in a way, because I met David again.'

The man in the next bed was calling to a nurse to help him pull a cracker. 'I've saved it all day just for you,' he cackled. On her way across the nurse pushed back the curtains round Nathaniel's bed.

'You closed them again.' She wagged her finger. 'We really do like them open, you know. Now you can see the tree too.' Clementine followed her gaze to the small plastic Christmas tree that stood on a small table at the far end of the ward. Outside in the corridor an orderly clattered past with a trolley. Clementine leant back against the hard chair, her eyelids drooping with exhaustion.

*   *   *

She ran through the town, elbowing her way through the throng of drinkers coming out of the Prince of Wales, stopping only when her chest hurt so much she could not go on. Bending double, her hands on her knees, she drew in great gulps of cold air until she thought her lungs would burst like frozen water pipes. It was raining, a spiky drizzle, and the tyres of the car passing her on the road squelched in the gutter, splashing her feet and ankles. She started running again and this time she did not stop until she was far along the canal footpath, past the last of the town's lights.

The water looked as black and deep as a forest mere and if she closed her eyes she could hear the River Man playing his fiddle.

'He sat on the rock where the river was at its wildest, playing like an angel on the Devil's errand, luring young maidens to a watery grave,' Aunt Elvira's voice had been low, not much more than a whisper. 'Such was the beauty of his music that the young girls could not help but dance. When they were quite dizzy from twirling and turning he drew them closer and closer to the water's edge, until unable to resist they tumbled to their deaths in the whirling current in the water.'

Two strong hands grabbed her shoulders, pulling her back from the water's edge. Her heart thumping, she twisted round and came face to face with David. 'What the fuck do you think you are doing?' His voice was pitched high with anxiety and his face was a pale blur in the darkness.

Clementine gave an awkward little laugh, but her heart was still pounding. 'Nothing. Nothing nothing nothing.'

Calming down a little, David sat down in the grass by her side. 'I thought I had problems,' he muttered.

They sat in silence for a while and then Clementine scrambled to her feet, looking up at the sky, feeling the cold rain on her upturned face. She looked back at David, barely distinguishing his features. 'Do you never sleep?' she asked him.

The boy too got up, hunched, hands in his pockets, shrugging. 'I sleep during the day. It's safer that way.'

He looked up at Clementine. 'What about you?'

'Oh me? Well, normally I sleep at night.' They walked on in silence, back towards the town centre. As they reached the High Street David stopped.

'I'd better go back,' he said. 'I don't like leaving my stuff for too long.' A street lamp cast its light in a circle around them, turning the rain gold, picking out the boy's pale face.

'You can't spend Christmas on the streets,' Clementine said.

'I've got the shed.'

Clementine ignored him, suddenly determined. 'I want you to come home with me and my sister. Stay over Christmas and then maybe we can sort something out with the council. I want to help.'

The next morning, 22 December, Clementine woke wondering how to explain to Ophelia about the skinny boy sleeping on the camp-bed in the boxroom between the pink rosebud-patterned sheets that had been a gift from Grace.

By the time Ophelia had sauntered into the kitchen, blond hair ruffled, eyes smudged by last night's mascara, Clementine had decided on a firm stance.

'You know the young boy busking in the square? Well, as it happens, he's got nowhere to live so I've asked him to stay with us over Christmas. I've put up the camp-bed for him in the boxroom. He's still asleep.' And taking advantage of the fact that Ophelia seemed incapable of speech just at the moment, she continued. 'We weren't murdered in our beds during the night, so I don't think there's anything to worry about.'

Her bravado dissolved before Ophelia's gaze and she shifted nervously from one foot to the other. 'It would have been a bit of a bummer if we had, I admit, but all's well that ends well et cetera, et cetera.' She crumbled. 'Maybe I was a little bit hasty.'

'Have you gone completely mad?'

'Aunt Mabel asked me that once,' Clementine said, 'and the answer now, as then, must be a resounding, I don't think so.'

'He can stay for breakfast and then he leaves.' Ophelia relaxed as she stretched across the table for a second slice of granary toast. 'Do you want me to wake him up?'

'I've asked him to stay for Christmas.'

'Well, you'll have to un-ask him.'

Clementine bit into her toast. She chewed slowly, thoughtfully, enjoying the sweetness of the honey on her tongue. She sipped her tea, Earl Grey this morning, and then she said, 'No I won't.'

Ophelia, who was spreading Flora on her toast, stopped what she was doing and looked up sharply. 'What do you mean, you won't? Look,' she dropped the knife back onto her plate and put her hand on Clementine's across the table. 'I know you've been through a lot and I know that for some reason you resent me being with Nathaniel, but now it's time to draw the line.'

Clementine looked back at her, quite kindly. 'You're a bully, Ophelia, and yes, you're quite right, I do resent you being with Nathaniel. I also resent being told what to do in my own house and if there's any line drawing to be done it will be my kind of lines.' In spirit if not in words, she added a 'so there'. 'Now if you'd excuse me, I'd like to read the paper in peace and quiet,' she reached over and picked up the *Independent* from its place by Ophelia's plate. Sitting back in her chair, she unfolded the paper and studied the first page. A moment later she leant forward again, passing the copy of the *Gazette* to Ophelia. 'Here,' she said, 'you read this.'

After breakfast she went over to the calendar and picked that day's note out of its pocket, then, without looking at it, she crumpled it up and chucked it in the bin. She felt she had done enough battle for one day.

David had showered and now he sat at the kitchen table dressed in an old track suit of Clementine's. He was almost as tall as her so it fitted him perfectly. His own clothes were tumbling in the dryer, on the delicate programme; they looked as if they would fall apart any moment.

'I'm sorry, they were pretty dirty,' David apologized.

'That's all right. They're clean now.' Clementine did not tell him that she had used rubber gloves when gathering them up and placing them in the washing-machine.

'Are you sure I can stay? Your sister seemed pissed off.'

'Don't mind her,' Clementine said. 'PMT.'

David's brow cleared and he nodded gravely. 'I know about that. Lots of the girls at school had problems. You really had to watch your step with them at certain times of the month.'

'David,' Clementine turned from the sink, a cloth in her hand, 'are you sure you can't go back home? I don't mean right now,' she added, hastily, as the boy's face clouded over. 'After Christmas. Maybe things weren't as bad as they seemed.'

David's face was set in stubborn lines and his chin, shaved of blond fluff, jutted. 'I'm not going back. If you don't want me to stay, just say so.' The fear in his blue eyes belied the belligerent tone of his voice.

'I told you,' Clementine said, 'I would very much like you to stay for Christmas. I'm simply concerned about later on. How long have you been living rough?'

'July. I dossed with a mate in Basingstoke for a while but I couldn't hang around too long because of his mum. I got up to London once but,' he shrugged his shoulders, 'I didn't like it very much. It got really rough and then there was this party on a boat and these geezers started beating up on this boy, bashing him on the head with those old-type beer mugs, the ones with the handles. And then one of them got up on a table and just jumped down on the boy's head and his mates who tried to help, they got beaten too, so I left. I like it better down here. Aldringham is good for money. I got twenty quid busking, the other day.'

'I don't suppose you'd like to learn to play the guitar properly?'

David gave her a bright blue glare. 'What do you mean, properly?'

Clementine squirmed. 'Maybe it was a while since you took lessons.'

'I've never had lessons.'

This did not come as a surprise to Clementine. 'I could give you some. I'm a piano teacher really, but I studied the guitar. My neighbour, Nathaniel Scott,' she paused before allowing herself the luxury of saying his name one more time, 'Nathaniel Scott,' she shook herself and concentrated on David, 'he plays wonderfully well and I don't think he's had that many lessons. It just helps to know the basics.' David looked unconvinced so she dropped the subject. 'I must get on,' she said instead. 'What are your plans for the day?'

'Dunno, the usual.' His face brightened. 'I'll give you some of my takings for board.'

'Have you gone mad?' Jessica was eating a piece of a toasted tuna sandwich as she spoke.

Clementine sighed. 'I wish people wouldn't keep asking me that.'

'Don't give them cause then. I was going to ask you to be godmother, but now I'm beginning to wonder.'

'You can't fight dragons in kid gloves.' She corrected herself. 'I don't mean that the dragons are wearing kid gloves, I mean that one cannot wear kid gloves whilst fighting them.'

It was Jessica's turn to sigh, but Clementine ignored

209

her. She was, after all, fighting for her life. 'It's the pendulum thing. You have to rush to the far end in order to reach the middle. By the way, why are you always eating tuna these days? I meant to ask you.'

'Because I like it.'

Clementine felt that the lunch was not going that well. 'I'm seeing Rosie Bray on the fourth. You remember Rosie?'

Jessica was still annoyed. 'Fat girl who sang a lot. No friends.'

'That's her,' Clementine admitted.

'Have fun.' Jessica put the last piece of her sandwich in her mouth.

I've changed, Clementine thought, and that annoys her. People expect their family and friends to play out their allotted roles. Assume a new character and you upset the balance of their universe, however slightly, and they don't like it. Clementine was cast as large, bumbling and scared, and she should have had the decency to remain so.

'David and I will be on our own on Christmas Day. I was going to go to Timothy and Janet's but they weren't too keen on me bringing him.'

'I can't say I blame them.'

'Why not?' Clementine had to ask.

'You haven't got a monopoly on caring, you know. Your brother and his wife have young children and they have to come first. Expecting them to welcome this young vagrant into the bosom of their family, and at Christmas time at that, it's really asking a bit too much.'

'That's why I didn't ask them,' Clementine protested feebly. Jessica was not listening.

'The point is you know nothing, nothing at all about this boy you picked off the streets on a whim. Does he do drugs?'

'I haven't asked him.'

Jessica signalled to Mrs Challis for the bill.

'Clementine, what's happened to you?'

Green eyes, black hair, dead old men, wasted lives, that's what's happened. Clementine shrugged her shoulders. The more she had to say the less she knew how to speak and conversely she was never as full of talk as when she had nothing at all to say. Then, she was not unusual in this. She walked back home from the Chocolate House alone, having kissed Jessica goodbye and handed over her present. She stopped off at the music shop and bought some guitar music for David. She had not seen him around town that morning. Maybe he had been driven out by the Aldringham Lions. Their sledge was parked on the centre island in the High Street, just outside Argos, belting out Christmas Carols sung in American accents from loudspeakers fixed like headlights.

Green eyes, black hair; Nathaniel was making his unsteady way out of the wine bar at the corner of the street. She hurried her steps and caught up with him, touching his elbow as if they were in a game of tag.

Nathaniel started and turned round, the expression of bewildered pain in his eyes making her gasp. 'What's happened? Did I give you a fright?'

Nathaniel shrugged her off. 'What do you think if you go around grabbing people in the middle of the street.'

'You've been drinking.'

'Might have.'

'I thought you were off on a job.'

'Well, I'm not.' He stopped and glared at her. 'What's this? Twenty questions?'

Clementine took his arm. 'Come on, I'll take you home.'

Nathaniel shrugged himself free, his face set in sulky lines. 'Leave me alone. Go away. Go off and abseil down a building or something.'

'I've only got two more bits of paper and neither of

211

them tell me to abseil down anything; I know because I wrote them. I can't remember everything I wrote, it's a long time ago, but what worries me is that I've got, *Leave the house for the night without going back inside three times to check whether the gas is off*, left, because there isn't really time to go away before Christmas, and then there's David.'

'Well tell the sodding calendar to butt out.'

'That would be cheating.'

'Who cares?'

Clementine stopped dead, right in the middle of the road. 'You must never ask that,' she said as Nathaniel grabbed her hand and pulled her out of the path of a silver-coloured Renault Espace. Unperturbed, Clementine carried on talking. 'We all know there's no point to anything. The trick is to carry on as if we think there is.'

They had arrived at her gate and Nathaniel gave her a little shove towards it. 'In you go,' he said impatiently. 'Chop, Chop.' He wandered off next door and after some trouble fitting the key in the lock, he disappeared inside.

The note for 23 December asked Clementine to *Speak your mind*. She blanched over her cup of tea. Had she really set herself such a task?

'I won't be going to Timothy's either on Christmas Day,' Ophelia slipped into her usual seat opposite Clementine. 'I'm cooking Nat a real Christmas dinner. He hasn't had one since his mum died.'

Then again, maybe it was not as hard as she had first thought. 'Right this minute I hate you and I might well go on hating you for the rest of my life, and it might well be a very long life dedicated to spiting you,' Clementine said.

'I really don't get you sometimes,' Ophelia raised heavy eyes above the teacup. 'So is David leaving today?'

'No, he is not. This is my house and David is my guest.'

Ophelia sighed and reached across the table for the crumpled note by Clementine's plate. Having read it, she crumpled it up again and placed it in the ashtray which Clementine had bought for Nathaniel's use a long time ago and that she still had not had the heart to put away. 'That explains it,' she said; 'you really are very childish you know. Or you're having a break-down. I can't quite decide which.'

'I can't either,' Clementine confided, 'but let's not talk about me. Part of all of this training is to free time for thinking of others.'

'Could you think about me? He soaks the floor in the bathroom and leaves his smelly socks all over the place. His ghastly playing is driving me insane, he stomps upstairs in the middle of the night waking everyone up, and loafs around in bed half the day. I really don't like him staying here. So, as I said, why don't you think about me for a change?'

'No,' Clementine said, 'you think of yourself the whole time. Your mother thinks about you. That's enough.'

'You're becoming a monster,' Ophelia said.

Clementine said she did not think so. 'I'm taking David out to lunch to The Mill today,' she added.

'That's great. Play dollies with him for a couple of days. Get him used to the good life and then chuck him back out onto the streets.'

'That's not what I have in mind,' Clementine said.

'So what did you have in mind?' Ophelia's eyes blazed a challenge across the table. 'I don't believe you've been thinking straight about anything since Toby Scott died and I certainly don't think you've thought out this thing with David. Admit it, you acted entirely on impulse when you brought him home, and now you don't know what to do next.'

'You're right,' Clementine said. It was easy really, speaking your mind; it really was.

'What did you say?'

'I said that you were right. I did act on impulse and now I don't really know what to do next for the best. But I'm working on it.' She got up. 'I'd better wake David.'

David slept, and sleeping he looked like a child. His eyelids were translucent, crossed with fine blue veins. His cheeks were flushed and one thin arm was flung across the pillow, almost touching the metal head-board of the camp-bed. Looking at him from the doorway, Clementine wondered what kind of woman his mother was to stand by while her child wandered the streets, homeless and alone.

'David, wake-up time,' she called. In the end she had to shout to wake him and even then he just lay back down, bleary-eyed and tousle-haired from all that sleep.

They walked together to The Mill restaurant on the edge of the town; David, smart in a navy sweater belonging to Clementine and a blue and red tie left behind many weeks before by Nathaniel. Even his worn jeans looked good, newly washed and pressed. Clementine was dressed all in black; it was that kind of Christmas.

The old mill house had been decorated to the last inch of its mellow red bricks, twinkle-lit, bedecked and beribboned. It reminded Clementine of Gustaf's old father going off, dressed as an elf, cross and humiliated, to a long-ago Christmas party. Inside the restaurant it was hard to move for Christmas trees and candles and office party revellers. Clementine turned to David, wondering if going there had been such a good idea. The answer lay in the concentrated smile of pleasure on the boy's thin face as he followed the waitress to their table. Once seated he spent a long time looking at the menu before ordering.

'I'd like the snails Provençale, and to follow, sirloin steak in green pepper sauce,' he said firmly.

Clementine asked for stilton tart and, after some hesitation, she tossed the menu down on the table. 'What the hell, I'll have the beef too.'

David, his mouth full of ciabatta bread, could do nothing but nod. When his snails came, steaming hot in a miniature cast-iron pan, he looked up at Clementine and said, 'My mum was always telling me to try new things. She used to cook all sorts of stuff.'

Clementine reached across the table and touched the boy's hand. 'Are you sure we shouldn't phone her? She's probably frantic.'

'No, she's not. She's relieved.'

It made Clementine want to cry, that laconic stating of painful facts. That was children for you: accepting, non-judgemental; what awful thing happened on the way to turn them into adults?

'It was different before, when it was only her and me. "The man in my life," she used to call me.' For once, the expression did not make Clementine wince, as a quick smile passed the boy's solemn face. He shoved a snail into his mouth, garlic butter dripping down his downy chin. 'Then we moved in with Jim,' David shrugged his shoulders. 'She doesn't need me now.'

'Have you no other relatives?'

'My dad's sister in Canada.'

'What about her? Would she take you in?'

Again David shrugged his shoulders, such square bony shoulders. 'Don't know. Anyway, how would I get over to Canada?' All at once he seemed bored with the whole subject. 'This is great.' He wiped the last of the garlic butter from the pan with his bread.

The steaks arrived on two larger versions of the sizzling pan on which David's snails had been served. 'Medium for Madame,' the waiter pronounced in suspect French tones. 'And well done pour Monsieur.'

Clementine's steak was cooked through and the

sauce was not nearly peppery enough. 'Yours all right?' she asked David.

The boy nodded emphatically. The head waiter breezed past, stopping fleetingly to enquire if everything was all right. He was already on his way, a pleased little smile on his face, when Clementine said, 'My guest's steak seems fine, but I'm afraid that mine is overdone and the sauce, in my view, is not peppery enough.'

'I'm sorry about that,' she whispered to David as the head waiter disappeared in a fog of insincere apologies. 'I hate making a scene, but I do think one has to speak one's mind. I don't normally, but today I do,' she added.

'It's cool,' David speared a chip with his fork.

They walked home in companionable silence, Clementine thinking that more than anything she wanted to bump into Nathaniel. 'And how are you on this fine day before Christmas?' he would ask. Well, of course he would not, but in her mind he did. 'I'm fine in small parts but mainly I feel like dying,' she would reply, smiling brightly. 'I feel like dying for all the good old reasons of having wasted my life and killed your father, but also because I love you with a passion I have never felt before and will, I know, never know again. I feel like dying because having known what it is to bask in the sunshine of your love, a life in the shade is unbearable. It has to be said that the thought of Ophelia lying in your arms, doesn't help.'

She would say all this because it was her day for speaking her mind. But David and she walked through the bustling, twinkling town meeting no-one at all whom they knew.

Chapter Nineteen

'That day on the footpath I dropped you as if you were a dirty syringe and my feelings for you no more reliable than some drug-induced vision of heaven. How could I ever expect you to forgive me for that, let alone for what followed?' Clementine spoke to Nathaniel in a whisper barely audible above the clatter of trolleys and the snoring and sighing of the other patients. She glanced at her watch. It was one o'clock in the morning. She had been at Nathaniel's bedside for most of the night, a night of being able to gaze at his face and of being close enough to him to touch his hand.

'I love you.' she leant across the bed and kissed him lightly on the lips.

*　　*　　*

Clementine arrived back from shopping on Christmas Eve to find David and Nathaniel together in the sitting-room. Clementine had not seen quite such a smile on David's face before. 'Check this out.' He got to his feet holding up a brand-new guitar for her inspection. 'He gave it to me.' David struck up a pose and strummed the guitar.

Nathaniel looked vaguely uncomfortable. 'I was passing the music shop,' he muttered.

Clementine beamed at them both, moving across the

room and taking the guitar from David, inspecting it, caressing the glossy golden wood of the instrument. 'You bought David this beautiful instrument?'

'Wicked isn't it?' David reached out for the guitar and began to play, badly, a rapt smile on his thin face.

'Why don't we all meet up for Christmas Day now you're not going to your brother's?' Nathaniel asked. They had fled to the kitchen, away from David's blissful, tuneless playing. Nathaniel perched on the stool; Clementine sat at the table, drinking him in.

'Oh yes, that would be lovely,' she beamed at him.

'I leave for Paris on the twenty-eighth, so it would be the last chance for us all to meet up for a while.'

Happiness comes and happiness goes. She sat back in the chair. 'You're going away?' she said finally, having achieved a model voice of polite interest. 'How long for?' A small discordant note of desperation squeaked into the careful tones.

'Oh, to live.' Nathaniel leant against the doorway and lit a cigarette. 'I'm going to work for this European agency. I need a change. As always I'll be travelling a lot of the time.'

Now why did she used to think that being the architect of one's own misfortunes would somehow make those misfortunes easier to bear? That to brush yourself down and say, 'Well, at least I have no-one to blame but myself,' would somehow be easier than looking up from the devastation at a disappearing hurricane or a pig dropping from the sky.

'How lovely,' she said again in a voice not much louder than a whisper. The day before she had had to speak her mind; this was another day.

A look of irritation swept across Nathaniel's face. 'What do you mean, "how lovely?" What exactly do you mean by "How lovely?"'

Clementine turned away, staring out at the garden so that he would not see her tears. She pointed to the bird table. 'Look, a Robin.' Then she said, 'By, "how lovely"

I meant, I'm sad at the thought of you going away and will Ophelia be going with you?'

'Will Ophelia be going where?' This was the whole child herself, appearing in the doorway with the immaculate timing of all bad fairies.

Clementine turned round slowly. 'To Paris with Nathaniel?'

'We haven't discussed it,' Nathaniel said, putting out his cigarette and chucking it straight in the bin, making Clementine think he might start a fire at any time. 'As I said, I won't be there much either. Now, what about tomorrow? Why don't you and David come over to me?' He reached out and took Ophelia's hand. 'Don't you think?'

Wanting to save everyone embarrassment Clementine was about to say she was very happy staying in, when Ophelia gave a tight little smile and said that it was a very good idea. If Clementine had wished to be awkward she would have smiled and gushed, 'Are you sure now?' but she did not want to stretch Ophelia's new-found insincerity any further.

'I'll check with David,' she said, 'and thank you both very much for asking.'

'Last day,' Nathaniel nodded towards the calendar. 'So what's on the menu?'

Clementine picked up the small piece of paper lying crumpled up on the table. 'It's a blank. I can do whatever I want as long as I'm afraid of it. If you see what I mean,' she added quickly before Ophelia's look of contempt.

'I just hope there's enough turkey,' Ophelia said.

After Nathaniel had left, Ophelia made some coffee and handed a mug to Clementine. 'Sit down,' she invited her, 'I think we should talk.'

In the sitting-room, David was attempting to play 'Hey Jude' on his new guitar.

Clementine settled back at the kitchen table with her coffee, wondering if there was anyone capable of hearing those innocuous words, 'Let's talk,' without a feeling of impending doom. Waiting for Ophelia to speak she tried to cheer herself up. Maybe 'Let's talk,' meant simply that. It would be unusual. Words, like people, seldom travelled baggage-free, but carried with them a weight of hidden meanings.

'Clementine, you never really loved Nathaniel.'

'Is there a little question mark type thing at the end of that sentence?' Clementine asked.

Ophelia sighed and shook her head; a reasonable woman, she seemed to say, thwarted at every turn. 'Be honest with yourself; for a while you mistook infatuation for something more serious . . .'

'I think', Clementine interrupted her, 'that infatuation is vastly underrated. It's usually where it all starts, after all. No, my problem was mistaking infatuation for something *less* serious.'

'Jesus, Clementine,' Ophelia paused as if she was waiting for Clementine to take her to task for blasphemy. Clementine was about to when she decided that she could not be bothered. It was not her responsibility. That had been one of her many other mistakes: seeing everything as her responsibility and doing nothing about the few things that really were.

'You can't just twist everything around,' Ophelia continued.

It was Clementine's turn to sigh. 'It doesn't matter now anyway.' She got to her feet heavily. 'I'm borrowing Jessica's car to drive over to Timothy's with the presents. Shall I take yours?'

'I haven't got them. I'm going out in a minute. But Clementine, what I'm saying is, you seem to resent me and Nathaniel being together and I mind that.'

Clementine, rinsing out her mug, turned and looked straight at Ophelia. 'Well tough titty.'

So much shaking of heads; it was Ophelia's turn now. 'God you're childish sometimes,' she said.

*

Clementine had ended up staying for supper at her brother's house. She had phoned home and David said he was very happy to look after himself for the evening. 'There are lots of videos in the cupboard in the sitting-room,' she told him, 'I won't be late.'

As it happened, it was past one o'clock when she drove back into Aldringham. She was tired; twice already she had nodded off at the wheel and once she had stopped at the roadside, winding the windows right down to let in the cold night air. It was Christmas Day already. And she had failed to carry out her last task. (Telling Timothy to mind his own business twice during dinner did not count, she knew that.) Blinking, desperately trying to keep her eyes open, she turned up the High Street. A gang of drunken teenagers reeled out from an alley-way when one of them, plump, pallid and with a tinsel wreath in his stubbly ginger hair, stumbled out into the road in front of the car. Clementine swerved violently to the left and the boy staggered back onto the pavement, unhurt. She had to stop the car for a moment her heart was beating so hard. She had been inches from causing her second death. Accident-prone, Aunt Mabel used to call her. Clumsy, her stepmother Grace used to sigh. At the time Clementine had felt they were unfair. Now she began to see that they had been quite kind in their judgements. Taking a deep breath, she brushed the hair from her eyes and drove on.

She smelt the smoke through the open car window as she drove up in front of her house. She got out quickly, hitting her head against the door of the car. Looking up at the cottage, inspecting it, she unlocked the front door and hurried inside.

She went from room to room, checking for fire. Ophelia and David were asleep in their respective bedrooms and all was peaceful. Yet the smell of smoke grew stronger, wafting in through the open bedroom windows. She went back out onto the street, sniffing the air and looking up at the star-studded sky. Then she saw it: smoke spiralling out of Mr Scott's attic window. She rushed up the path to the front door and pressed the bell, keeping her finger on it for what seemed an age and all the while the smoke grew thicker, billowing from the window in great sheets. There was no reply to her ringing. She stepped back onto the path and stared up at the attic. A gust of wind blew the smoke clear and in that moment she saw the outline of a figure slumped in Mr Scott's chair. She threw herself against the door, hammering it with her fists, shouting for help.

'Ophelia!' she screamed, turning towards her house. 'David!' She took a run at the door, shoulder first, trying to force it open. It remained closed. For a moment everything was still as she listened for sounds; any sound, any sign of life. But the town slept on. She looked around her, sobbing, when she spotted the hedgehog boot brush on the doorstep. Picking it up with both hands she carried it to the hall window and lifted it above her head, smashing it right through the glass. Mindless of the jagged pane slashing her arm, she reached in and opened the latch. Within seconds she was through and inside the house, calling Nathaniel's name as she ran up the stairs.

As she reached the attic the smoke was so dense she had to struggle for breath and, eyes streaming, she pushed the door open. She stepped back with a yelp of anguish as the heat from the flames hit her face. She half ran, half fell back down to the landing, grabbing the phone on top of the chest of drawers and dialling 999.

She replaced the handset and for a moment she stood motionless, staring as the smoke around her got denser. With a small shudder, like someone waking from a deep sleep, she walked through to the bathroom and grabbed a towel, soaking it under the cold tap. Then she ran. She ran back upstairs, through the smoke, covering her nose and mouth with the towel. It seemed to take an eternity, but at last she reached Nathaniel, slumped unconscious in his father's chair. The curtains were on fire, the flames reaching up to the wooden rail above, and the other chair, the chair which Clementine had sat in that long night back in the summer, that too was burning, black acrid smoke billowing from the stuffing. Eyes streaming, she made her way across the room when the curtain rail snapped in two, sending one half crashing down, hitting Nathaniel.

She shouted his name, stumbling over the decanter left sitting on the floor by the chair, sending it rolling across the floorboards and crashing into the small portable heater.

She pulled the burning curtain cloth away from Nathaniel and covered his face with the damp towel, before grabbing him under both arms and dragging him from the chair. She held him tight, inching backwards, his legs and feet trailing the floor. She backed out through the smoke and flames, her eyes stinging, every breath a struggle as, choking and close to vomiting, she fell to her knees, tears streaming down her hot cheeks. He seemed to grow heavier with every second and there seemed to be no air left, only thick smoke. They were going to die up there. That's how it would all end; Clementine and Nathaniel, dead ever after.

'Nathaniel, oh Nathaniel, I'm sorry.' She lay down, shielding his body with her own.

Chapter Twenty

Nathaniel opened his eyes, looking straight at her. 'Hello, you.'

She looked back at him and then she smiled and she went on smiling as if she had forgotten how to stop.

'I thought you might never wake,' she whispered.

'You old optimist you,' he whispered back before his voice broke into a cough. A nurse came hurrying over to the bed.

'Good morning.' She smiled. 'I'll call the doctor, she'll want to look you over now you're back with us.'

Clementine followed the nurse's disappearing back with her gaze, while, almost nonchalantly, she put her hand over Nathaniel's. She sat like that for a while, pretending that he was hers, then with a little sigh she turned to face him, withdrawing her hand.

'Don't! Don't take your hand away.' He shifted in the bed, wincing. 'I remember arriving here, but before and after that, nothing.'

'You were in the attic. You must have fallen asleep. They found an ashtray in the other chair, the one that was on fire, so you must have put the cigarette there and then it tipped onto the seat, something like that. The fire brigade will tell you, I expect. I was on my way home and I saw the smoke. You were unconscious when I got up there and then I blacked-out too.' She pulled a face. 'You were so heavy. I tell you, if the fire engines hadn't arrived when they did . . .' she shuddered.

'I was drunk.'

Clementine nodded. 'I thought you might have been.'

'I could have killed us both.'

'We all make mistakes. Oh, and Ophelia came to see you. I told her to go away and that if she didn't, my heart, weakened by the smoke in my lungs, might stop. I exaggerated a little bit there.'

'That's all right. You saved my life. You can exaggerate as much as you like.'

'Are you in love with Ophelia?'

'No.'

'You shouldn't have led her on.'

Nathaniel sighed. 'Probably not.'

'Never mind. We all make mistakes.'

'You just said that.'

'So I did.'

*   *   *

'What's going on?' Ophelia asked, gimlet-eyed as Clementine arrived back home from the hospital on Boxing Day morning. 'How's Nathaniel and what's all that crap about your heart?'

'Questions, questions, questions, so many questions,' Clementine muttered, nursing her right hand in the crook of her left arm.

'Is he all right?'

'He'll be fine. He's got mild concussion and some first and second degree burns on his hands and arms. They're keeping him in for a couple more days and then he'll have to go back every day for a while as an outpatient to change the compresses, but all things considered, he's doing very well.'

'Well, I'm visiting this morning whether you like it or not.'

'Good,' Clementine wandered past her into the sitting-room. She stood in the middle of the room, a smile on her lips. The dragon in the corner of the room was a tiny creature now, all floppy and with just one shamefaced head on his scaly neck.

As Ophelia appeared behind her, Clementine turned around. 'Where's David?'

'Asleep as usual. He didn't seem overly worried about what had happened.'

'That's good then. Now I must get on,' she said, more to herself than to Ophelia. 'I've got a million things to do.'

She began with Aunt Elvira's notes, bringing the whole stack of them, balanced on her left arm, across to the sofa. She made herself some milky coffee, using her left hand all the while. It hurt just carrying the biscuit tin so she had to go twice to the kitchen, once for the coffee and the other time for the biscuits. She read for four hours, pages and pages of Aunt Elvira's notes, pausing now and then to make notes in the margin. Luckily she could still hold a pen. When she looked at her watch it was almost one o'clock.

David had just got up and she went to join him in the kitchen, giving him a hug hello. 'I'm sorry, it wasn't much of a Christmas for you,' she smiled at him.

'I had a good time,' David smiled back, adding quickly, 'I was really worried about what had happened and everything, but once I knew you were going to be all right I had a really nice time.'

'Did Ophelia cook you something?'

The boy nodded. 'Yeah. We didn't have the turkey but she took some chops out of the freezer and we had sprouts and roast potatoes; she did them in olive oil, really nice.' He bit into a slice of toast. 'I suppose I should be off soon.'

'There's no hurry.'

'Is it sore, your hand?'

226

'A bit. Not too bad. Now you mustn't worry. Everything is going to be fine.'

She wanted to clean the house. She managed fine, although everything seemed to take twice as long as she avoided the use of her right hand, careful all the time not to knock it against the compress. She was careful with the house too, cleaning it as gently and as thoroughly as if it had been a baby, bathing the window-panes in clear warm water, going from room to room wiping every corner and crevice, rubbing the wood with greasy polish.

'I'm off out buskin',' David called from the hall.

Clementine called back goodbye before returning to her cleaning. She dusted the books as best she could, and every now and then she put one down on the floor rather than back in the bookcase. They soon formed a small pile at her feet. Later she packed them in a small leather holdall. She checked through her paperwork and paid her bills. When she finally sat down to rest it was dusk. Ophelia had come back from the hospital some hours earlier, saying nothing and going straight to her room. Clementine dozed in the chair in front of the unlit fire when the phone went. It was Jessica and she was, she said, horrified.

'You could have died and a fat lot of good you would have been as a godmother then.' It took Clementine a good five minutes to calm Jessica down and she only managed then by saying that it could not be comfortable for the baby to have such an angry mother. Jessica's voice changed. She had felt the baby move the day before, on Christmas Day, and if that was not a good omen, what was? Clementine began to worry that Jessica was taking the adoration of her unborn child a little too far.

'Don't hang everything – all your love and hopes and plans – on this child, or its little neck will break from the weight and you yourself will be far too vulnerable.'

'Oh, and Abby Challis had her baby this morning.

June Challis called me,' Jessica said. 'Apparently the baby is beautiful, just like Abby was when she was born. Derek was there at the birth videoing the whole thing.'

David came back just as they finished the call and Clementine was starting supper.

'You shouldn't be cooking, not with that hand,' David said. 'I'll take care of it.'

She watched him as, frowning with concentration, he cracked four eggs in the mixing bowl, whisking them with a fork, adding a carefully measured spoonful of water.

'You know you should always keep a separate pan for eggs,' he said as he knelt down, pulling out Clementine's only frying-pan. 'Now do you want plain or cheese?'

Clementine was far too restless to be hungry but she ate every bit of her cheese omelette. 'That was quite delicious,' she said. 'Thank you.'

David looked quietly pleased. 'I used to make them for my mum sometimes when she was tired after work,' he said. He nodded towards her hand. 'Were you scared?' he asked.

Clementine nodded. 'It's nature's little joke,' she said. 'However miserable you might be, however much you might think you'd like to just die, when the crunch comes, you're still scared. Something in you, something beyond your control, fights for you to stay alive.'

David searched her face, his own creased in a frown. 'You don't want to die do you?'

'No,' she said, 'of course not. I'd like to give living a go first.'

She went to bed early, but exhausted as she was, she could not sleep; she tossed and turned, sitting bolt upright in her bed one moment and the next lying down clutching the second pillow, the pillow on which Nathaniel's head used to rest, back when he was still sharing her bed. It was morning when she fell asleep and then it was only to be woken by Ophelia some minutes later.

'I'm off to get some food and things for Nathaniel when he gets out and then I'll go over to the hospital. I'll be there most of the day. You'll be all right on your own won't you? Oh, and I almost forgot. Your mother phoned yesterday. I managed to calm her down, but I promised you'd call.'

Clementine sat up in the bed. 'Ophelia, wait a moment. Listen, I've decided to let David stay for a while longer. He might find a job now he's got somewhere to live and then he can save up to rent a room or something. And I've written to his aunt in Canada, if the letter gets to her – David knew only her name and the name of the small town where she lives. Anyway, I told him he can stay until he's sorted himself out one way or the other.'

'You must be joking.'

'No.'

Ophelia glared at her. 'I haven't got time to argue,' she said, 'we'll talk about it later.'

'What you mean is, you'll talk me out of it later,' Clementine said.

Ophelia disappeared downstairs with a 'Don't be silly' thrown like a pinch of salt over her shoulder.

Clementine stayed in bed until noon. She bathed, holding her right arm high up above the water, soaking in jasmine-scented bubbles, and dressed with care. She spoke to her mother on the phone before settling down to write a letter to Beatrice. When she had finished she folded the pages and placed them in a long white envelope, sealing it and writing Beatrice's address on the front. She put the letter on the hall table on her way out to the shops.

The town was packed with shoppers restocking their fridges, returning unwanted gifts, cashing in tokens, queueing up for the sales. Clementine just wanted some food for her's and David's supper. He was home by the time she got back.

Clementine left the carrier bag in the hall and disappeared upstairs to her room. She returned with a small brown leather case.

'Here,' she handed it to David. 'I want you to have this. It's my father's watch. And before you say anything, it's not that big a deal. He was a watch freak so we all, each of his five children, had one when he died. I want you to have mine.'

She was in bed already, dozey from having taken two sleeping pills, when Ophelia returned home. 'He'll be out tomorrow evening.' Ophelia appeared in the doorway. 'I said I'd collect him around six.'

Clementine was grateful for those pills that kept her sleeping until morning.

The day passed, slow as a childhood church service. At quarter-to six she was already at the window, and there she waited, her arm raised and pressed against the glass, as if she was ready to wave. It was almost seven o'clock when the street light picked out Ophelia's white Golf. She watched it slow down outside her house, only to drive on the few yards to Nathaniel's front gate. For long moments nothing happened, then Ophelia opened the door and climbed out, walking round to help Nathaniel out from his seat. He stepped out onto the pavement a little unsteadily and walked up to the gate. There he paused for a moment, one bandaged hand on the latch, raising his head and looking straight up at Clementine. Ophelia appeared at his side, and with a quick upwards glance, she pushed him gently through the gate. Clementine looked after them until they disappeared through the front door, her face pressed against the window.

'Nathaniel,' she whispered, tears running down her cheeks, 'Nathaniel, please. I've carried out my tasks, I've come to your rescue, please come to mine.'

She slumped to the floor, resting her head on the

230

window-sill, and there she fell asleep. In her dream a bell sounded, shrill and persistent, but she was too far away to answer it. Hail stones scattered against the glass, whilst outside the wind raged at the trees. She woke as a smattering of pebbles hit the window and she stumbled to her feet, opening it and leaning out.

Nathaniel stood on the path, his undamaged right hand raised. As he saw her his hand relaxed into a salute and a scattering of pebbles fell to the ground. Clementine held out her arms and he dashed forward, making as if he was going to climb right up to the window. Smiling up at her in the light from the bedroom, he said, 'I'm afraid this is as far as I go.'

Laughing, she withdrew her hands and ran downstairs to let him inside.

'I love you, Nathaniel,' she said, holding her arms out to him once more. 'I love you and I want to come to Paris with you.' She pointed to the suitcase standing by the mirror. 'See, I'm packed already.'

Chapter Twenty-One

The sun shone in through the window of the tiny
bedroom. Clementine woke and stretched, sitting up
in the brass bed. After a moment she got up and
padded across to the open window and leant out over
the small courtyard. She closed her eyes, enjoying the
feel of the sun on her face, drawing in the mild air with
its familiar smell of cat's pee and baking bread. She
opened her eyes again, blinking against the light, and
turned back to the bed.

*   *   *

'What do you mean you're going to Paris with him?'
Ophelia stood in the kitchen doorway, small and
vengeful, her arms folded across her chest. 'You can't
do that.' And Clementine, large and determined, saw
that her sister was close to tears.

'Oh, darling, I'm sorry. I'm so sorry.' She put her
hand out and touched Ophelia's shoulder.

'What is the point in being sorry?' Ophelia shrugged
off the hand.

'You're right,' Clementine pulled back. 'You're
absolutely right.'

'And what about the house? What about me?'

'You can stay in the house as long as you like. But
please allow David to stay too, at least until he's able

to get a place of his own. I've been in touch with the social services and they'll help out as much as they can.'

Ophelia wandered into the kitchen and sank down onto her chair. 'I would never have believed this of you.' She looked up. 'Are you sure you've told Nathaniel? This isn't any of your fairy tale crap?'

'But he told you it was over between you before he left hospital, didn't he?' Clementine said gently.

'Of course he did,' Ophelia snapped, 'but he didn't say you were going to Paris with him.'

'He didn't know then,' Clementine mumbled.

'I really believed I could get him to change his mind,' Ophelia said plaintively. 'Let's be honest shall we; I'm younger and prettier than you, I've got a career. How could he choose you?' She looked so forlorn in her chair, the stark winter light emphasizing her pallor and the dark circles under her eyes.

Clementine sat down beside her and said gently, 'It's a mystery, I can see that, but that's love for you. How can you hope to explain why of all the people you meet, one and one alone holds the sun and the moon and the stars in his hands? Why one pair of eyes is so infinitely appealing when another pair, just as pretty, leaves you cold. How can you hope to explain love?'

'When do you think you're leaving?' Ophelia asked, turning her face away, as if Clementine's very countenance was abhorrent to her.

'We're going to London to stay with a friend of Nathaniel's tomorrow; he can have his treatment there, and then on to Paris in two weeks' time.'

'Well, I hope you have a thoroughly miserable life.'

'You didn't really mean that,' Clementine said.

'Try me.'

Early the next day Clementine closed the front door behind her and stepped out onto the street. She had said her goodbyes; to David, whom she had given an envelope with £200 and a contact address in Paris, and to Jessica. She had phoned her mother, her sister in Israel and her brothers to tell them her plans. She was ready to leave.

Nathaniel was waiting for her at the gate and when he saw her walking towards him he smiled, as if nothing in the world gave him such pleasure.

He held out his arms and then, remembering his injuries, put them down by his side. 'I couldn't sleep,' he said, suddenly looking anxious. 'I kept thinking you'd changed your mind.' He took her left hand in his right. 'You're sure aren't you? Leaving everything behind for goodness knows what. There are no guarantees.'

'What are you trying to do, put me off?' She pulled away gently, looking at him, her hands on his shoulders. 'You know me, a risk-taker from way back.' She put her suitcase in the boot of the car and slipped into the passenger seat.

Beatrice sat curled up in her favourite armchair in her parent's sitting-room, munching on an apple and reading her letter.

'I'm enclosing the name and telephone number of a teacher who can take my place. He is a marvellous musician and I think you will like him very much,' Clementine wrote.

'And what do you know but I found the ending to the story I told you about many months ago when you first came to see me. You remember the little creature who lived her life expecting a catastrophe, how she could never relax and enjoy her beautiful house filled with treasures because she was so frightened of losing it? How she used to stand by her bedroom window in the white and yellow wooden turret looking out at the blue sea, her face all elongated with anxiety; waiting, waiting, always waiting, blind to the sun shining in the blue sky, deaf to the birds singing in her garden.

234

'And what do you know? Finally it happened. The catastrophe she had feared for so long arrived. It was night and the little creature was sleeping her uneasy dream-spun sleep, when she was woken by a sound like a huge train hurtling through a tunnel. Terrified, she leapt from her bed and raced across to the window. Outside the black night was wild and the seabirds were fleeing towards the wood for shelter, their wings battling against the wind. And what a wind. It hurled itself against the lovely house, battering it until there was nothing left but a heap of bricks and sticks of wood, and then, sated, it died down to a soft breeze. Morning came and never had there been a more beautiful dawn as the sky turned pink and gold in celebration of the rising sun. If you had happened to walk along the seashore you would have seen the little creature alone amongst the ruins of her home, dancing, her skinny legs flying, her arms raised towards the sky. You see she was happy at last. The worst had finally happened, but she had seen the sun rise in the sky and the birds still sang, only now she heard them, and for the first time in her life she was free.'

In the bedroom on the ground floor of the old apartment house, Clementine crept back into bed and lay down next to Nathaniel, her arm across his chest. They had been in Paris four months now, living together in the small apartment in the 8th arrondissement. Clementine taught music at an American school and, when she could, she travelled with Nathaniel. When they first moved in, Clementine had turned round from unpacking her case and said, 'Getting to know each other before you make a commitment is for whimps,' showing off her new-found courage as if it was her first-born child. But by now they knew each other rather well, and still they loved each other.

She admired his loyalty and warmth, his energy and

his commitment to his work. He relaxed in her endless capacity for loving him and for forgiving. There were his moods, of course, the days of self-imposed isolation, and his drinking; and Clementine's daydreaming and inefficiency, and her infuriating habit of never finishing a sentence. But they believed that their love might defy the odds and conquer everything, even their own frailties, and that perhaps they would live happily ever after.

THE END